ROSE SANTORIELLO

DANCE

FOR

DEMONS

HEL'S CARNIVAL BOOK ONE

Editor: Heather Nix

Cover Art: Amira Naval

Graphic Design (Typography) and Map: Eternal Geekery

Chapter Headers and Dinkus: Fallnskye

Developmental Editing and Formatting: Rae Douglas

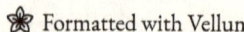 Formatted with Vellum

CONTENT WARNINGS

Dance for Demons is a Paranormal Romantasy with (darker) rom-com energy. Although it's generally a good time, it will still take you on a roller coaster *(or should I say Ferris wheel)* of emotions. If you have any questions/concerns, please email me rosesantoriello@monsterromanceauthor.com, or reach out on my socials @rosesantoriello.

- Adult language.
- Alcohol consumption and mention of drug usage.
- Consensual sex between adults including: edge play, knife play, public/semi-public sex, and grinding.
- A main character with chronic migraines.
- Sexual wrist slitting/blood play (not between the main characters)
- Physical assault and sexual harassment (not by love interest)
- Attempted murder (between main characters)
- Lots of violence including: murder, stabbing, and throat slicing.
- Vehicular accident and injures (to an adult, they survive)

- Residential fire and injures (to children, they survive)
- Mentions/memories of: patricide, teenage r*pe, parental abuse (mental and physical, including wing mutilation), and suicidal ideation.
- Mentions of: serial killers, serial r*pists, drinking blood, political revolutions, war, and controlled substances.

Reader discretion is advised.

PRONUNCIATION GUIDE

Haeresis - hi-ruh-sis
Gemma Marino - gem-uh muh-ree-no
Draven Orzath - dray-ven or-zath
Luc Morningstar - loose morning-star
Raph Morningstar - raff morning-star
Reina - ray-nuh
Absinthe - ab-synth
Una - you-nuh
Po - poh
Quinn - qwin
Robyn - rob-in
Rowan - row-uhn
Leo - lee-oh
Lyle - lie-uhl
Baelor - bay-lore
Yasmeena Al-Khalifa - yahs-MEE-nuh all-kah-leaf-uh
Khalid Al-Khalifa - KAH-lid all-kah-leaf-uh
Aida Ali - eye-e-duh ah-lee

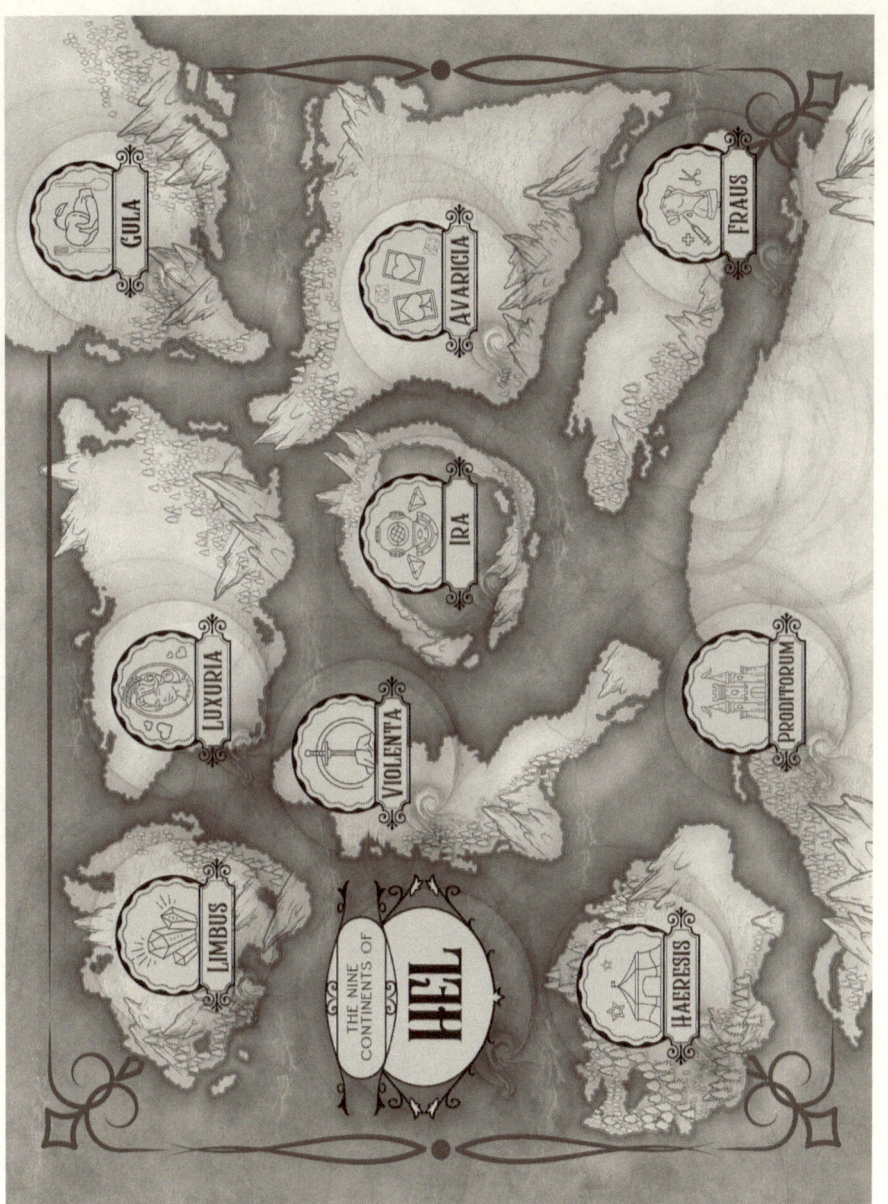

Playlist

Prick! Goes the Scorpion's Tale - The Devil's Carnival
Freak Show - Set It Off
New Girl - FINNEAS
Body - Rosenfeld
Sick Obsession - Landon Tewers
Around My Neck - FINNEAS
Pale Moonlight - Dayseeker
In All My Dreams I Drown - The Devil's Carnival
If I Killed Someone For You - Alec Benjamin
Die With A Smile - Lady Gaga, Bruno Mars

DEDICATION

For the ones who yearn to forget.

PRELUDE

Welcome to Hel, where your earthly morals no longer apply.

Symphony No. 1
Gemma

Green light flickers through my lashes as I pry my eyes open, my body waking. The air smells sharp as I inhale; a metallic tang mixed with magic. My head pounds, everything is strange and technicolor. How did I get here? Where even is *here*?

Neon lamps adorn the streets, each one brighter than anything I've ever seen before. A cambion walks by, an umbrella in one hand and a tiny horned baby cradled in her other deep red arm, but her outfit is odd. Her waist is cinched, the fabric of her skirt bustled in the back. It reminds me of old photos of Earth prior to The Convergence. The way the fabric was sewn is almost Victorian—or maybe Edwardian—but it's definitely not modern.

Did I get drunk and end up in some sort of poorly done historical reenactment?

Buildings loom above me, their structures cold and unfamiliar. Everything is dark and busy, and as I look up at what appears to be a late night sky, there's some*thing* over me. A monorail. A tram flies by at an incredible speed, bright light glowing from underneath, where the tracks lie.

Welp. Wherever this is, it's definitely not Sunspell City.

I can't remember where I was before I woke up. I can't even

really remember who I was—who I *am?* I rack my brain, trying to think of anything—whatever I can recall—but my thoughts are sluggish.

My name is Gemma, I do know that. Gemma... Marino. I'm a human. I remember my neighbor was an elven mage, but I don't have magic, because I am an unlucky loser.

I live in Sunspell City. I don't remember what I do for a living, what my home looks like, or if I live with anyone, but I can remember Magia Island. That's it, though. That's all I've got. *Shit.* This isn't good.

I know I'm supposed to have preferences for things and child-hood memories, but my brain seems to only want to recall things about Earth, not myself. How does one forget so much about their life? I must've hit my head or something. Or maybe I was kidnapped and drugged? There's no other explanation. I mean, my head is fucking *empty.*

Scanning my surroundings, I search for any indication of where I am. Signage, a landmark, anything I recognize, but I draw a blank. Wherever I am, magic is definitely favored over technology. It's everywhere I look. The lights, the tram, everything seems to run on this glowing green magic like nothing I've ever seen before. Even the sparkling taste on my tongue is foreign, crisper than the magic from home, and it terrifies me.

It's not like I'm unfamiliar with magic. Ever since The Convergence, magic is fairly common. When galaxies collided, depositing new fragments of continents and powerful beings like elves and orcs onto our planet, magic became the norm. I'm used to it, even if I don't have any of my own. Earth feels safe, familiar. But this place? It's new and different. I don't like it—I don't enjoy this feeling of not knowing, especially when paired with the loss of my memory.

My hands are shaking, my skin slick with sweat. I don't remember much about who I am, but this level of fear *feels* wrong—as if it isn't like me to be scared. And yet here I am, my heart rate pounding like an EDM song right before the beat drops, my skin slick with nervous sweat even though it's chilly outside.

Anxiety is a vise around my chest, squeezing until it is impossible to breathe or move. The fear of the unknown is overwhelming and all-encompassing, and I want to free myself of it. I want to shake it off, or let it burn away like an infection, but the feeling continues to take hold of me, forcing me down.

I would rather feel nothing at all than feel this. This pit of pure panic. My thoughts spin like a runaway merry-go-round. Beings waltz by me without a care in the world as I stay planted to the cold, wet ground. Nobody stops to ask me if I'm okay, or to tell me how I got here. Not a soul cares.

Which leaves me with one option: I have to fix this myself. Whatever mistake got me here, right now it's up to me—and me alone—to make it right. I'm going to figure out what happened, and more importantly, who I am.

Taking deep breaths of cool air, I try to steady my still-racing heart. I stand up and brush the dirt off my jeans as cambion with large horns and skin in shades of red and pink travel past. There are no elves in sight, which is weird. On Earth, elves are everywhere. I haven't seen an orc or satyr either. Fragments of memories glint like twinkling stars in an onyx sky, but I can't reach them; they're trapped lightyears away.

Could this be a city dedicated to the half-demons? I'd once read about pockets of the Earth that hold tight-knit communities of mages who tend to stay amongst themselves, but most places are far more integrated between species. Magia Island buzzes with mages and humans alike, and hybrid babies are born every day. Elflings and orclings, too.

Fuck. Where the hell am I? It's oddly chilly, but there could have been a cold front. My fingers fumble with the zipper of my jacket and I pull it up, hugging my arms close to my body as I force myself to walk. There's a metal fence with posters for various events, including a large one that reads *come enjoy The*

Sinner's Circus—The Greatest Show on Hel. I get closer to read the small line of text underneath. *Sanctuary for the strange.*

My chest tightens, the wind torn out of me as I reread the bottom lines over and over again. *The greatest show on Hel. Sanctuary for the strange.*

Hel. The planet, Hel. Is the universe fucking with me? The gears in my brain turn, grinding against the impossibility of this reality I've stepped into. Maybe this is a simulation? Could this all be a dream? I pinch myself until it stings, but nothing happens. Just a raw, aching feeling of my bruised skin left behind.

Rationale, Gemma. Given everything I've seen today... tonight... whenever it is... being on another planet *could* make sense if I squint and don't think about it too hard. But it doesn't explain *how* I got here, or more importantly... *why?*

I massage my temples, working to clear my mind of my racing thoughts, but it's no use.

I need answers.

I climb the fence and charge directly towards the large red and white tents emerging in the distance. If it's truly a sanctuary, maybe they can help me find my way home from this nightmare.

Looking around, it appears the carnival is split down the middle. To the right, there's a Ferris wheel, a carousel, and other random tents and stands. Fliers stick to light poles above, advertising a myriad of wholesome side shows. A strong man, an acrobat, a young child on a tight-rope, horse riders, and even a pianist. My eyes linger on the musician's muscular frame, the way the corset cinches his back and waist, and the golden gleam of his eyes.

The carnival glows, lit by flickering lights that cast strange shadows against the dirt-covered ground. It's vacant, void of any of its daytime excitement, and my hair stands on end, made uncomfortable by the eerie emptiness.

To the left must be The Sinner's Circus.

It helps that there's a giant sign saying exactly that; it's fixed to a gate made of twisted iron, shaped like bones, separating the two spaces. Everything about the circus is darker and more sensual, with posters of lewd acts and a wall of hanging weaponry. There are no kiddie rides, and the closer I get to the fence, the fainter the smell of popcorn is.

Here, it smells like sex and decay—not rot, no, but like old costumes and building rubble. Bloodred lanterns flicker across the field, casting long, distorted shadows across the cobblestone ground. Although only a metal fence separates the carnival from where I just came from, this place is nothing like that roaring cityscape of innocent entertainment.

The Sinner's Circus is a relic from the past.

Squeezing myself through a gap between the bars, I'm grateful the fence is more decorative than protective.

I hope someone here will have a definitive answer for me about who I am and how I got here.

Faint strings play in the background. The melody is warm and low, resonating through the still, cold air. *A cello?*

I think I know how to play. The skill feels far out of reach—coming from the deepest caverns of my mind—but my fingers can feel the strings against the fretboard. They know the shape they need to make to hold a bow. It's distant, yet familiar. Am I a musician who lost their soul in a bet?

A massive sign sparkles outside the sprawling tent.

Come one, come all, if you dare, a world of wonder waits in there.

Heed this warning, loud and clear, for the acts you'll see may strike some fear.

Nudity, erotics, violence, and more. If this disturbs you, see the door.

Blood and guts may even spill, but join the crowd, enjoy our skill.

The night is young, and you're a winner. Enter the tent, become a sinner.

Wonderful. I don't need a sex show, I need a sanctuary. A few hundred feet away, I spot a grouping of smaller tents, and I head in that direction.

Nobody is out and about—the lanterns hanging outside each tent are extinguished—and as I cross towards the largest structure, a feeling gathers at the base of my neck. Fear takes hold, choking me, while goosebumps prickle across my skin.

A faint clicking noise echoes from within an open tent.

Come on, Gemma. You can do this.

Finding whatever mental strength I've got, I peer inside. It's mostly empty, but there's a shiny, gleaming piece of metal, and a cambion sharpening a blade. A dagger.

He's handsome—his body built of sculpted muscle, white hair shining in the dim lights of the tent. The cambion looks up at me, and his eyes instantly darken. Every hair on my arms is standing up, and I fight to catch my breath as he lunges towards me.

On instinct, my legs start moving before my mind has the time to absorb everything. I know I came here seeking sanctuary, but this seems to be anything but that. Adrenaline rushes through my bloodstream. Every part of my body is telling me I'm in danger, and I fucking listen. I don't know much about myself, but I do recognize this instinctive feeling churning in my gut—I don't want to die. I want to live, if even just to learn and understand the missing pieces of myself.

If I die here, I wouldn't even be a big-time news headline. I'm a stranger. I'd be a picture on the back of a milk carton that reads *twenty-four-year-old Gemma Marino: MISSING*.

I don't even think I like milk.

Propelling past the tents and back beyond the iron gate to the less whimsical part of the carnival, I run to find a place to hide while I come up with a plan on how to escape, because I refuse to be tortured by a killer clown. I've seen that old horror movie Terrifier—I will not go out like this.

Oh my goodness, a memory.

My mind flashes to sitting on a big leather chair with an elderly man, watching horror movies as an older woman bakes us macaroni and cheese. My grandparents, maybe? I'm not sure, but I can remember the taste of the cheese as it hit my tongue—the gooey warmth and the delicious flavors—and for now, that'll have to be enough.

Hauling myself onto the carousel, I shift past horses and crawl into a chariot adorned with little cherubs. I duck inside, peeking up only to look for my killer.

There are many ways this could go. I could run straight toward the fences, but I'm not sure if I'm a fast runner, and if the person trying to kill me has a better cardio game than me, I might be screwed. I need to keep hiding until I'm close enough to the back fence that I can clear it.

A large building with a wooden clown face on the door sits a few hundred steps ahead of me, and I see a route that might work if I weave through the stands.

Go, Gemma, I urge myself, working up the courage to run for it.

Jumping up, I dart for the building.

"If I catch you, I will kill you," a deep, masculine voice shouts my way. Its accent sounds almost English, which is odd, but I don't have time to think about anything other than running for my life right now.

Shadows trail behind me, but I don't dare look back. I keep running until I touch the door, and I shove it open before I'm surrounded by icy darkness.

I slam into something cold and hard. *Why can't I—oh great, it's a maze.* Running my fingers along the wall, I find a seam and continue my way through.

Flick.

There's a young woman, and I almost punch her before realizing she's standing still. She's pale with long, wavy brown hair.

Her eyes are big as she stares back at me, clearly frightened. I move, instinctively reaching for her, when I realize...

It's me.

The lights flood my vision and I blink, realizing I'm in a house of mirrors. Golden eyes lock with mine, and the sexy cambion smirks at me in the reflection. *Is that the guy from the poster?*

I can't tell how far away he is, but I continue past the warped mirrors, a reflection staring back at me a thousand-fold. *My* reflection. Those are *my* jeans, *my* streaky eyeliner, and *my* zip-up jacket sliding down my shoulders. I look like someone who is about to die in half a second if she doesn't get her shit together.

My heart pounds in my chest, crawling up my throat as the cambion draws nearer, the glass walls closing in. I'm not sure if I've ever been in a house of mirrors, a fun house, whatever the fuck this place is called, but it's not exactly my vision of *fun*. Fear glistens in my big brown eyes, but I tamp it down. I can be scared and confused later when I'm not running for my life.

There's a metal bar halfway down the wall, and I push it, the darkness of night greeting me like an old friend as I escape the building and haul ass towards the fence.

It can't be more than a hundred feet away.

Fifty feet.

Twenty-five.

Ten.

I climb, my boots pushing against the chain link as my fingers fit in each opening until I reach the top. I jump down, but my body won't budge, my clothes snagging on an isolated wire in the fence.

Turning, I see him reaching for me. I unzip my jacket, take in a deep breath, and free myself from the fence before my feet hit the ground. Before I even have the chance to look back one last time to see if the golden-eyed hunter is still tracking me, I'm in a new part of this sprawling city. The circus tents are out of sight, blocked by the skyscrapers and monorails that take their place.

Although it's only a few streets down, everything looks different here—shiny, modern, and bureaucratic.

Fuck me. This place really is hell.

Coming across a bench outside a restaurant, I curl my body onto it, resting my eyes for just a moment. I'm not sure exactly who I am or how I got here, but one thing's for sure: I have to find a way home.

Symphony No. 2

Gemma

"Hello human, could you loiter somewhere else? I'm about to open up shop, and I don't have time to make sure you don't get robbed while you're sleeping," a voice says from behind me.

Sitting up, I open my eyes and stretch, turning to see a petite cambion jangling a set of keys in front of the building. To my surprise, there's a sign that reads *Haeresis Bakery*.

"That sign is in English," I say, stating the obvious.

She furrows her brows. "English and Latin."

Why would the people of Hel speak English or Latin? I know I'm not on Earth anymore. I can feel it in my bones, but I ask all the same. Just to make sure. "Can you tell me if this is Earth or not?"

"No," she replies.

"Why not?"

She shakes her head. "No, it's not Earth. You're on Hel. Here, you might as well come in."

I follow her inside the shop, which is much warmer than it is outside. It doesn't look much different from the bakeries you'd see on Earth.

"Why would any of you speak English?"

She shrugs, but doesn't dismiss my *probably stupid* question. "The most common languages on Hel are English, Latin, Ombrano, and Vietnamese. But there are other languages here, too. Earthly ones you'd recognize, and ones from other planets as well."

"That's convenient."

"More of a coincidence, I'm afraid. Parts of Europe and Asia made it onto our planet during The Convergence. It's basic history." I can't tell if her tone is more *this chick is stupid* or *aw, this poor pathetic girl.*

She pulls out a metal container from a drawer and places it on the table, pouring some ingredients into the openings. It's different from any of the baking tools I'm used to, but it looks helpful. This entire bakery looks like a weird, otherworldly version of the bakeries on Earth. Metal lines each cabinet, and all their containers take unique shapes. They remind me of beakers from old cartoons of science experiments. Some are full of powders, others liquids. The smell of freshly baked goods, however, is completely the same. "So you're a... human?" she asks.

"As far as I know," I say. "Though I don't know much of anything."

She squints at me before opening a door and grabbing what looks like dough. "Did you hit your head or something?"

"Or something," I say, scratching the back of my neck.

"You should be more careful, then. If you aren't a part of our society, you won't have anyone to protect you," she warns, and I recognize her accent as faintly French. "And that... well, that can land you in big trouble."

I wish I could remember more from my history or solar geography classes. This whole amnesia situation is a real kick in the ass, but at least I remember something about school, I guess.

"What do you recommend I do?"

Her fingers press into the dough as I hover in front of the counter.

"You should go home. Go to the Earth Embassy and see what

they say. But please, I have children to feed; I cannot help you."
There are dark circles under her eyes, and it's clear she's a hard-
working woman. I don't blame her for not wanting to help.

"Understood."

She nods. "It's the tall building a few blocks away."

I give a small smile. "Thank you."

Exiting the bakery, I take a deep breath.

Cambions buzz about, walking up and down the street with
purpose, reminding me of big cities on Earth. There are casually
dressed beings, sure, but lots of suits. Fancy suits, colorful suits,
even weirdly historical suits. Styles I've never seen before, too.

The air is cold. Not biting, not frigid, but simply cold. I long
for a nice, warm sweatshirt. Too bad I lost my jacket at that stupid
circus.

Earth's embassy is... strange. The architectural design of the
building itself is simple—it honestly just looks like an office
building—but the ornamentation is unique. There are statues out
front depicting famous buildings from Earth's past. Some that
still stand, like The Colosseum, and others that don't, like The
White House.

I try to conjure up more memories. My parents, if I have any
siblings, my favorite type of pasta, but everything else in my mind
goes fuzzy.

*Why can I remember random historical buildings, but not my
own middle name? Or who my parents were? Was I fucking cursed?*

Walking up the steps to the building, there are no handles on
the doors, just panels of glass and a small, silver button. Hesi-
tantly, I press it.

"Are you a citizen of Earth?" a shrill, feminine voice asks
through a hidden speaker.

"Yes." That's maybe the only thing I'm certain of.

"You may proceed."

The glass doors slide open, revealing a large, well-lit room.
The Earth flag—a blue flag with seven white loops overlapping in
circles to form a flower—hangs from a pole leaning against the

wall. An ornate gold picture frame hangs nearby, containing hundreds of miniature flags, likely representing the flags of past countries. A second frame is simple and black, containing a treaty between the leaders of Earth and the King of Hel.

Earth's had a lot of leaders. One per each continent, plus all the smaller islands. It's one of the few things I can still recall from school. Hel seems to only have one leader, at least on the surface. Maybe they have mayors or governors. Or Prime Ministers.

Walking up to the desk, I stare into a feminine cambion's golden eyes. Her hair is tightly pulled back into a high ponytail. She looks serious and sleek, the way her nails tap against the counter.

"Can I help you?"

"Yes. Two things." I pause, but she gestures for me to continue. "First, I'd like to report an attempted murder."

"Attempted murder?"

I shrug. "It would be better classified as a physical assault, but he did *say* he was going to kill me. Or maybe it's better labeled as a threat?"

"Were you holding a small child or caring for the elderly?"

I squint my eyes. "No?"

"What were you doing that caused him to want to murder you?" Her tone is sharp and berating. Cambion are the half-human, half-demon species. She seems to be leaning into her demonic roots.

"Does it matter?" Jeez. *Is this the murder equivalent to asking me what I was wearing?*

"If you were inflicting harm upon him, stealing from him, or trespassing on his property, it was perfectly legal for him to attack you," she explains.

I shake my head, unable to fully comprehend her words. "*Murder* is legal here? Or do you mean it was legal for him to defend himself?"

"Was he defending himself?" she asks.

"No," I say, a bit exasperated. "It was unprovoked."

"Still legal," she replies, her tone bored.

"Murder?!"

"Welcome to Hel," the woman—no, the *demon*—at the front desk says, adjusting her scarlet lapel. "Here, your earthly morals no longer apply."

The baker wasn't lying, this place really is Hel. I'll be damned. "You're serious? He can just play around with a knife and do whatever he wants?"

"Yes. We've established that the laws here are different. What was the second thing you needed assistance with?"

I take a deep breath, not allowing this revelation to shake me. "I'd like to go home, please."

She purses her lips. "Okay?"

"I don't have any money here," I say. I don't mention that I don't know if I have any money at home, or where home really is. I just know I belong on Earth, and once I'm back, I'll find my way to Sunspell City. All my answers should be there somewhere.

"Tickets to Earth are one hundred thousand crown. The spacecraft, which is primarily for trading supplies and delivering mail, comes once a year."

"When's the next shipment?" I ask, hopeful it's in a few weeks... or months. I give her a small smile, in case it helps.

"It just left yesterday, so, one year."

My smile falters just a little. "I'm not lucky enough for a year on Hel to only be thirty days, am I?"

"Thirty? Try three hundred," she replies.

Well, at least it's less than Earth years.

"And seventy five," she gets out, her voice even slower than before. "And our days are slightly longer."

I have to live here for *over* an entire year. Shit. "Can someone on Earth pay for my ticket?" It's not like I have anyone who could help me, but I ask anyway. Just in case I remember something, or someone.

She shakes her head. "I'm afraid not. And besides, the ticket is equivalent to one hundred thousand dabloons. Most people on Earth don't have that much money saved."

Oh great, so I'm fucked then. "What do I need to do? I mean, realistically."

"Hel is very different from Earth. While you gasp at our lack of laws, you'll find that the benefits outweigh any cons. An apartment and a card for basic foods will be provided to you. Water, electricity, and laundry are all included. If you'd like non-necessities like internet, entertainment, or a flight out of Hel, you'll have to get a job."

"That is kind of you all." It could definitely be worse.

"Name, age, and species?"

I almost smile. "Gemma Marino. I think I'm like... twenty-five. Human."

"You think?" Slowly, she crosses her arms.

"Yes, that sounds about right."

"And to confirm, that is in human years?"

I nod, exasperated. "Yes." Wait—how old am I here?

"Excellent. Here are your key fob, food card, and law book." The booklet she hands me is solidly three pages, which is wild if you think about how the Multi-Continental Earthly Peace Constitution is like... four-hundred-plus pages.

Tucking the key fob and food card into my back pocket, I bow my head, unsure of how to pay my respects. "Thank you." Turning, I make my way towards the door.

"Ms. Marino," the cambion says.

"Yes?"

"You'll need your apartment number and a map. Here, I've circled it for you as well as the tram you should take to get there. It's the second stop in the residential district. Your place is #67."

I'm such a dumbass, I almost left without this pertinent info. "I appreciate that. Thank you again."

She tucks a strand of black hair behind her ear. "No problem. Just doing my job." But her smile doesn't reach her eyes.

Does she dislike humans? I wonder why they chose her for the

Earth Embassy. She doesn't dress like someone from Earth, but that could be me just making assumptions. She does *sound* like people from the Americas and the Isles of Magia. If I meet her again, maybe I'll ask her.

Probably not.

Exiting the embassy, I make my way to my new home.

THE TRAM RIDE to the residential district was short and easy to navigate, and now I'm outside government housing... which is surprisingly nice. On Earth, most areas with government housing are run down because the residents can't afford the upkeep, and the Earthly government officials don't care to help. They think providing an empty building is enough, even if that building is falling apart. It's fucked up.

This place is different. Colorful murals of cambion families and circus performers make me smile as I walk closer. The landscape is beautiful, lush green with small flowers I don't recognize. There are silver stones trailing through the grass up to the doorway, each one decorated with little designs that look like they were drawn by children. It feels utopic to be here after how confusing and terrifying the last day has been.

I think I'll like it here.

Climbing up the stairs to the third floor, I make it to apartment number 67. I unlock the door in anticipation of an empty apartment, but there actually is furniture and even appliances. Not a lot, but enough to comfortably get by. There's a small loveseat, a mattress on the floor, and what looks like a refrigerator and microwave.

There's no projector or flat screen TV, no family photos, and no friendly pet to greet me... but this is a proper home. It's livable; I could even get used to it. At least for the year.

But ultimately, I know I need to get back to Earth and figure out who I am. Better the devil you know than *the devil* you don't.

Symphony No. 3
Gemma

I knew it wouldn't exactly be *easy* to get a job on a different planet, but I didn't think it would be impossible. Seventeen businesses. Over the last three days, I have gone into seventeen different places looking for work, many of which had *Now Hiring* signs on their front doors.

The issue? Well, me. I have no references, no proof of any previous work, and little to no memory of my past. I might as well be a pile of meat with how useless I am to these people. Why hire a human with no skills who knows next to nothing about your planet, let alone the product you're selling or service you're providing? I truly get it, I do.

But as I exit the eighteenth building, I'm at a loss. Moving down the busy street full of cambion and demons walking and flying to their next destination, I stop outside a building, exhausted.

Except it's not just a building, but a massive, all-consuming skyscraper. It's tall, taller than anything else on this avenue, and I glance up at the sign written in small, gold text. *One Haeresis Plaza.*

What the fuck is this place? Clearly it's important. Maybe it'll be good for something, 'cause I'm desperate for… anything.

Pulling the door handle, I take a step inside. There's just a long, narrow hallway. Walking down the brightly lit space, I look around to find... nothing. It's oddly simple, reminding me of a dental office *minus the creepy pictures of perfect smiles that are usually everywhere.*

I turn a corner, and a very old cambion sits at her desk, looking down at something. Her sizable horns point upwards, much like a goat, and her red skin is creased and wrinkled.

"Haeresis Plaza, how can I help you?" she asks, the words coming out slow and raspy.

"My name is Gemma Marino and—"

"Do you have"—she starts, her mouth moving at an almost painfully slow pace—"an appointment with the devil?"

I freeze. "*The* devil? Like, the devil from Christian Mythology? Hell and everything?"

"The devil as in the King of Hel, yes," she says slowly, looking at me as if I have *dumbass* written on my forehead. I know CEOs love power dynamics, but having your employees call you *The Devil* and *King* is just fucking weird.

"Just confirming. Yes, I have an appointment," I lie. She could easily check the computer sitting in front of her, but she doesn't, and I get the sense she doesn't need to. There's a weird air about this place, like something is watching us.

"13th floor." Her hands shake as she points down the hall. "First door on your right."

My eyebrows scrunch together. This feels too easy, but after three days of no job offers, I decide *fuck it*. I'm going in. I head to the elevator and wait for the silver doors to open. We don't have 13th floors on Earth. I've always found it to be a silly superstition, but it's tradition. And apparently it happens to be one of the useless factoids about Earth my brain chose to remember.

I hit the up arrow, and the elevator immediately opens.

The door closes, and I press number 13, leaning against the wall and letting my muscles relax as I wait for the elevator to crawl its way up to the 13th floor. Soft, classical music plays over a speaker, and I'm almost certain it's Liszt. Dante Symphony, to be exact. As the brass comes in over the speaker, my body begs to move. To sway. I close my eyes and allow myself to wander through memories. Everything is blacked out or blurry, but as I search for something, I find myself in a dance class.

No, a recital. A recital with some brat who decided to dance to Dante Symphony when she *knew* I was dancing to Totentanz. I can remember the immature, childlike rage I felt. The shaking of my fists, and the movements of my little feet. But wait... this is *The Devil's* office.

Does *the devil* know this composition is about him? I mean, he has to, right? It's thousands of years old.

Maybe this is just another part of the bit.

The elevator door opens, and I step onto the marble floor, my boots squeaking as I follow the old woman's directions to the first door on my right. I knock, half expecting it to open on its own.

"Come in," says a charming, deep voice with an unrecognizable accent. Almost Italian or Spanish, but neither is quite right.

I sniff myself—not great, but not horrible—and open the door to find a very simple office, and my eyes probably pop out of my head with surprise at his droll response.

"Not what you expected? What's missing—walls seeping with human blood? Or perhaps a circle of flames? A chamber of ice shards?" he asks, and I still. "Please, take a seat."

Oh, wow. He's *really* committing to this. I honestly don't know what I expected, but I guess something more lavish. "You're *the devil*," I say. It's a statement, but it's also a question.

The devil sits at his desk, his feet propped up, and I lower myself onto the leather chair across from him. His skin is a deep red, much like the cambion I've met before, but something about him is different. It's his eyes—they're an almost icy-white blue. And the way he smells and moves, it's just not the same as everyone else here. His magic smells... stronger. I think he's a full-blooded demon, like the ones we learned about in history class.

He's wearing a sharply tailored suit with an M embroidered onto the lapel. And ironically enough—he is *hot*.

"You're in here and you don't know that?"

I shrug. "If I'm being honest, I don't know much about anything. I seem to have lost my memories."

"I was wondering who would have the gall to step into my office unannounced like this. I'm surprised Baph let you in, but I'm sure she noticed me watching. It figures it is someone unaware of my power."

I knew it. I knew someone was watching us. "Baph?"

"Baphomet, my receptionist."

"Oh. I told her I had an appointment," I admit. "This is kind of a last ditch effort on my part."

"Why would you do something so reckless? What if I stuck you in a dungeon for eternity for this?" he asks.

"First off, I won't live an eternity, and second, I highly doubt if murder is legal, lying will land me in a dungeon," I say, shocked at how cavalier I'm being, but I figure, what is there to lose? Worst-case scenario is probably what, he kicks me out? Best-case scenario, he sends me back home or at the very least gives me a job. Heck, maybe he makes me his queen, like in those old romance books.

"How do you know I'm not an evil dictator?"

There's a quiet yip from under his desk, and the devil puts his feet on the ground, reaching down and retrieving a fluffy, tan creature.

Specifically, a corgi.

"I don't," I confess, trying not to laugh at the juxtaposition of his question with the adorable dog on his lap. "But you give more businessman or governor vibes to me. What—or should I ask *who* exactly, are you?"

He smiles, seemingly entertained by my idiocy. "I'm a demon, but more specifically, I'm Luc Morningstar, the King of Hel."

My mouth gapes open. I thought I was fucking with a CEO, not a supreme leader. A creature of legends, this man sits before me as if he might've had Cheerios for breakfast. "Lucifer Morningstar?"

"No, no. That was my grandfather. I'm simply Luc," he says.

I squint. "Loose?"

"L-U-C, Luc."

"That's Luke," I say, trying not to laugh.

"I can assure you it's Luc," he says, and I fight the smile that threatens to spread across my face.

"So. Your grandfather could shapeshift into a snake and is a fallen angel?" I ask.

"No and yes. Sort of," he says, as if that's not the wildest thing I've ever heard. I amuse him, and I'm not sure if that thrills or terrifies me. "My grandfather Lucifer was a defector from the League of Seraphim. He took power from Deus, Hel's first devil. Lucifer established a monarchy to replace the oligarchy that had developed. When he grew too old, he let my mother, Lucile, rule until I was born, and now I am the devil."

"Did you guys mean to base all your names on Christian lore?" It was probably bold and irresponsible of me to continue speaking like this, but the look in his eyes tells me he doesn't mind, which is all the fuel I need. *I guess I'm impulsive. Or suicidal. Or idiotic. Who knows? Definitely not me.*

"Oh sweet child," he chuckles. "You think we named ourselves after some religious figures from Earth? We are the things of legend your people were so obsessed with."

Saying my mind is blown would be an understatement. This should be a catastrophic revelation, but I guess there are some perks to only having a tenth of your memory intact. I'm uniquely interested in learning more about the other things we have wrong. And what other myths are real? "So you know the song playing in the elevator is Dante Symphony?"

"Indeed," Luc smiles from ear to ear. "You're the first to recognize it. Inspired by my grandfather, of course. I think it's ironic."

I let out a little giggle. I genuinely like his sense of humor. "It is."

"So, what are you here for? I'm assuming it's not to ask for my easily searchable origin story."

"I need a job." I need a lobotomy, but a job will do.

"Have you applied for one?"

I squint my eyes. "I know I'm a human, but I'm not stupid. This is my eighteenth attempt this week, nobody wants me. You're the ruler, I'd like to send in my formal complaint. I don't know... isn't this species-based discrimination or something?"

"We don't have laws against that."

"What?"

"We don't have many laws at all, human."

"Gemma," I say, appalled. "Gemma Marino. And that's severely fucked up." Isn't the point of a government to create and uphold laws? Or at the very least, protect its citizens? I might be stupid. Crazy, even, to be talking like this to a planetary leader, but even I know that much.

"I don't disagree, but I cannot change the laws."

I cock my head and cross my arms, unsure of what to make of this. "You're the devil and you can't change the law?"

"I don't expect you to understand the intricacies of our governmental system, Ms. Marino."

"Whatever. Can you give me a job?"

He laughs, and I almost think he's enjoying how frank I'm being. "What was your line of work while living on Earth?"

"I'm not sure. Like I said, I lost my memory. I have no idea the kind of person that I was."

Luc gives me a puzzled look, like I am the strange one out of the two of us. "What do you remember?"

"I remember dancing."

"Were you any good?"

"I'm not sure."

"For your sake, I hope you were. I don't have any positions

open here, but I have something else in mind. Give me a moment to make a call," he says and pulls a landline off the wall.

I'd heard of landlines. They were something people used before The Convergence and magic and monsters roamed the Earth, but I would think the people of Hel would be more advanced by now.

Noticing my stare, Luc flicks his wrist, shooing me out of his office.

And with that, I step out and pace the hall. I can hear the hushed sounds of a conversation, but it doesn't sound like English. It doesn't sound like Vietnamese either.

A few minutes must have gone by, but I don't have a watch to check as the door swings open and Luc gestures for me to come back in. Except, he's still in his chair, his expression sterner than before. *How the fuck did he open the door? Is he a charms mage?*

I don't recall the complexities of magic, nor does it seem like I can wield it, but I do possess enough knowledge to know there's different types of magic. Or at least there was on Earth. I wonder if magic is the same here, or if the people of Hel use it differently?

Luc's sharp tone snaps me out of my train of thought. "You're being given an audition for a position as a dancer. There might be other tasks assigned to you, but your main job, should they accept you, will be to dance. No harm will come to you from the other carnies while you are assigned there. If you fail to perform your duties, or bring harm to anyone else in the carnival, the protections granted by me will cease and it's likely you'll be eliminated. Do I make myself clear?"

Gone is the man I was laughing with about human music, and now all I see is the sharp leader of this planet. I'm making a deal with the devil.

"Yes," I say and swallow. "Wait—carnival?"

"Hel's Carnival. That's where you'll be headed."

Back to the Sanctuary of the Strange.

Oh, I'm fucked.

Symphony No. 4

Draven

I might be the only being outside of the Morningstar family who understands Luc, yet with every step he takes lately, I find myself more and more uneasy.

A human.

He says he's sending us a human and there's a decent chance it's the one who broke into the carnival the other night. Humans are a rarity on Hel, and based on his descriptions, I highly doubt there are two *perky brunettes* that just happened upon Haeresis.

It was a terrible idea. Humans have no place here. Not even pretty ones.

I tried explaining to Raph just how bad of an idea this is, but his hands are tied. Raph may be our ringleader and governor, but Luc is still king.

Fingers crossed this silly human is a terrible performer, so I can dispose of her before she becomes an issue.

Exiting Raph's quarters, I head towards the hall so I can greet our guest alongside the others.

The hall is a fairly large tent, though not as large as our big top, situated in the center of camp, which is the fond little term we call our sleeping quarters. It's where we congregate for meetings, meals, and plan aspects of our show, and it is also home to me.

Long draping curtains and a metal structure hold up the place. Wood panels create the floor where we watched Po take her first steps. It smells of sweat and hard work, of leather and spray paint. Yet there's an unfamiliar quality to the air, and some part of me thinks it's my senses telling me there's an intruder.

The carnival has always been a sanctuary, a place where weirdos can live and grow with other misfits, but it is a close-knit group. We never hold auditions. Raph has never even mentioned wanting to open up to more people, but with the way things are going with The Legion, I fear we're close to things changing, and this is just the first step of many.

Still, I cannot comprehend his choosing a human of all species. But it would make for quite the spectacle, I'll give him that.

I give Robyn a look as if to ask *is Raph serious,* but she nods sagely. Robyn is one of the only beings who has been a part of the carnival longer than I, and she's like a second mother. Raph, Luc, Robyn, and Quinn were the village that raised my damaged teenage self. They made sure I maintained some of whatever goodness was left inside me, but some of them also cultivated the monster that I have become. None of them made me a killer—that was set in stone before we ever met—but Luc and Raph did nothing to quell the rage inside me. No, instead, they encouraged it. Directed it towards those they thought deserved a quick, painful death.

It was I, however, who perfected it. Nobody else gets to take credit for that. My strength, my wit, it's mine.

"Ms. Marino should be here any moment for her audition," Raph states as he enters, already wearing his attire for tonight's show. He adjusts the glitzy buttons of his vibrant red coat before looking directly at me. "You, Robyn, and myself will vote on her admittance or rejection."

I grind my teeth, my jaw tightening, but give a curt nod. He knows I don't like this, and I know we don't have much of a choice, so here we are.

"This is exciting," Robyn says, trying to ease the tension brewing in the air. "A real life human."

"Will the human be nice?" Po asks, her big eyes staring up at us.

Po is seven, and doesn't understand that this human is a stranger. That she could be dangerous. She could be working with The Legion, plotting against our leaders, which would put us all at risk.

Luc and Raph are not without flaws, but the alternative is terrifying. Luc's other siblings could take over Haeresis—or worse, Hel in its entirety—and that's something I cannot allow.

"I don't know, but we won't be here to watch, just in case," Quinn says, gesturing for Una and Po to follow. Po heaves a frustrated sigh before nodding her agreement. The two girls tag behind their parent, Po grabbing onto Una's hand, much to her teenage dismay.

"Well, *I'm* looking forward to the show," Reina says from her chair, grinning with fangs on full display.

The twins move close to me and place their hands on my shoulders. "We are going to get ready for tonight," Leo says.

"But we wish you luck," Lyle joins in, and they exit out of the hall.

Taryn and Aida are nowhere to be found, so that just leaves the eight of us. Lilian is sitting in Baelor's lap, the two giggling into each other's necks, and I watch Reina's eye roll with a smirk.

I'm happy for them, truly I am, but I don't think Reina or I will ever like Baelor. When the girls—my chosen sisters—joined the carnival, we became a pack. Reina, Absinthe, Lilian, and Taryn, in that order. We were essentially Robyn and Quinn's kids. Baelor disrupted that. He was always fixated on Lilian, always gaining her attention, but he wasn't always faithful.

If he weren't who she chose to spend her life with, I'd have probably put him in the ground by now, but as it stands, I am playing nice. Kindness toward him is just one of the many masks I wear.

As if feeling our disdain, Baelor pushes Lilian off him and stands. "We're awfully busy, so we'll have to miss this one. Let us know how it goes, though," Baelor says with a cocky smile as he takes his wife by the hand and leads her out.

Six. That just leaves the six of us.

Absinthe stands up from the dining table and skips towards me.

"Not you, too," I say.

"No, silly, I'm one. Number one." Both corners of her mouth turn up, her light gold eyes wide and sparkling with amusement.

"Why is everyone leaving?"

"They don't want to see a potential bloodbath. It kind of kills the vibe," she explains and boops me on the nose.

I take a seat next to Robyn, and Raph saunters towards the entrance of the tent. "I believe our guest has arrived," he says, giving me a chafing look.

The human walks in wearing the same clothes from the night we met, but they're more worn down now. Purple mars her dark brown eyes, and her skin is pale and ghostly. Even though she's clearly exhausted, she is still quite attractive. Well, I don't know human beauty standards, but to me, she is.

Attractive or not, she's still an unwanted pest.

"Raph Morningstar. I'm the ringleader. It's a pleasure to meet you. Please, come stand in front of the table. Let's get a good look at you," Raph says, gesturing for her to follow. He takes a seat by my side, giving me a single pat on the leg. "Tell us about yourself."

She breathes deeply and schools her features, losing any sign of fear or vulnerability. It's fascinating. "My name is Gemma Marino. I am a human from the planet Earth, and I'm here to audition as a dancer."

"Great! What kind of dancing do you do?" Robyn asks. "Our chimera, Reina, dances as well as plays the cello."

The human seems to falter for a second, as though she isn't

sure, before she reinforces her smile. "I've done a lot of styles. Lyrical, mostly, though."

"Burlesque?" Raph asks with a grin.

"I'm not sure," she answers plainly.

"Well, that's alright. Reina, could you provide Ms. Marino some music?" he asks, then turns back to the human. "I hope you like the cello."

"I do. I played a bit when I was young," she says, removing her boots.

Reina crosses over towards where her cello rests on its stand and pulls out its endpin before tightening her bow. There's a hushed silence before the music starts, and the human moves.

Her limbs are lean and graceful, her body delicate as she glides across the floor. Only a few of the tents have wooden floorboards covering the dirt, and the hall happens to be one of them.

A part of me hoped she'd be bad. It would make it easier for me. But as she moves, her hips rhythmically swaying, I can do nothing except watch. Her hands extend, fingers tracing the air as if she's grabbing the notes while the cello crescendos into a more lively allegro movement.

The human's beauty is a palpable force, her body and the music articulating emotions that words often fail to convey, and for a moment, I let myself enjoy it.

Reina stops playing, her bow coming off the strings, and everyone claps. Rowan, Robyn, everyone. Absinthe even lets out a high-pitched cheer, but I don't move. My arms remain fixed in place across my chest.

"She's amazing," Absinthe says from the edge of her seat. "Really, truly good."

"Let us take it to a vote, then." Raph sounds serious, but there's a joyful gleam in his eyes. "I say yes. She's in."

"I completely agree," Robyn nods, looking at the human and smiling.

Everyone turns to me, but there's no point. We have always done things by majority rule. Raph has never used his veto power over Robyn, Quinn, or me, but ultimately he and Luc have the final say. So what does it matter how I'd vote now? She's in. She's one of us.

I just hope she's too stupid to realize what she saw the other night and put the pieces together. With tensions growing on Haeresis, I cannot have her fucking up our operation. I can already feel my head start to pound.

"Congratulations, you're officially a carny," I say, the words bitter on my tongue.

Symphony No. 5
Gemma

I got the job. I actually got the job.

I'm pretty sure Draven 'The Scorpion' wants to kill me, but at least I've made another step toward getting home and regaining my memories. With the exception of Raph, I only know the other carnies by the names on their posters. So far, everyone has been polite as they congratulate me on my acceptance.

"I know it's a lot, but why don't we all introduce ourselves," a feminine, English-sounding voice offers. She's one of the three who had the power to accept me, and I'm grateful for her approval. "I'm Robyn."

Robyn has ram-like horns and mauve-colored skin. She's smiling at me, and her kindness reaches her eyes, crinkling them at the corners. "This is my partner Rowan. Our other partner, Quinn, is with the children."

Rowan stands, walking over to greet me, and he might be the most massive being I've ever met, with broad, muscular shoulders, and a familiar set of tusks.

"Wait—are you an orc?" I ask, perplexed.

He nods. "I'm orc and half-demon."

"I didn't realize other species lived here. I thought it was just cambion and demons," I say.

"Many of us are something other than demon or half-demon," Robyn explains. "Hybrids, if you will. I am part satyr. You will meet a serpentine and a mermaid as well."

Wow. This place is so different from what I can remember of Earth, and yet so similar. The Convergence must've caused a lot of planets to have similar developments. We call half-demons cambion, but the beings of Hel seem to have developed different terms. It makes sense, but it's still jarring to hear aloud.

A young, feminine clown jumps out of her chair, her movements much like a marionette as she rushes over to me and grabs my hands. "I'm Absinthe," she says. It's hard to tell the color of her skin under the white face paint, but I think she's pink. "You look like a human."

"You look like a clown," I say.

"I am a clown," she nods, her face beaming with joy.

I let out a soft laugh, barely more than a sigh. "I am a human."

Her brows furrow. "You appear much less delighted with your humanness than I am with my clownness."

"I guess you're right. I am neither happy nor sad about being human, it is just what I am." And it's true. Happiness, sadness, none of them are ample descriptions of how I feel. Lost, confused, and determined are much more accurate. Everything I am doing is just a way to get home—to regain my sense of self.

"If it's any consolation, most of us are at least a quarter human," a sultry voice cuts in from back at the table. Absinthe pulls me towards her, excited to show me off. It's the cellist.

This is the first being I've seen with human-like skin since leaving Earth. Humans, elves, and some of the other species on Earth come in shades of cream, beige, tan, and brown. Cambions and demons are all red or pink. But like Robyn said, many of these carnies are hybrids—a combination of three or more different species.

"I'm Reina," says the tan, feminine being. She's one of the only beings here who sounds like where I'm from. "I'm who they call The Chimera."

"That is... something," I reply, not sure of an appropriate response. She's both striking and terrifying.

"I am human, demon, and vampire."

"Vampire? What is this place?" I ask. I don't mean to say it out loud, but I'm starting to feel like I'm losing my mind at all the revelations.

"The carnival is an important part of Haeresis society," Raph begins to explain, his fingers pulling the curly edges of his mustache.

"Due to the nature of what we do, we're a sanctuary for the *unique and strange.* Cambion with genetic differences, or individuals who don't exactly fit in with any species, come here to find a family. Some of us just have quirky personalities. Regardless, we're a community. Nobody here is strange, because we are all different," Robyn adds, her tone light.

"This is also how we pay for everyone's basic necessities," Rowan says. "That is the carnival's purpose. We perform for some to provide for the many."

I stare at all of them, overwhelmed and intrigued with how open they're being. "Why are you guys being so... kind and transparent with me?"

"Because you're one of us now," Raph replies, as if the answer was obvious. "That is what the carnival has always been about. A sanctuary for the strange."

From the corner of my eye, I see a cambion shift in his seat. I was wondering when he'd speak. "And because The King required we audition you."

"Oh?" I'm not sure why the devil would do such a thing for me, but I'm not going to look a gift horse in the mouth.

The cambion—my attempted murderer, the being who clearly didn't want me to join—stands and traipses towards me before reaching out a hand. Heat forms in my lower body as he approaches, something about him setting me on edge. "I don't believe we've met. I'm Draven Orzath, it's a pleasure." The charming smirk on his lips could end friendships and start wars. And frankly, I can't stand it.

I can't stand *him*.

"Alright, troupe. This was fun, but we've got to get ready for tonight. Reina, could you show Ms. Marino to your room?" Raph says, his voice so similar to his brother's, and Reina nods. "Draven, let's go." He starts to leave the room, but stops and turns to look at me. "Gemma—you're officially a carny."

I give a genuine smile and turn to Reina. I am truly, actually grateful they're accepting me. I'm not sure what I'd do otherwise, especially with my lack of memory, but something gnaws at me all the same.

Why doesn't Draven want the others to know we've met before? It's possible they wouldn't react well to his prior treatment of me. A group of people who claim to be so welcoming and open might not agree with threatening to kill the first human to step foot on their grounds.

But then again, if a person I didn't recognize broke into my home, I'd probably reach for a knife, too.

Reina takes me by the hand and drags me out of this larger tent to a series of smaller ones—ignoring them all until she brings me into hers. *Ours, I guess.* "I've got to get ready just in case, but luckily I shouldn't have to go on tonight, since it's my night off," she shares.

"What do you do?" I ask.

Although Reina's skin is similar to mine, she arguably looks the most different from anyone here. Her hair, which is up in a high ponytail, is long and straight, coming down nearly to her ass. Her eyes are red too, but her scleras are... well, black.

She looks more stereotypically demonic than any of the demons I've met so far. Her teeth, when she smiles, also showcase a sharp set of fangs, and I wonder where she gets her blood supply from. Maybe it's best I don't know.

"At The Sinner's Circus, or for the carnival?"

"Both? I guess. What's the difference?" I ask, sitting on the empty cot.

"This whole place"—she says, gesturing to the air around us —"is Hel's Carnival, but the daytime show is simply called the carnival. It's the big wheel, games, as well as food and sideshows. At night, however, things change. The Sinner's Circus is an adult show."

"So, what's your act? You play the cello?"

"During the day, I'm a cellist. Draven and I are a duet of sorts," she explains. "We also all take turns manning different games and booths. At night, I do erotic Boleadoras."

That's an Earth-style of dance. "Were you born on Earth?"

"No, I was born on Ombra, but one of my grandparents was from Earth. My father was born here, though. He was a demon. What about you? What styles of dance do you do?"

"A few different types. I'm not really sure..." I say, trailing off. I try not to stare as Reina strips off her clothes to a see-through lace bodysuit. She's covered from head to toe, but somehow looks entirely too naked. My mind backtracks to what she said about duetting with Draven. "Are Draven and you... romantic partners as well?"

Reina sits at her vanity and gives me an incredulous look in the mirror before swiping on some eyeliner. "Absolutely not. Draven and I grew up together with Lilian and Absinthe. Taryn too, honestly, but she was a bit older than us and had more responsibilities."

"Is Taryn still alive?" I ask, thinking of all the tragedy that must happen on a planet where murder is legal.

"Yes," Reina answers with a laugh. "You haven't met the entire troupe, some of them were getting ready for the show. Taryn sometimes unwinds in her spring or one of her tanks."

Tank. She must be the mermaid, then. "How many others are there?"

"I think seven? Including Taryn. You should get to see everyone tonight. You're coming to the show, right?"

My eyebrows raise. "Am I?"

"You should come with me. We can sit in the stands instead of backstage," she says before standing to show off her outfit. "Grab yourself a coat, though."

Using Reina's makeup and closet, I doll myself up enough to feel comfortable attending The Sinner's Circus. There's a small part of me that's terrified to be the only human in a room full of demons and cambion, especially because I'm still learning the intricacies of society here, but Reina reassured me that no harm can come to the carnies while we're on the property, and I am a carny now.

"Here, you're going to need this," Reina says as she hands me a mask. It's shaped like a monarch butterfly, but black and red. She places a masquerade mask on herself as well, the style gothic and pretty, and we continue walking.

The Sinner's Circus is held inside a large big-top tent with a red and cream-colored canopy. Everyone in attendance seems to be donning their most sensual outfits. Leather, lace, and other suggestive clothing is everywhere I look. Many of the people here are wearing masks or other disguises, and I can't help but wonder why. In a society in which things like murder are legal, why do they feel the need to hide their identities and desires? The people of Hel strike me as anything but repressed.

Raph comes down to the front in a red coat and top hat, stepping up onto a podium and speaking into the microphone. His presence is both captivating and electrifying, and the crowd falls into a hush. "Demons, half-demons, felion, lupion, hybrids and humans alike, thank you for joining The Sinner's Circus—a night for the erotic and disturbed. Step right up! You're about to view a daring couple. Witness The Pretzel *bend* your beliefs of what is possible."

Reina's face lights up, and it's an expression I know all too well. Pride. My brain momentarily takes me to memories of riding bicycles, but it quickly reels back to the present, much to my dismay. Every time a new memory threatens to surface, part of my brain seems to lock it away, and I'm afraid I'll never find the key.

Lilian moves gracefully towards a small metal box and bends backwards onto it, making difficult shapes with her body in the center of the room. As we all stare, I realize her bodysuit is made of a mesh fabric, exposing her nipples and... everything else. She's gorgeous and curvier than the contortionists I've seen before, and like the rest of the audience, I find myself captivated by the way she moves.

Though her body bends, her wings are sprawled out behind her before she snaps one, folding it in on itself, and I cringe in horror.

Is she breaking her wings?

The audience cheers loudly, but I hold my breath as she commits to the first bend of the other wing and then continues on, making them smaller. Her wings fold in on themselves like a piece of paper. It looks incredibly painful, but her smile remains.

From the entryway in the back, I see the shadow of a figure holding a small, slender object peek out from behind the curtain, and I turn to Reina, whose cheerful expression drops.

"Be warned, tonight's next act is not for the faint of heart. This performance will carve its way into your heart. Give it up for The Clown," Raph announces.

Pushing open the curtain and crossing towards Lilian, Baelor bends to kiss her before he shifts over into the audience, climbing up the stands. She continues her contortion, bending in ways I've never seen before. It's captivating, and yet I find my eyes following Baelor instead, anxious to see what he has up his sleeve.

A young cambion woman holds out her arm, and he lightly trails his blade over it, making a razor-thin cut across her forearm. Blood trickles down, and he uses his finger to paint it across her face, making her into a clown of his own accord.

The audience oohs and aahs, but something churns in my gut as I watch him play with another woman's blood as he grinds his body against hers.

What is exciting about this? Or sexy? He seems to only bring pain, while remaining completely clean. I'm not here to knock anyone's interests, but this just doesn't do it for me. It makes the hairs on my neck stand at attention.

When he's finished, he returns to Lilian, and mocks as though he's going to slit her throat.

"Why do people enjoy that?" I let slip, and I almost cover my mouth when Reina laughs.

She shrugs. "Why do people enjoy anything? But no, I don't get it either. He's always given me the creeps."

Raph and two others I don't recognize begin moving set pieces around during what appears to be some sort of intermission, the audience whispering to one another.

"When did he join the troupe?" I ask.

"A couple years after I did. But he was a lot older, so it felt different. Draven, Lilian, and I were all teenagers, and Absinthe was just a kid," she explains. "Everyone else obviously accepts him, but to me, he's still an outsider."

"I'm an outsider," I point out, and the corners of her mouth tick up.

"Yeah, you definitely are, but I'm not afraid of you," she admits.

My eyebrows shoot up. "I'm not sure if I should be insulted or not."

"It's a good thing. I trust people based on vibes, and yours are excellent," she says, which might be the nicest thing anyone's ever said to me.

The lights flicker, signaling everyone to take their seats. Rowan comes out pushing a tank, taut biceps on display, while Raph jumps back onto the mic. "Welcome back, welcome all. This next act will surely leave you wet." Raph winks. "Let us take you beneath the waves, where The Siren will dance her sensual rhythms from the sea, before The Goliath brings you back to land, wheeling you towards ecstasy."

"That's Taryn," Reina says as my jaw drops at the being

before me. Taryn is a mermaid, with blue skin and large fin-like ears. Gills contour her cheeks, and her body is made of dreams.

Sensual music plays in the background, and the lights shift to shades of aqua and purple as Taryn takes off her clothes one article at a time.

I have to force my jaw to close, but I open it again. "She has perfect boobs."

"Don't feel bad. All the best boobs come from Fraus. Mine are fake, too. Taryn didn't have any, and mine were incredibly small, so we both went there together."

"Fraus?"

Reina gives me a look that screams *really, bitch* before schooling it back into a smile. "It's one of the continents on Hel. Man, we should really give you a map or something."

Rowan throws a metal ring into the air, and The Siren jumps, slipping her body through.

"I've got one of Hel's Carnival, but I'd appreciate a globe," I whisper.

"Every continent has their thing, their moneymaker to provide for the people. Fraus has a surgical hospital," Reina explains. "We have the carnival."

I nod. The Siren's dancing has turned into an all-out strip-tease, her breasts now on full display, and Rowan has stripped some, too. They're both incredibly attractive—everyone at the carnival is. I'm practically frothing at the mouth, but I try to tone it down.

He turns away from the crowd, unzipping his trousers, and The Siren tosses a ring of her own in the air. It lands and starts swinging back and forth, my brain slow to process that Rowan is flinging the ring with his dick.

"Holy shit," I say, astonished. "Doesn't that hurt?"

Reina shrugs, but the crowd watches, awestruck. All the eyes I can see are glued to the performance, though not all eyes are visible. Some faces are completely covered, and I wonder if they can even enjoy the show.

"Why do people here wear masks? Are they ashamed?" I whisper to Reina, my voice barely a whisper.

"You sure do ask a lot of questions. No, it's more complicated than that."

I sigh. "Explain it to me like I'm five?"

She smirks, her gaze dancing across the crowd. "The people here don't experience shame like your people do, but we do have a hierarchy. Demons are on top—they are the monarchs and the oligarchs. Then there's half-demons, which are the majority of the population. There's also felion and lupion, and then there's beings like you and me," she explains, and I look around at the assortment of horns and ears. "Outside of these walls, there are societal expectations of who you love, who you associate with, and they're all based on class and species. Here, you can just be free."

There's a beauty in this carnival I would've never expected. A sanctuary for the strange and the damned, indeed.

Rowan ends their act on something I've learned is called a Cyr wheel—a large, round metal apparatus that reminds me of a hula hoop. He's sprawled across it, his limbs spread out like the Vitruvian Man, and it's astonishing—the sheer strength and flexibility of his body. The Goliath.

Raph returns to the stage again as Rowan and Taryn take a bow, the crowd's applause a roar in my ears. "Tonight's finale will be from none other than The Scorpion himself, give it up for an act that's hard to swallow."

Draven steps out from behind the curtain, and a knot forms in my throat. His shirt is unbuttoned, and a purple sash crosses his body. He's carrying a long, slender sword, which he holds high up in the air before lowering it down into his mouth.

I watch the strong column of his throat, waiting for any sign that he's uncomfortable, but he's perfect as he takes the sword in its entirety. This is somehow the most erotic act I've seen all night, and my eyes remain fixed on him.

We're not too far from the center, and it's close enough for me to see the droplets of sweat beading down his neck and chest. I don't like that my mind flicks to visions of licking them off. Licking *him*.

Reina stares at me, and as if she can see my thirst, offers me a bottle of water. I take a sip, nodding my thanks.

He pulls the sword out and winks at a masculine looking cambion in the audience. "Just remember, I swallow."

And at that, I almost spit.

Symphony No. 6
Draven

Getting up from a night of restless sleep, I grab a pair of trousers and a tunic. I can't seem to shake the pesky human from my thoughts, and how, out of the entire crowd, my eyes couldn't help but be drawn to her in that butterfly mask.

I pull on my trousers, pissed at my own brain, and exit out of my tent and into the main part of camp.

Before I even enter, the smell of whatever breakfast Robyn and Quinn are cooking hits my nose and I inhale deeply. Something—or someone—tugs on my shirt. I look down to see a very excited Po clinging onto my leg.

"Uppies!" she says, and I laugh, scooping her up and throwing her over my shoulder. Una follows behind as we make our way into the hall.

Everything I do, every decision that I make, I do it for my family. My chosen family, and Phaelyn—my sister by blood.

Pale skin and long brown hair greet me with a rictus smile. I knew the human would be here. She's one of us, of course she's here, but my hairs still stand up at the sight of her in my space. It feels like an invasion. I put Po down next to Rowan and take my seat between Lilian and Reina, eagerly waiting for Raph to come give us an update.

From what I overheard of Raph and Luc's phone call yesterday, the human is here to work. If she doesn't work, she cannot stay.

A familiar tuft of dark hair comes into my line of sight as Raph walks in with some of the others, and Quinn passes out breakfast to everyone, filling our plates with meats, cheese, and bread. My stomach growls, and I take a bite of some fruit.

"Gemma will be joining one of the sideshows today," Raph states as he sits on one corner of the long wooden table, an empty plate before him.

I figured they would have her perform on her own, but perhaps someone wanted to dance with her. I take a sip of my coffee, allowing the hot liquid to burn my tongue, only a little. In some sick and twisted turn of fate, I've come to enjoy pain in small doses.

"She'll be dancing during Draven and Reina's performance."

I nearly choke.

"Pardon?" I ask, blindsided that Raph would stick this on me. I'm not scared of the human, but I don't trust her. I'd rather keep my distance.

"Yes, it was Reina's idea, actually," Raph explains. "Gemma's a talented dancer, and so we decided she will perform during your songs. We're finally going to get use out of the wing prop."

I sigh, understanding dawning on me. A few years ago, Absinthe began making wings for those who do not have any, including herself. My reaction was not what she anticipated. There were a lot of raised voices and hurt feelings, and she locked the wings away, never to be seen again.

We all feel guilty about it, but nobody fully *gets* it. The phantom pains Absinthe and I feel. I understand her longing for wings more than anyone, and yet I was the first to shut her down. Raph is just trying to make up for it.

Absinthe grabs the wings out of a bin and brings them to the human, who eagerly puts them on. Any negative remark I had is swallowed as I watch the absolute joy on Absinthe's face as she shows off her work.

"These are beautiful," the human says, slipping her arms into the loops and twirling the wings around.

"You look like a butterfly," Po says, placing her palms against her cheeks and giving us a wide smile.

"That is what we'll call you," Raph states, and everyone nods their approval. "The Butterfly."

Traitorous bastards. She's not a butterfly, she's an infestation. A *pest*. Maybe she's a butterfly after all, swarming me, ready to consume my rotting flesh after she kills me.

Breakfast continues as usual, though some of the troupe doesn't join us. Leo and Lyle are late risers, always sleeping in until the last moment. It strikes a chord of envy in me, to be so lacking in responsibilities. But they joined the carnival only a few years earlier, and I think their youth lends them to not taking things quite as seriously.

"I'm curious," Lilian says, and props her head up, her chin resting in her palms. "How'd you end up on Hel?"

It's a question I've wanted to ask plenty, but haven't gotten the opportunity to pursue yet. I considered calling Luc just to find out what he knew—or more importantly, what he didn't know.

"I don't actually know," the human answers, her shoulders rising as her palms face up. The wide-eyed look she gives everyone appears genuine, but I'm not convinced. She's an incredible dancer, who's to say she isn't an incredible actress, too?

"You really don't know?" Lilian asks. "Do you remember anything from before you wound up here?"

The human nods, her voice a little choked up. "Bits and pieces of memories. Mostly general stuff. I remember a lot about Earth, and super basic facts about myself, but nothing personal or recent, really."

"Oh, honey," Robyn walks over and rubs a hand down the human's back, gently comforting her. "That sounds awful."

"It's terrifying, but there's not really anything I can do. Things are slowly coming back to me, though. I remembered a song when I was in Luc's office. I remembered I could dance. I'm hopeful that between now and when I return home, I'll be normal again," she admits.

"I hope you are able to return to Earth," Aida says at once. Though she's been a part of the carnival for as long as I have, our serpentine rarely speaks unless she's telling your fortune. "It is my intention to return as well, for a visit... Perhaps we can go back together."

The human gives her a wistful smile. "I would like that."

"Let's place some bets," Absinthe shouts across the table. "I think Gemma was cursed!"

Reina shakes her head. "Has Earth's magic advanced more than ours? Maybe you drank a potion that sent you to Hel?"

"Earth's magic has *not* advanced more than ours. Don't they still use electricity?" Raph says, and I consider this for a moment.

I've never paid a ton of attention to the people of Earth, even though they're a part of my history, and I'm coming to regret that decision now, because I want to learn everything there is to learn about this human.

"Yes." She laughs. "We use electricity."

What was that human phrase my mother taught me as a child? Curiosity killed the cat, but the satisfaction brought it back.

THE CARNIVAL OPENS like any other day, with everyone heading towards their usual locations. Raph uses his magic to man the rides while the rest of us take turns between performing our sideshows and operating games and food stalls. Aida and Taryn are really the only ones who stay in one place the whole day, as they have lines that often stretch outside of the carnival grounds.

The smell of popcorn and candy floss fills my nostrils as I walk past Robyn and Una, who are manning one of the food stalls. I make my rounds, checking in on all of my favorite carnies before my one o'clock show.

Even more than the thrill of killing, I live for the thrill of performing, because only then do I feel completely in control. When my fingers grace the piano, I am the one orchestrating melodies. No object or obstacle can get in my way, not even the constraints of my own mind.

It took me a long time to get used to the idea of performing with someone else. When my little sister and I were very young, our parents used to make us perform together. Phaelyn on the violin, and I on the piano. The pressure got to be too much for Phaelyn, absorbing her whole. It broke my heart because, just like my father, I expected perfection. I was one of the people destroying her.

I thought I would do the same thing to Reina. I never wanted to feel that way again — that I could be anything like him. The idea chills me to my bones. But we trusted one another, and I realized I'm not him. And Reina, well, she's amazing. She actually makes me a better musician, constantly pushing me to the edges of my capabilities, forcing me to improve.

I'm afraid throwing the human into the mix will only mess up the balance.

Walking up to the sideshows, Reina greets me with a shit-eating grin.

"Hello there, sunshine," I say teasingly.

Reina's blood red hair is neatly tied up in a high ponytail, and it swings with her movements, back and forth like a metronome. "How're you feeling?" she asks, but I read between the lines.

"Like a human is about to ruin our show."

She crosses her arms. "Gemma can't ruin the music; if she doesn't dance well, she'll only embarrass herself."

"But?" I say, knowing damn well there's one on the way.

"*But* I'm confident she's going to do well. Or at least halfway decent," Reina says and picks up her cello case, unzipping it to retrieve her instrument.

I can play the piano. I might even be the best pianist on Haeresis, but Reina *is* the cello. When she plays, the skin of her body and the wood of her instrument fuse together as one, her hand moving as gracefully as a ballerina across the fingerboard, muscle memory finding each and every note with perfect precision. It's a kind of magic one can only aspire to have. Even more than the literal magic flowing inside me, it is a gift. And one hard-earned, at that.

"So where is our beautiful butterfly?" I ask as I prop open the lid of the piano and take a seat on the bench.

"I'm sure she's—" Reina can't even finish her sentence as Gemma strides towards us in full force, her wings shimmering even in the bright light of day, and I have to give Absinthe credit.

Those wings are bloody fucking brilliant. At night, they light up, but in the day, the sun's rays bounce off of the iridescent fabric, making beautiful spectacles of light around the wearer. Raph used tape to section off part of the floor beneath the platform, which is where the human stands, posed and ready for us to begin.

Reina nods, and I begin the piece, sound resonating from the piano alone. After eight measures, the cello joins in, and our butterfly starts her dance.

I can't watch her, at least not entirely, but I find my eyes wandering over to the human when she moves within my peripheral vision. Her body is fluid and strong, and for the first time in many years, I am somewhat distracted—enrapt in her beauty.

I close my eyes and let the music envelop me, the dynamics of this allegro movement animating more than just my hands. My fingers pound against the keys, my shoulders tightening and rising as I crescendo, then falling and relaxing as my body eases into the next movement. I try to stay focused, but my mind drifts, and I find myself envisioning what it's like to be in the audience.

To watch the cellist use her bow with swift, agile movements, her instrument purring beneath her touch. To hear the pianist, and to see how he plays with his entire body. To witness the dancer, and the allure of her choreography.

In my mind's eye, the human is not standing on the floor, moving the prop wings. No, she is soaring, allowing the fabric to propel her over the audience. She is a butterfly, freed from her gilded cage, and I realize I likely helped turn the key.

When we finish, the audience roars its applause, and Reina and I stand to take our bow. My gaze traverses over the human's sweat-slicked body, and my blood feels heated, my heart rate accelerating to an uncomfortable pace as the muscles in her arms flex with her curtsy.

Get your shit together, Draven. But as she turns back to me and winks, I know I'm a fucking goner.

Symphony No. 7

Draven

Everyone corrals around the dinner table, taking our seats as Raph reminds us of where we are in our rotation.

"Tonight we'll have acts from The Pretzel, The Scorpion, The Chimera, and The Phantom," he says, gesturing to himself. "I've got a real showstopper planned for the finale."

Gemma whispers something over to Reina, who seems pleased with this admission, and I want to ask what they're giggling about, but I refuse to come across as interested or prying. It might bother me that my family-by-choice is so willing to open their hearts to someone we all barely know, but I don't need them to be aware of that.

One of the twins enters the hall and hands something to Lilian, and I realize it's Leo from the tiny, almost nonexistent scar above his brow.

"I'm going to get the floor ready for Raph, but I will see you all tonight," he says, and I give a single wave.

"See you tonight, sexy," I say and wink. Leo and I are both shameless flirts.

I watch Gemma to gauge her reaction, but there is none. Her eyes stay fixed on Leo as he exits the room, but her face remains still, and she doesn't ask the other carnies about him.

Rowan serves us dinner, and Absinthe begins to ramble about her newest inventions. Gemma listens intently, engaging on occasion, but mostly leaves the talking to everyone else.

Fascinating. She seems confident, but cautious.

Lyle enters, sauntering over to an empty chair before taking a seat. He's so relaxed I think he's about to kick his feet up when Gemma's eyebrows scrunch together.

"Didn't you just say you had to prepare for something?" she asks, and Lyle shakes his head.

"No, I don't recall saying anything. I just got here."

Gemma goes to speak, but stops herself, nodding as if she just accepts what he's saying as truth. Does she not trust her own memory?

Leo returns from wherever he went, the smell of smoke lingering on his body, and he crawls beneath the table. Nobody says a word. I keep quiet, curious to see where this is going.

"Gemma, do you like what Taryn is wearing?" Lyle asks, pointing to the tank. Taryn's in a flashy burlesque outfit. "Absinthe could make you something like that, if you wanted."

Gemma turns to look at Taryn, and Leo pops up behind her. She nods. "I would love—fucking shit. You scared me," she says, but stops, her head cocking to one side. "Twins?"

"I'm Leo."

"And I'm Lyle."

She laughs and makes polite conversation with them, asking about their acts and their time spent at the carnival. They give the information away freely, and it grates on me. Does nobody here have an ounce of self-preservation? For all we know, she could've been sent here by The Legion. But then again—wouldn't Luc have figured that out by now? I've just got to trust in him and his vision.

My pager pings. *Speak of the devil.*

I step away from the table and out of the hall, pressing to listen to Luc's recording.

"I have a job for you," he says into the mic, and I have to

wonder if it's for the spy or the executioner. "Male, half-demon, age thirty-four, serial rapist. His name is Josh Molyneux. I've got a tracker on him, but it's currently only visible on your server. He should be at Sinner's tonight. Take care of him."

Executioner. Understood.

Slipping back into the hall, my eyes meet Raph's. "I'm seeing someone tonight," I say, and waggle my eyebrows suggestively. "Please have Absinthe perform in my place."

"Really?" Absinthe jumps out of her seat. "I've been working on my knife throwing." She beams, and I place a hand on her shoulder.

"You're going to kill it," I say, and wink at Raph, who groans and rolls his eyes. I choose not to look at the human; I can't be distracted tonight.

With thirty minutes to show, I head back to my tent and grab my computer tablet. I run my fingers down the edge until I activate my connection into Luc's private server, and the screen glows magicite green. There's a mask on the table that looks like the lower jaw of an animal, and I grab it, allowing myself to blend in more with the crowd.

Where are you, Molyneux? Clicking onto the map, I watch as tonight's victim gets in line for The Sinner's Circus. I'll need a way to lure him in. It would be a lot easier if half-demons still had access to our magic.

Every version of myself is just a mask I wear. They're all a means to an end. The Scorpion is who I am when I perform. He's a scoundrel, a showman. The Spy is for when I need information. He's quiet and reserved—a fly on the wall. And The Executioner is who I am when I kill. That mask feels like taking a drug, the way it sinks its teeth into me, creating the version of myself I recognize the least.

Compartmentalizing the different facets of my identity is what allows me to still be Draven Orzath at the end of the day. It's how I can still look Po and Una, Reina and Lilian, Taryn and Absinthe in the eyes, and know that I do it all for them. That the vile, most vicious parts of me stem from a love more true than any story told before.

Grabbing my daggers and sai, I slip one blade into my boot and another up my sleeve before walking out onto the carnival grounds, heading towards where I'll perform the kill. My sai looks like a trident, and I hang it on a hook on the wall in Taryn's tent, to be used later.

As I head back to The Sinner's Circus, I make sure to smile as I walk in. On the back wall of the big top, is a booth where we sell drinks and drugs—whatever tickles your fantasy—and I spot Molyneux waiting in line.

Getting behind him, I cough before adjusting my trousers. "The Siren sure knows how to use that pretty mouth of hers," I say. The line nauseates me, but as Molyneux looks my way, eyes hooded with lust, I know it was the right choice.

"I thought she wasn't here tonight," he says, running a thumb over his lower lip. "I know The Pretzel and The Chimera are, though. Admittedly, The Siren caught my eye at a previous show, but The Chimera isn't half bad, either."

My pulse roars in my ears, but all I do is raise a single brow. "Why don't you try her out for the night? I'll see if I can send The Chimera your way after the show."

He grins and pats me on the back. "Thanks, Scorpion."

The thing with my reputation is I've got many. The Scorpion is the performer. I can portray myself as a cocky asshole, an abuser, anything, really. These sickos eat it up. I pay the right people to spin webs of lies about me. The Spy and The Executioner, however, are more accurate to who I am. And fortunately, thanks to carefully calculated moves, not many know where the dots connect.

This man knows that I'm venomous, but he thinks we are the same, and he is sorely mistaken.

I keep my feet grounded as I allow him to exit the big top. Once I think we're in the clear, I walk outside and monitor from afar as he moves past the gate and onward towards Taryn's tent.

Except Taryn isn't there.

When he's close, I sprint towards him, careful to keep my footsteps quiet as I sneak up on the tent, carefully opening the flap. Molyneux stills, but there's no fear in his eyes. Only annoyance and confusion, his brows carefully knitted together, and the heat simmering in my gut rises in temperature.

"Did you think I was going to let you fuck her?" I bite out. Beings like him make me sick, the way they use their strength to take advantage of the weak.

"You said it yourself," he laughs and shrugs like this is all some game. "She's got a pretty mouth. What, are you suddenly possessive?"

I untuck the blade from inside my sleeve, and his amusement swiftly turns to fear.

There was a long time where I couldn't confess to myself how killing made me feel. The raw, intense power I felt taking a life, especially when it was someone who didn't deserve the privilege of living. It's almost unmatched, second only to performing.

These are highs no drug could ever provide. Even now, I want to believe I'm righteous—want to believe that if I found out ten seconds from now that Molyneux was the wrong half-demon, and that he wasn't a perverted abuser, I'd stop.

But as I grab my sai off the wall next to him and stab it straight into his heart, I know my answer.

The tent is silent except for the sound of Josh Molyneux taking his last breaths in heavy, rasping sighs. Pulling my weapon out of his chest cavity, I watch as he drops to the floor and his blood spurts out, synchronized with the rhythm of his barely beating heart.

RAPH EXHALES into the phone on the wall before handing it to me.

"Why the fuck did you send that human here, Luc? What if she works for The Legion?" I ask, grilling him before he has time to make whatever ridiculous command he's gearing up to give.

"We both know she doesn't," he says, as if that's an acceptable answer.

"Okay, so she's just some human that coincidentally got zapped onto Haeresis and ended up on your doorstep, alright. Fine. Why would you send her to us?"

"Do you dare question your king?"

I knew it. He sent her to fuck with me. I wish he could see the glower on my face right now. "And what if I do, your infernal majesty? Are you going to have me execute myself?"

He lets out a chuckle. "No, but I'm going to pocket that idea for later. Honestly, I felt bad for the lady. And it doesn't hurt that she reminded me of Zada."

The human does have the gutsy, brazen attitude of the Duchess of Luxuria, I'll give her that, but that's not good enough. A king can't just allow anyone access to his inner circle because they remind him of his sister. I suppose a king can do anything he wants, but it's a bloody stupid move if you ask me.

"Now, can we discuss why I called?"

"Kill confirmed." I like to get to the point.

"Excellent. I would like to meet with the troupe to discuss some ideas I have for you all. Is tomorrow a good time?"

"Anything you want, my liege," I say sardonically and hang up.

Raph's thick brows raise, his forehead wrinkling, and I pinch the bridge of my nose. "It appears we're expecting a visitor."

Symphony No. 8

Gemma

Watching Reina on stage is like watching a statue of a goddess come to life. She dances across the floor with nimble grace. One of the twins stands in the background, pounding a drum, but I'm not sure anyone else in the audience notices him. We're all captivated by The Chimera and the way her body moves to the beat.

Her arms and hands rise and fall in rapid succession, the bolas hitting the ground creating complicated rhythms. Just like how she plays the cello, Reina seems to embody everything she performs. Boleadoras is a dance I'm not incredibly familiar with, but from what I know, she truly has a gift.

I want to dance like that. I am so glad I was gifted this job, and that I can work and save to buy a ticket home, but I still want more. This is a chapter in my life, and I want to experience it to the fullest extent. I crave dancing in a way that is sexy and sensual —not this sanitised version they have me doing in the day, but I'm afraid of saying something and sounding ungrateful. Or like I'm trying to take someone's act, which I most definitely am not.

After Sinner's ends, Reina and I make our way back to camp in comfortable silence. She's likely exhausted, and I've got my own problems to think about.

If I'm going to make this place my home for at least the next year, I might as well try to make it worth my while. Why not use this as an opportunity to learn about a world and culture completely outside of my own? To make friends and connections —and to dance.

When we get inside our tent, I sit on my cot and practically twiddle my thumbs, unsure of what to bring up first. I have so many questions, but I decide not to dig too deep. At least not tonight. "It's interesting you don't have wings or horns," I say offhandedly as I try not to watch her change. Her body is lean and firm, clearly the body of someone who's been doing this a long, long time.

"A lot of us don't. Taryn and Aida have tails instead of legs, Una and I were born without wings, and Draven and Rowan, well... they lost parts of themselves."

"Parts of themselves—*what* parts?" I ask, my mind flashing to the most inappropriate of places. After seeing Rowan's performances, I was pretty sure that part was *fully* intact.

"*Gross*, Gemma. Draven lost his wings, Rowan lost a horn. They've both still got their dicks, though Rowan is very, very married," Reina says as she slips into a little romper. "They're a triad, but they're closed."

I blush. "Sorry, I'm not interested in—I'm just curious. I mean, you're all different species than me. I don't know how any of your bodies work. Honestly, I don't know how much of anything works here. The magic. The government. I know jack shit."

"Oh," Reina gives me a small, empathetic smile. "Most of us would be willing to answer any questions you have, but let's start small—the government, our monetary system, how we pay our taxes—y'know, something *other* than my family's genitals." She drops her voice down to a whisper. "Though I'm sure Draven would be willing to show you his if you asked nicely."

My face flushes crimson, my mind trying to do anything but think about the attractive half-demon who tried to kill me. "I think if I'm ever alone with Draven again, he'd be more likely to kill me, so I'll pass. Do you guys... Wow, this is such a weird fucking line of questioning," I say, and it's true.

"We work at an erotic circus. Ask your questions, darling."

"Does everyone on the planet have human-like genitals?"

"For the most part, I believe so. Half-demons and demon-hybrids have human-*ish* genitals, but with a few extra parts. You'll honestly probably see everyone's shit if you end up performing the night show with us at some point," she says, and it's a little spark of hope.

Even Reina is thinking about me performing in The Sinner's Circus. "Probably?"

"Merfolk have slits or pockets—similar to serpentine—and Taryn isn't comfortable talking about what she has with anyone she isn't going to be intimate with, so please don't ask her. She's pretty introverted in general. Other than that, most of us are pretty open. Sex sells and all that," she explains. "Oh! And Quinn doesn't do the whole gender thing."

I give a nod of understanding. "And demons?" I cock my head.

"Demons don't even have to have corporeal forms, so I think they can change their genitals at will, but I wouldn't know. Demons don't typically just go around sleeping with us."

"What the fuck do you mean they don't have to have corporeal form?"

She shrugs. "I'm not an expert on any of this stuff, so I'm just going off of what I've seen or heard. Demons, as a race, are older than humanity. They don't have physical forms, but ever since The Convergence, they started using their magic to create bodies to make humanity and other species more comfortable."

I don't even really understand what she's telling me—it all sounds fabricated, like a story you'd read in a fiction book. I know elves and serpentine are older species, but they at least are physical beings.

Reina pulls a blanket up over her body, and I do the same, feeling like we're two young girls at a sleepover chit-chatting away.

"Demons make up the upper echelon of society," she says. "They used to have carte blanche on who they could sleep with, which is how half-demons came to be in the first place, but now the oligarchs recommend they all stick together. It's complicated —even I can't comprehend the complexities of it all—but that's just how it is here. Raph is the only kind demon I know."

"What about Luc?"

Reina's muscles seem to stiffen, her entire body language changing, and I fear I may have overstepped. I read in a history book once that some leaders of countries used to require their citizens to only speak highly of them—maybe this place is like that. It kills me that I can remember that, but not who my parents were.

I flip through my brain like a reference book, looking for something else to ask her to change the subject before it hits me. "I hope this isn't violating, but do you menstruate?"

"Unfortunately," she says and gives me a little pout. "Pretty sure my reproductive organs think I'm fully human or something."

"That fucking sucks," I say, and we both shake our heads in disdain.

"That it does. We've got a long day tomorrow, better get some rest," she says before turning off the lantern. Like everything else, it seems to run on magic, and the crispy, bright smell dissipates as darkness takes hold of our tent.

Symphony No. 9
Gemma

I'm getting used to my new routine, the way the days ebb and flow, and with the exception of the seventh day of the week, we all perform or run stands at the carnival. When the sky is only lit by the moons, whoever's turn it is in their rotation performs in The Sinner's Circus.

If there are two moons, does that mean we're in a different solar system altogether?

During the day, I perform my sets with Reina and Draven. His glimmering eyes linger on me longer than I'd like, him using my dance routine as an excuse to drink his fill.

I think he sees me as prey—weak and unaware—but I won't let him fuck up this life I'm building, regardless of how temporary it may be. He has no right to make me feel uncomfortable or afraid when I didn't ask to be here in the first place. Hel, I'm not even sure how I got here.

Robyn exits her booth to perform her sideshow, and I watch her body move with grace and strength as her horse takes them around a small obstacle course. There are targets and rails to jump over, and they nail each one with precision. Her bow and arrow are just extensions of her limbs, and it's breathtaking to watch it all come together.

I move closer, my eyes narrowing on the horse's mane, and I realize he isn't an average stallion. Flame-like shadows ripple where a mane and tail would be.

"Helhorse," Reina says, as if that's answer enough, before continuing. "We have some earthly animals, but we also have helhorses and helhounds."

I'd like to see a helhound one day, I think. I wonder if that's what Luc' dog is, although I imagine it would be something a lot scarier than a corgi.

Raph comes around to everyone's booths and platforms to dismisses them early, letting us know that the King of Hel would be here soon. Draven and I are the only two to not shudder at the announcement, and I wonder what I'm missing.

Luc didn't seem like a big, scary guy. Quite the opposite, actually. He was nice and funny. Cute, even. But everyone here seems to balk at the mere mention of him.

"What don't I know about Luc?" I ask Raph. "He's your brother, right?"

"Yes," Raph answers with a smile. Robyn and Lilian are running around like chickens with their heads cut off, Rowan and the twins following close behind as everyone tidies up the hall.

"Why does everyone seem so anxious? I get that he's the king, but he seemed like a nice guy."

Raph cocks his head and crosses his arms. He's stout, much shorter than the rest of the troupe, but there's a robust confidence to him all the same. Unlike Luc, his blue eyes are deep, not icy. "His Highness is a... tough leader. Some say he rules with an iron fist. Personally, I'd be more inclined to use brass knuckles for the analogy."

Raph has been nothing but transparent with me, yet something about his answer feels very PR. He's telling me what he wants me to hear, but not how he truly feels, and it shows.

"The Devil should be here any moment," Draven announces as Absinthe runs past, giggling and mopping the floor.

As if on cue, an umbral figure appears in the entryway to the tent. Shadows swirl, the smoky tendrils curling as they transform into something more defined. Tangible. They twist like limbs, smoothing out until they are no longer transparent and spectral, but red. In the blink of an eye, Luc is here in his cambion form, and I realize that Raph is like this, too.

Raph has another form that I've never seen—that I may never get to see. It's exciting and scary all at once. I just hope learning about myself is as interesting as learning about this planet and its citizens.

"Hello brother, come and join us for dinner," Raph says, turning to face where the rest of us are seated at the table.

Rowan is grilling some kind of meat, while Quinn serves salad and hors d'oeuvres. Luc, Raph, and Draven all sit on one side, the rest of the carnies filling in after them, and I sit between Reina and Lilian.

The energy in the air is palpable, everyone's shoulders tensing, their foreheads creasing, and I begin to wonder if my entire previous interaction with Luc was a fabrication of my clearly broken mind.

Robyn helps Rowan as they pass out the main dish to everyone except the two demon leaders, and everyone digs in. Una helps Po cut her meat, and the little cambion thanks her repeatedly, a nervous shake to her voice.

It's silent other than the clanking of forks and knives for too long.

"Hello, carnival troupe," Luc begins. It's weird. Raph sometimes calls us the troupe, but usually he just refers to everyone as carnies. Sinners, even. Carnival troupe sounds obnoxiously formal.

Everyone stands and takes a bow. "Hello, our Infernal King," a few reply in unison.

Oh my—this *is* a formal meeting between a king and some of his citizens. I realize we might as well be government officials without decision making power. We provide the funds, but Raph and Luc get to choose what's done with them.

"We are having a bit of a problem. I'll cut to the chase. The amount of money Raph has reported to me as of late is lower than what's necessary to provide for the population of Haeresis"

We're broke? Raph and Draven look at us, and it's clear they knew this was coming. There's a guilty gleam in Raph's eyes, and I put down my fork, no longer hungry.

Luc adjusts his tie. "Raph and I are left with three possible solutions. Remove citizens—"

"Not an option we're actually considering," Raph interrupts.

Robyn and Aida sigh in relief, grateful for the explanation.

Luc nods in agreement. "Stop providing as many resources for our citizens—"

Reina crosses her arms, and Taryn furrows her brows, both clearly pissed off by the heartless suggestion.

"Also not an option," Raph clarifies.

Luc looks us all in the eyes. "Which leaves us with one choice: make more crown."

"And how do you expect us to do that?" Draven asks. Everyone stills, not knowing what to make of their friend's question to the king.

"Easily. I'm sure you'll think of something. You've got a human at your disposal," Luc gestures towards me before looking back to Draven. "You're welcome, by the way. I'd suggest bringing in more members, as well as coming up with some new acts. Fuck someone on stage, fake someone's death—do whatever you need to do."

You have no other choice goes unspoken.

"I will be suspending everyone's pay until a solution is found," he adds. "I look forward to seeing everyone during tonight's performance."

Tonight, they dance for the devil. Fuck my chances of getting off this planet, I guess.

Everyone walks out of the hall on edge, but still head towards their prospective places for the show. Reina and Lilian are both off tonight, and the three of us put on masks before we file into the audience.

"So, is he single?" I joke, trying to lighten the mood.

"The Devil?!" The pinched look on Reina's face can only be described as horrified with a pinch of exasperation.

Lilian waggles her eyebrows. "Or were you asking about Draven?"

I sigh. "I was kidding. No to both, thank you."

Everyone makes a spectacle of Luc's arrival to The Sinner's Circus. He is a shadowy figure, his eyes glowing white instead of their usual icy blue as he enters, but he transforms once seated. Not a single eye in the tent isn't fixated on him, and it takes the audience a moment to look away from their king to the show before them.

As The Phantom steps onto the stage, I people-watch. I'm not sure if I can call it that, since everyone here is demon or part-demon, but I observe everyone all the same. Their reactions to the show—to the madness. It feels somehow the same as every other night, yet eerily different.

It's oxymoronic at best. The audience, all dressed up and masked, still oohs and aahs, still screams and provides lustful looks, but there's tension. Static, magical energy filling the space that isn't there.

It feels a lot like rage. Discomfort.

Turning to Lilian and Reina, I realize neither of them is watching the show, but instead, stare Luc down.

"Do you guys have a personal vendetta against him?" I ask in earnest.

"No. He just... frightens me. The amount of power he holds. He could probably fix so many issues with the snap of his fingers, and yet he doesn't," Lilian explains.

"And you?"

Reina's eyes widen as if to say *later*, and I nod in understanding.

"I just hate the government. Doesn't matter the planet or

place, it's always the same; full of useless idiots who would rather fight over who's right than actually help the people they've been put in charge of caring for," Reina says.

The show continues, each act stranger and sexier than the last, and I try to gauge Luc's reactions. There's a strip tease, and axe throwing. Lilian and Baelor even fuck on stage—or at least they *appear* to be screwing behind the curtain—and the crowd goes wild with applause and laughter and lust. I think Luc is enjoying himself, but it's hard to tell with the way he's schooled his features.

For the final act, Draven walks through the audience while juggling three knives. His body prowls like a panther as he stalks his way up and down the aisles before pulling something out of his pocket and throwing it into the air. Before I've blinked twice, he's chucking a knife at it, and the apple lands on Luc's head.

"That was a bold move," Lilian whispers to us, and I hold my breath.

I don't care about Draven. Really, I don't. The dude tried to fucking murder me, but I don't want anyone to die, and with the way everyone's playing up the devil, I'm afraid Draven's going to leave in a casket.

Luc Morningstar laughs. It's a sound I've heard before, but the audience seems stunned. "Good show." He picks the apple up, takes a bite, and tosses it back to Draven as he exits the tent.

What the fuck is going on?

THE CARNIES all pile into the entrance of the hall, everyone frantic with unchecked energy.

"Was Luc trying to show off that he can eat our resources?" One twin asks as the other paces the tent. "Was that a sign?"

Lilian, Reina, and I all take our seats, while Absinthe and the twins remain standing. Draven is leaning against the table, scratching his chin as if in thought.

"And why would he come in demon form?" the twin asks, clearly distressed. "Was his goal to agitate the audience and drive fear into us after the earlier threat?"

The other twin stops pacing.

"Might I remind you, Leo, that Luc might be our king, but he is also Raph's brother. He's not trying to scare us. Today was a reality check. Do you even know what you're talking about?" Draven asks. "Or are you just running your mouth?"

"He runs his mouth just like you run away from all your problems," Lyle says.

Draven stands up straight and squares his shoulders, crossing towards the twins, and my heart drops into my stomach. They were fine all week, why is everything haywire now?

"What is that supposed to mean?" Draven asks, threat lacing his tone. If his voice was a liquid, I would drink it.

"Nobody seems to know what you do when you disappear, but I'd bet crown you spend it running errands like the king's little bitch." Lyle points a finger against Draven's chest, and Reina stands up, quickly striding towards them.

"Why don't we all take a deep breath—" Lilian says, and Baelor stands, balling his fists as if he's ready to join the fight, too. I'm not sure whose side he'd be on, though. His wings and nostrils flare in tandem.

"I think we should—" "Take a swing and see—" "I'd love to—"

"*Enough*," Raph shouts from the entryway, disrupting the cacophony of rage that was manifesting between everyone. "Sit down."

Everyone does as they're told, the twins sitting at the opposite end of the table from Draven, who winds up directly next to me. His chest rises and falls with his heavy breaths, and I almost put my hand on him to try and ease his anxiety, but I don't—remembering he doesn't like me.

"Regardless of the meaning behind what just happened, do you really think fighting would change a damn thing?" Rowan asks from behind Raph.

I don't really get how magic works here, so I'm not sure who is the strongest. Magic is everywhere, yet nobody seems to be using it. But physically? Raph and Rowan are the most intimidating. Mostly because Raph is a shapeshifting demon, and Rowan is, well... big. Taut muscles attach to broad shoulders as he crosses his arms against his chest.

"I believe it was my brother's intention to send a message," Raph starts. "But the message was that we are protected. Draven threw a knife at his head, yet our king laughed and tossed it back. Took a bite of the apple, even."

"Showing he knew we wouldn't poison him," Absinthe says, and I almost forgot she was here with how quiet she's been, likely still riding the high of performing.

Leo gives Raph a look, and I notice the scar on his brow. *That's* how everyone can tell them apart. "I'm not sure the audience saw it that way."

"At the end of the day, Luc relies on us. All of us. He's not using us to send a message to the people. We are the message, and we are his people," Raph explains, though I'm not sure everyone buys it. "We might be a family, but I am still the governor of this continent. Now, go get some rest."

The twins storm out, Lilian and Baelor on their heels, and everyone leaves. I follow Reina back towards our tent, feeling more confused than when I left our bedroom this morning.

"I have no idea what just happened," I say, sitting down on my cot.

Reina sighs. "That conversation at dinner—Luc was essentially saying we need to figure out a way to attract more guests, or the lives of the citizens of Haeresis are on us."

I shake my head. "Well, that's not fair, but why are the twins fighting with Draven? Doesn't everyone want the same thing?"

"They're pissed that Draven didn't fight back more," she

explains as she grabs a comb, pulling it through her long strands of red hair.

"But how can he? That's his king—that's *our* king." And it's one of the first times I've ever thought about him in that light. This is my home now, therefore Luc is just as much my king as anyone else's.

She shrugs. "Draven receives more lenience than anyone. I think Luc sees Draven as like a son or younger brother. The twins think he has to utilize this. I don't know. I'm honestly afraid they might be becoming sympathizers of The Legion. I'm pretty sure Baelor is too."

"The Legion?"

"They're a... uh... political group inspired by the original leader of Hel from before the rebellion. There's a lot of history and weight to the term, but essentially they want to overthrow the government."

"And that's a bad thing because? I thought you hated the government?"

"I do," she says quickly. "But I'm not sure they're the answer, either. What if they put someone worse into power? I think Luc is a lazy leader, but he's not inherently bad."

"That's hard. I'm sorry." Part of me doesn't want to care. I don't want to stress over the politics of this planet, because once the year is over, it's not my problem anymore. But my brain doesn't work like that. I may not truly know myself, but I know enough to know I'm not heartless. I want whatever's best for these carnies I'm beginning to truly care about.

I just don't know what that is or what I can do to help, but I'll sure as Hel try.

Reina yawns, and our lantern goes off. The darkness swallows me whole.

FLUORESCENT LIGHTS FLICKER above me as I sit in this chair. The room is cold, so cold, and the only sound I hear is the monitor's incessant beeping. People are shouting, and my legs twist and turn.

There's a woman on the hospital bed who looks just like me, and tears burn my eyes as someone presses something against her chest, her body jumping with the shock. Someone pulls me into their arms, a familiar cologne warming my senses.

My eyes shoot open, memories flooding back to me as I sit up and stretch my sweat-slicked arms. Out of all the things my mind could choose to recall, it decided on my parents' death. I wanna know if I went to college, or what my favorite childhood movie was, but no. This is what I fucking get for remembering.

Grief is all-consuming, isn't it? The way it slowly poisons you, bit by bit, until you are nothing but rotting flesh. A husk of the person you once were. The beauty of living always leads to the pain of dying—of watching death absorb those closest to you.

Tears threaten to fall but I blink them away, reminding myself that I've already grieved this. There's no use in doing it all over again.

Getting up from bed, I quietly slip out of the tent, careful not to wake Reina as I tiptoe towards the hall to see if I can find something to snack on or anything to distract me from this hollow ache in my chest. There are voices coming from inside, and I halt.

"We need new acts," Raph says.

"So we'll hold auditions," Draven replies. "I've already put up fliers."

"That won't be enough. We need to think of something new —what about what you did today to Luc—impalement arts?"

"I'd need a partner. Who is going to agree to that?"

I don't know where I get the guts from, but I walk in and make my presence known. "I'll do it."

"What?" His forehead creases, and I consider taking back my words, but choose to will confidence into my voice instead.

"I want to perform in The Sinner's Circus," I say, and it's

true. I've been thinking about it since I joined the carnival. "I can start our act with some burlesque, and then you join in and throw some knives at me. We could make a real show of it."

Raph's eyebrows shoot up, and it's clear he's at least considering it. "Draven—"

"Don't," Draven interrupts. "The problem with impalement arts is that if you flinch or move, you could die, human."

I don't like the audacity of this half-demon. He's part of a carnival that is meant to bring community and confidence to those who are different from the general population of Hel, yet he treats me like shit because of my species? Or is it just because I'm me? He doesn't fucking know me. *I* don't even know me.

What I do know is that I'm a talented fucking dancer, and an orphan, so what is there to lose? "What do you care? Worst-case-scenario is I die on stage and everyone talks about it, bringing more attention to the carnival. Best-case-scenario, I'm good and we continue working together. It's a win-win."

"Luc will not be happy if you die," Raph says.

"Then don't kill me," I respond with a smile, my eyes locked onto Draven.

He glowers, crossing his arms over his chest as he walks past me. "Auditions are first thing tomorrow morning. Don't be late."

SYMPHONY NO. 10
DRAVEN

T he problem with Hel is that we keep track of other planets and their cultures and governments. We have textbooks on the history of Earth, Barac, Moonflower, Ombra, and many other planets in this galaxy and the neighboring ones. It plants the idea in individuals that what worked for other places will work for us, but that's not how it goes.

Every planet, continent, and nation came about differently. We have different histories and morals. Look at how lawless we are on Hel compared to Ombra and Earth. Why would anyone think that our population can be controlled like theirs?

And yet The Legion wants a democracy. Described as *a government by the people, for the people.* Except *the people* are demons or half-demons, and not all of them are bright. Even fewer are good.

Centuries ago, this planet was monstrous. It's said that there were no laws, just powerful demons who sucked the life force from any sorry creature that wound up in this place. The Convergence changed us for the better. We formed societies and created new paths for the species that came about. *Why is that not enough?*

As I walk towards the lavatory, I ponder this. I threw my

dagger at Luc to send a message—that we are powerful, and that the carnival should not be overlooked. We are just as important as our governor and king—but somehow it was twisted into something it was not.

Leo, Lyle, and Baelor thought it was Luc's message to send, and they were sorely mistaken. I genuinely worry that if we became democratic, someone like Baelor would end up schmoozing his way to the top and misusing his power.

Maybe it isn't my place to decide, though. If I stopped helping Raph and Luc, the carnival would fall apart—Hel, our government would fall apart. They could elect whoever they want and reap what they sow. People would starve and suffer, and maybe then they'd feel an inkling of what I've felt.

I step into the stone-covered shower pod, allowing the warm water to envelop me.

Unfortunately, my mind won't let me give up on the citizens of Hel. Not because I give a damn about them, but because of my family.

The faces of Phaelyn, Reina, Absinthe, Lilian, and Taryn flash through my mind. Po, Una, Robyn, Quinn, and Rowan. Aida. Raph and Luc. The twins. Even arsehole Baelor. *They* are why I fight tooth and nail to make Luc a better leader, and to help him stop this slow crawl of an uprising.

I finish washing my hair and scrubbing my face, exhausted before the day has even begun. Holding auditions is fine, but if anyone is actually good enough to join, that'll be the real headache. They could have ulterior motives, or be a part of The Legion. There's no telling what kind of sickos might join us today. My last kill was a man clearly obsessed with my sisters. I can't allow someone like that into my space again.

Getting dressed, I head back towards the hall to start auditions. There's a short line of folks standing outside the entryway, and a clearly frazzled Quinn playing the dulcimodia to distract everyone while they wait.

The human is nowhere to be found. It's not like I was looking forward to seeing her, but I did *expect* her.

Robyn and Raph are already seated at the table, and I pull up a chair beside them.

"Good morrow," Raph says with a smile.

"*Morning*. I counted four candidates. Is that truly it?" I ask.

Robyn shakes her head, her curls bouncing with the movement. "No, Gemma took one of them to set up their apparatus in the big top. We'll have to move there to see their auditions."

Great.

Quinn peeks their head through the entryway, and Raph gives them the thumbs up to send the first auditioner in. A young, muscular looking half-demon walks in with no props. He's covered in tattoos, and his taut pectorals and biceps show through his sheer tank top. He spreads out his wings, showcasing his large wingspan. I wonder if his talent is strength like Rowan, or perhaps he'll do something with flight.

He stands there, smiling at us, but doesn't say a wink.

"Introduce your side act and begin," I say, gesturing for him to hurry up.

"I'm Edoardo *The Bubbler*," he says and begins breathing heavily from his nose and mouth. It's quiet for a moment, and I look at Robyn and Raph, who shrug.

Edoardo makes a strange sound before something appears in his nose, showing us exactly why he's called *The Bubbler*. There is a giant snot bubble coming out of his nose. I can't make this shit up.

Robyn claps, the movement frantic and quick. "Thank you, thank you. Please wait outside. We will inform everyone after auditions are over."

I rub my face with my hands, wishing for the sweet release of death. "What the ever-loving-fuck was that?"

We stare at one another for a beat before a very masculine, very human-like individual walks into the tent, and I almost don't spot the cat tail trailing behind him. He has two sets of ears—one pointed, but human, the other fur-covered and cat-like—and I try not to stare at them.

He's a felion. They're not as common on Haeresis, most of their species living on Ira, but with underwater minerals being their main export, I can imagine the cat-demons don't appreciate diving. Haeresis is a good continent to seek sanctuary on, and it's nearby, too. Raph is a much more forgiving governor than Cavan, and it helps that we have the protection of the king as well. Hel's Carnival is truly going to need to expand and grow if we want to continue caring for citizens from other continents.

This place started as just a carnival, nothing more, nothing less. It was merely rides and kiddie games. Robyn and Quinn started the side acts, and Aida began telling fortunes. I was the one who suggested The Sinner's Circus when I turned twenty, and it feels like it's been a lot longer than seven years. This won't be the first time Hel's Carnival has made improvements and added new members, but it is the first time it's been demanded of us. Unfortunately, this is a necessary evil on Luc's part.

"Khalid Al-Khalifa," the felion introduces himself. "The Pyro." He winks and throws a blade into the air. When he catches it, he sticks his tongue out, and I think he might be a sword swallower.

Though it's not my main skill, it's a craft I've worked heavily on, perfecting the art of not having a gag reflex. I'd hate for all that work to go to waste, although I suppose I could find other uses for it.

Everyone gasps as the felion's tongue catches fire. He pours a canister of oil onto the sword, and then touches it to his tongue, lighting it a flame. There are endless opportunities he could use this fire magic for—we could truly cultivate this felion into an all-star act.

I just wonder where he got the magicite from. Or perhaps his people have another method to use as conduits for their magic. Although Aida will never share hers, I know she doesn't rely on the crystal.

The true difference between all of us half-demons and hybrids, is that we require a conduit. Demons don't, they can just wield magic as they please. This is exactly why they're still in power. If every half-demon on Hel was given magicite, The Legion wouldn't have ever needed to even form. There's more of us—we'd have so much power, all Hel would break loose. It would be glorious and horrifying. There are some rare nights where I dream of a revolution, but most nights I know it would become too hard to protect the ones I love.

When his act is finished, he bows and takes his leave, and I look at Raph and Robyn, who are grinning ear-to-ear.

"What?" I ask.

"He's good," Raph says, and waggles his eyebrows.

"You're not allowed to sleep with the cast," Robyn reminds him.

He gives us both a look, his ocean blue eyes shining at us. "He isn't one of us, yet."

"He's in," I say, casting my official vote. "The Bubbler is a hard fucking pass."

"Agreed," they both respond in unison as our next candidate steps into the tent.

He's a tall, lanky half-demon with no particularly striking features. His eyes are gold, his skin red, and his hair slightly darker than his complexion. His horns aren't a unique shape, or very large, just small points coming out of his head, much like Absinthe's. In all honesty, he's bland, which is what makes him interesting. *What sort of secrets is he hiding?*

"Bryan," he says, as way of introduction.

"And your act is?" Raph asks, and the half-demon's brows furrow in confusion. "Your stage name. I'm The Phantom. He's The Scorpion." He points to me.

"I'm The Stallion," Robyn shares.

"Oh." Bryan nods in understanding. "I'm... The Water Spout."

If I had a drink, I'd have spit it out, my eyes wide with surprise.

"Er—no. I'm The Climaxer—nope," he corrects himself. "How about: The Satisfier," he finally says with confidence. I cannot possibly begin to imagine what this weirdo has in store for us.

"Sure," Raph says, his eyes a bit pained. "Take it away."

Bryan *The Water Sprout-Climaxer-Satisfier* lifts his hands up in the air, keeping them far away from his core. He closes his eyes, and Robyn points to the bulge emerging in his trousers.

"What is he—" Robyn's question is interrupted by the moans coming from his mouth. His whole body shakes, muscles twitching in waves as a scream comes out, followed by a wet spot on his crotch.

What fucking sins have I committed to deserve this? Not even murderers should be subjected to these horrors.

He smiles, the only being in the room satisfied, and bows before us.

"That's it," I say, and stand. "I'm fucking done."

"Draven, don't be ridiculous, we have three more candidates," Raph starts, but I'm already halfway out the door.

"Khalid," I say, looking at the felion, who is standing beside the other twats. "You're hired. Everybody else, go home." I turn, frustrated that I even have to hold auditions, when something grips my shoulder. A clawed hand.

"I won't join unless you also accept my sister," Khalid says, and I look at Raph, whose eyebrows shoot up.

"Excuse me—are you negotiating when our offer is already incredibly generous?" I ask, shocked at the gall of this guy. But if he has fire on his tongue, I suppose it's no surprise there's fire in his words as well.

He gives me a sour expression. " I am bargaining, yes. You either take both of us, or you get neither of us. That's the deal."

"And where is your sister?" Raph asks, genuinely considering the felion's offer.

This is absurd. Luc has put us in such a tough predicament, we're genuinely bargaining with a being we just met in hopes that he and his sister can help us perform better. We look *desperate*, which is not something I'm willing to be.

"She's in the large tent with the human woman," Khalid says, pointing to the big top.

The human woman. Fuck me.

Raph, Robyn, and I follow Khalid towards Sinner's. Once inside, I see a lyra hanging from the ceiling of the tent, a feminine felion sitting inside it. She must be an aerialist.

Everyone watches as the cat-demon moves her body into different figures, showcasing her flexibility and strength. That is, everyone except me. My eyes remain fixed on the human standing by another apparatus, stretching her bare legs.

"She's amazing," Raph says, his neck craned upwards. "See, Draven. There was nothing to worry about. We can accept Khalid and his sister...."

"Yasmeena," Khalid clarifies.

Robyn seems to track my eyes, and she looks me up and down, giving me a knowing glare. "We should audition the human, too."

"Fine," I say through gritted teeth.

I. Do not. Fucking. Like this.

The human waltzes towards us as Yasmeena gets off the aerial hoop, shaking hands with Raph and Robyn. She's curvy and muscular, with deep tan skin, short hair, and fur-covered ears on the top of her head.

Yasmeena is downright beautiful. And so is her brother.

"Draven," the human says, her voice like an electric charge to me. "I'll need you for this."

I groan, but oblige, and follow her back towards the wheel of death. I'm not sure if this was in our prop shed, or if it was a special gift from the devil himself, but it's different from anything else here. Hel's carnival is lots of pretty shades of black, red, and orange—this apparatus is minty, with a blue and white star and red leather straps exactly where the human's body should go.

She climbs onto a stool and places her arms up into the straps, and I follow her, tightening the restraints against her pale flesh. I'm sure she can feel the warmth of my breath—I just hope she can't hear the raging beat of my heart as I secure her to the device.

The human looks like a perfect doll, like porcelain. I just hope she doesn't shatter.

Pulling a dagger from where it was tucked into my boot, I go to aim at her, but she shakes her head.

"Strap my legs in, too."

"We shouldn't be doing this at all. This act isn't safe. If you flinch—"

"I won't," she interrupts me. "And besides, my limbs will be strapped in. I just have to control my neck. That's easy."

There's a confidence to her that borders on suicidal, but I remove the stool and kneel down, gently tucking her ankle into the leather before tightening it. I grab her other leg and do the same, my fingers traipsing down her skin before securing her.

"Now spin me."

Placing my hands on the wheel of death, I turn it, backing away as I watch her spin round-and-round, until I finally throw one of my blades. It's rare I'm anxious about doing most anything —spying, murder, impalement arts. I've done it all, and I've done it well.

Throwing a knife—Hel, just about everything about this human puts me on edge.

It lands right between her head and her right arm, and I sigh a little in relief. I chuck another, straight between her legs, and she doesn't flinch.

She's dynamite in human form.

There's a quiet fire simmering inside me at the way my body reacts to her. I'm fucking drooling at the sight, desperate for her safety, her attention. Hel, I might be desperate for her affection at this point.

I refuse to let this human take over my thoughts for a minute longer tonight.

Even if she's explosive.

Symphony No. 11
Gemma

I'm not sure if there's anything strong enough to get me as high as proving Draven wrong. He was surprised with how well I handled my impalement arts audition the other day, and to be fair, I was surprised too. I had no idea if I was going to be capable of any of that—I just acted on instinct.

But what shocked me even more was him telling me we'd have to rehearse for a few weeks before debuting our act. I figured he wouldn't care to perfect it, because if he fucks up, well... I'm dead. He'd get exactly what he wanted from the start. I also didn't expect him to agree to spend extra time with me. Alone. Yet here we are.

"What do you think of Yasmeena and Khalid?" I ask, genuinely curious.

I spend the majority of my time with Reina. Absinthe and Lilian talk to me in the hall, but it's rare I get the chance to speak to anyone one on one. I like Yasmeena from the interactions we've had so far. She's tough—even tougher than Reina—and it's refreshing. Khalid and I haven't gotten an opportunity to speak yet, but he's caught the eye of a particular vampire. I'm itching to know what Draven thinks about the newest two members.

"I hope they'll bring in a crowd," he says, not meeting my eyes as he sharpens his blades.

"Sure," I say, nodding my agreement. I'd love for us all to bring in a crowd and get our pay suspension revoked. "But what do you think of them as individuals?"

We stare at each other for a long beat of silence, the air dripping with tension. The hairs on my arms stick straight up, and I take in a breath, trying to calm the uneasy feeling churning in my gut.

Draven stands up and stalks towards me, clearly irritated. He grabs and pins me to the wooden wheel. One of his arms is pressed against my face, holding up my wrists, while the other holds a dagger directly against my neck.

"What, now that we're alone, you're finally going to kill me?" I tease.

But there's not an ounce of humor in his expression as he stares back at me. "Do you work for The Legion?" he asks, his eyes gleaming with rage, and my blood runs cold.

I shake my head, stifling a breath. "No. I'm not a part of some fringe group—"

"How the fuck do you even know who they are, then? I thought you were a useless human with no memories?"

"Reina mentioned it."

His brows furrow further. "Do Yasmeena and Khalid work for The Legion?"

"No," I say, struggling to shrug my shoulders under his vise of a grip. Somehow, I don't think I'm doing a very good job at convincing him of the *truth*. "I mean. How should I know? I met them for the first time the other day."

The blade is cold, almost pinching as it presses into the lean column of my throat. My head is pounding, my heart thundering, and it feels like I'm going to choke from a lack of oxygen. There's nothing preventing me from breathing, but it's like my breath is caught in my chest. What if I die like this? What then? My brain takes me out of the present. Flashes of a man—my nonno—

coming to the forefront from the recesses of my mind. He's got strong arms and he smells like whiskey and amber cologne.

Never show a man you're afraid. Or that you're weak. Fear is a shadow that fades when you create your own light, he says in my memory.

I blink, coming back to the present. Not because I want to, but because in this moment, I *need* to. Steeling my gaze, I don't allow a single tear to fall. Maybe my memories will all return the moment I need them most.

"And you don't work for one of the other governors? You weren't secretly put here to distract me—to manipulate me?"

The fear in my belly is churning, turning to rage. He *still* doesn't fucking trust me? Over the past two weeks, I've worked hard. I do everything that's asked of me. I can barely remember my favorite movies, and he thinks I'm some government spy from a continent I'd never heard of until I woke up here?

"No, asshole, but good to know you find me distracting," I say, and crane my neck closer to the blade. It nicks the skin of my throat, just the smallest amount. Draven watches the blood drip down, his eyes widening in horror for only a split second before returning to normal.

Two can play at that game. Taking a page from Absinthe's book, I lick my lips and give him a devilish grin. His grip on my wrist loosens as though he's ready to back away.

"Is the Crown Prince of the Carnies afraid of a little ol' human? Why don't you just zap me with your magic? Why resort to weapons when you're all-powerful?" I mock him.

"I would if I could," he confesses, and a ripple of surprise shoots through me.

"What do you mean? There's magic literally everywhere."

Draven's golden eyes meet mine, and it's deadly quiet for a moment. "The demon leaders... the Morningstar family... they limit our usage of magicite. It powers our cities, but that's it."

Magicite is what some of the cambion on Earth used. It's a pretty green crystal.

"Why? And why are you telling me this?"

"I'm telling you this because it's no secret. As for why, I haven't the slightest idea. I theorize Luc fears it hurting everyone. A bunch of half-demons running around with powers they don't know how to control. It would be madness."

I shake my head. We're so close he could kiss me if he wanted to, but for obvious reasons, he does not. "On Earth, we have schools for that. Universities dedicated to teaching people magic," I whisper. There's a quick flash in my mind of camphor trees and laboratories, but I force myself to stay in this moment with him, and a realization hits me. "Oh my god. I thought you were using magic when you threw your knives at me, but you were really just hoping for the best, huh?"

Blade in hand, Draven pulls back, and I suck in a breath, bracing for him to stab me. Instead, he shoves the dagger into the wooden wheel right next to my waist, ripping some of the fabric of my bodice in the process. He presses his body into mine, his neck bending as his mouth makes its way to my ear. "You're a fucking pest."

I wish I could say this isn't turning me on. Or at least, I wish I had an explanation for why these terrifying, almost deadly encounters make me want to bend over and beg for it, but I guess the most twisted memories are yet to come.

Literally.

Silently, he unties the straps and my body relaxes against him. He finally lets go and backs away, exiting the tent without another word, and I'm starting to believe he wants to do more than just kill me.

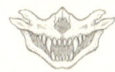

ABSINTHE IS STITCHING the ripped side of my bodice, carefully wielding her needle as Reina and Lilian talk about our newest members.

"Yasmeena is somehow harsher than you," Lilian says to Reina, who lets out a laugh. "She scares me."

"She's not harsh, she's just tough. She had to be. Ira makes all its citizens dive for minerals. Yasmeena and all the other felion were probably miserable going underwater." Reina is defensive of Yasmeena in a way that's admirable.

"Draven had to be tough, and he's still nice," Lilian says, and I almost break my neck from craning it so far.

"Draven is everything but nice," I say. "He's an absolute ass."

"To be fair, you are like... a punishment sent to him from The King," Reina says. "By the way, I got a salve to heal your throat. The scratch should be gone in a day or two."

"Thanks." Am I really a punishment? It feels more like an equivalent exchange. Hel's Carnival gets a human to use and display, and I get money until I've saved enough to go home. That feels relatively even.

"Draven *is* kind of a dick. In like a cocky, full of himself sort of way. He'll die for us, but he'll also... piss us off and make us cry," Absinthe finally says.

The sound of laughter sings through my ears, causing my heart to flutter for a moment, before it dissipates into silence. I should be having fun in the moment I'm in, yet I can't help but feel grief for the friendships I cannot seem to remember.

"You okay?" Lilian asks and walks over to plop down beside me. Reina quickly follows suit, and then we're all sitting on the bench, squeezed together, while Absinthe finishes the final stitches.

"Eh," I confess, shrugging my shoulders. "I am starting to remember bits and pieces of my life, but it just brings me a deep sense of sadness."

"Are you sad because you remember, or sad because you can't?" Reina asks.

"Both." Remembering death has forced me into a weird stagnant mental space. I'm stuck between wanting to grieve and knowing I already did. But not remembering things seems to bother me even more.

What was my favorite color? What did I used to do to calm myself down? It's maddening to think that I remember so much about Earth, but not myself. Who even am I?

"Instead of focusing on what you can't control, why don't you just try and create new memories?" Lilian suggests.

"I second this. Your old memories will come back, but there's no point in dwelling on them while they're out for the count," Reina says and gives my shoulder a squeeze. "Let's do something wild."

"Like set things on fire? Or learn to juggle knives?" Absinthe asks, her eyes lighting up.

Lilian and Reina shake their heads. Absinthe is only a few years younger than me, but her youth shows at times. Or maybe she's always going to be this chaotic.

"Hey," a voice says from the entryway. Yasmeena. "I don't mean to intrude, but I caught the tail end of your conversation and I might have a fun suggestion."

"Let's hear it," I say. I like this. I like these women—beings? Individuals? I don't really know how to classify other species. I can't recall what was common courtesy back on Earth, or maybe I didn't spend a ton of quality time with non-humans. I'm sure I went to school with some, but when I try to take my mind back there, it's all blurry.

"Have any of you ever tried pole?" she asks, crossing her arms. I notice the claws on her fingers, but two of them have been shortened on either hand, and I can't help the blush that spreads across my cheeks.

Reina furrows her brows, her bright red hair cascading down her back. "Pole dancing?"

"Yeah. We could ask Rowan to install one and practice. Not for an act—just for fun," Yasmeena replies.

My mind flashes for just a moment to my body in a mirror. I've got on high heels and fun, floral pasties, but I lose the memory just like so many of the others. Instead of sulking, though, I choose to smile. "Let's fucking do it."

We all stand and head out of the entryway, following on Yasmeena's heels.

Absinthe reaches over to Lilian and whispers in her ear. "Can we set the pole on fire?"

"No," the four of us answer in unison.

Symphony No. 12

Draven

I decide to do what I should've done a long fucking time ago.

"This is... the office of... Luc... Morningstar," Baphomet says on the other end of the line.

"Baph, sweetheart, patch me over?" I ask and immediately hear the click.

"Luc Morningstar, King of Hel speaking—"

I take in a deep breath. "I want magicite."

"Huh?"

"I'm supposed to spy for you, perform for you, *kill* for you, and you won't even grant me access to my own magic. I could find another way. Aida, or maybe one of our newest members could teach me other means of conduction," I threaten.

"I take it things are going swimmingly, then? Bringing in more ticket holders?" The sarcasm dripping from his tongue is less than appreciated.

"Yeah. I mean, Khalid has access to magic and nearly caught his sister on fire, but other than that, everything's going great. I'm even working on a new act with your favorite."

"Lilian?"

Fucking Hel, he's obsessed with her. I shake my head. "No." *What a fucktwat.* "Your little pet, the human. We're doing impalement arts, but I would feel a lot better about it if I could use my magic."

"What, are you suddenly growing soft?" he chuckles, clearly amused by my misery.

"Luc, if you don't get me some magicite, I'll ruin you. I can make every single member of that carnival walk," I say. It's more threat than promise, but I know I could make it happen.

"Raph and Gemma would be loyal to me," he says. "But I understand your frustration."

"Do you?" Half-demons and hybrids have never had free access to our magic. Some find other methods—there's a special tea the serpentine use. Orcs, satyrs, and some other hybrids often use familiars, but many of us can't tap into our magic without magicite. The Morningstar family controls all of it.

Though demons don't require magical conduits, it makes them stronger, and so they covet the crystal. Only the half-demons that run our cities and infrastructure can use it for work. It's how we have lights and power, phones and tablets. Running water. Other than that, it's a luxury of the rich.

My father had a magicite ring that I stole before I took his life. When Raph and Luc took me in under their wings, they confiscated it from me. Now, I want it back.

"I can't just give everyone magicite. It would be chaos. So many beings with unchecked magic—what about those with malicious intent? Or someone who struggles to control their magic?" Luc says, and it grinds my gears.

"We could be like Earth and build schools, or like Umbra with their competency exams," I suggest. "And besides, it's not like all the demons use their magic properly. Look at your siblings and how they misuse their powers to abuse their citizens."

"Might I remind you that *we* are working on that," he says, clearly frustrated with the early morning grilling I'm putting him through.

"And *I* would work a lot better and *faster* if you granted me magic," I reply firmly.

Luc's end is quiet for a few moments, the silence between us a heavy anchor, threatening to drag me down.

A golden, shimmering ring appears on my right hand with a large chunk of magicite in the center. *My father's ring.* What should've rightfully been mine this whole time.

"Do not tell a single soul I gave you that," he says as he hangs up. Not a problem, because I didn't intend to.

Heading out into camp, I search for Khalid. He's sharing a tent with his sister, which is unfortunate for literally everyone here. They're both *incredibly* fuckable. But that's not why I need to see him—I need to ask about his magic.

Today, I am both The Scorpion and The Spy, wearing masks split in two, much like Raph when he is The Phantom.

My ring seems to glow, though I'm not sure if it's real or if I'm seeing things, and I follow the path until I slam directly into the felion himself.

"Hey." He gives me a wicked smile. "I was just looking for you. I wanted to say I'm sorry for the scare. Yasmeena wasn't actually at risk of being burned, I was just messing with her."

"Apology accepted," I say without a second thought. "Accidents happen, but make no mistake, if you burn this place to the ground... I'll kill you."

"Noted."

"Actually, Absinthe would probably kill you first. All her props and costumes suddenly gone? You'd never see a clown more murderous than that," I say, and he laughs. *Good. Let me wear down your defenses.*

He leans against the prop shed, and I do the same. "I think Yasmeena would kill me first. She's so glad to be out of Ira."

"Good. We're happy to have you two. Listen, I've got a few questions about your magic. How are you able to wield fire?"

Khalid gives me a scrutinizing glare, and for a moment, I don't think he'll tell me. "It's tattoo magic—Yasmeena and I both have runes tattooed down the center of our backs," he shares.

"Yasmeena has magic too?"

"Eh. Yes and no. She's not nearly as proficient. We have different runes anyway. Mine helps me wield fire." He sticks out his tongue, and a small flame appears.

"And hers?"

He shrugs. "She'll have to tell you herself."

"So if I tattoo a rune on someone, it'll give them magical abilities?" I say, trying to will casualness into my tone, but my heart races with anticipation.

"No, you need atra. It's a powderized mineral. We used to drink some before going underwater on Ira, helped us to breathe underwater. Honestly, I wish I understood it more, but it's an old process that belongs to the vampires and the lupion," he explains.

"That's sick, dude. You're so lucky," I say, making sure to sound as mindless as possible. It's easier if everyone thinks I'm a fool. It's all just an act—I know exactly how to play the game.

I wrote the rules, after all.

"TIME FOR OUR LAST REHEARSAL," I say to the human as I enter her and Reina's tent.

Nipples. Those are human nipples with fleshy pink areolas. *Fuck.*

"*Hello,*" I say directly to her perfect rosy buds before I can even think about the words coming out of my mouth. It shouldn't be a surprise to see her newest costume. Absinthe has been making them more and more scandalous, but I'm used to looking away in horror to avoid seeing more of my sisters than I'd like to. This is an incredibly different and new experience altogether.

But we have our first show together tonight, and I do not have time to process the unchecked and *very frustrating* amount of sexual energy that's been charging between us for the last couple of weeks. It's as palpable as the magic humming beneath my skin.

There's no rule saying that we can't fraternize within the carnival, with the exception of Raph, as that would be an abuse of power. Robyn, Quinn, and Rowan are married. As are Lilian and Baelor. But even though I now know she isn't a threat, there's some feeling in my gut telling me to run.

I'm positive she felt the same when we met. The difference is —she *should* want to run from me. I am predator, and she is prey. It's fundamentally who we are.

So what about her causes my heart to jump into my throat?

"Where do you want to rehearse?" she asks, totally still, and for a second I wonder if she too can hear the blood roaring in my ears.

"We're less likely to be disturbed in our tents than in the hall. Mine is a bit larger, if that helps," I offer, and she moves towards me.

"Lead the way."

We walk out of her and Reina's tent, and it's just a short distance until we're outside mine. The sun is shining high in the sky, and everyone else is still finishing up their shifts at the carnival. We were let out early, of course, to practice.

Opening the entrance to my tent, I take her inside, and we stand here like two fools, silently staring at one another.

"I feel confident in my ability to throw knives at you." I don't tell her it's because I can access my magic now. Too risky.

"Oh good, I'm so glad you don't think you're going to kill me." She crosses her arms. "We still have a problem."

"And what is that?"

She plops up onto the top of my dresser. "We have no act." She looks mad, like *I've* somehow wronged her when *she* is the one constantly making my life more difficult.

"Are you dense? We are literally doing impalement arts," I say.

She shakes her head. "Everyone has... drama. A hook. Baelor does that gross—but oddly captivating—thing where he walks around talking to the audience. Taryn goes through hoops before stripping. Everyone's act feels like a show, but you just go out there. I'm afraid if I do the same, I'll look mousy and awkward."

I'm not sure if she could ever look mousy or awkward, but I try and listen to her. "I understand. How would you like to proceed?"

"Well, I think we should make it... sexy. I mean, that's what The Sinner's Circus is all about. Eroticism and violence. We should go all out," she explains.

I shift closer to her, until her legs are almost wrapped around me, and it's the most torturous thing I've ever done to myself. "So what, we fuck on stage? Is that what you want, human?" I'm trying to make her feel an ounce of what she does to me.

She gulps, wringing her hands with nervous energy, and then lets out a laugh that borders on maniacal. "No thank you. I was thinking I would dance?"

"I'm not a good dancer," I say, and place a hand on her thigh. Clearly, it's working. "Shocking, I know."

"I'm not going to dance *with* you, I'm going to dance *on* you."

I don't give her a reaction, my face carefully neutral. "Oh? Show me."

She pushes me off and jumps down, searching the room for something. Her eyes land on my radio, and she turns it on, changing stations until she finds something to her liking. I can't help but wonder how different our music is from the music from her planet.

There's a bashful gleam to her eyes, but it's gone in a flash. Perhaps the pest is more like me than I thought—perhaps she wears masks too.

"Sit," she commands, gesturing to a chair, and I obey, curious to see how this goes. If there's one thing this woman has taught me, it's that she's full of surprises, and is not to be underestimated.

Slowly, she crosses towards me, like a cat hunting a mouse. She moves gracefully, her body on the very tips of her toes, before she lands into a split in front of me. Just when I think that's it, the human sensually kicks her legs out in front of her and lies on the floor, and I can't look away. The vision of her is magnetic.

She's upside down from my perspective, her body on full display. Gemma is somehow soft curves, taut muscles, and lean lines rolled into one, her pale skin glittering in the dim light of the lantern. Pulling onto the bottom bars of the chair, she hoists herself up onto me, her perfect ass practically in my face, before she uses the strength in her legs to pull herself completely up.

Gemma is sitting in my lap, grinding against me, and I can't move—can't give any indication that this is enjoyable.

She stops and turns to face me. "At this point, when I get up, you'll push me against the wheel of death and strap me in," she explains.

"I can do that," I say, donning another mask. Whatever this one is, it allows me to pretend like every cell of my body doesn't yearn for hers.

Symphony No. 13

Gemma

"Tonight, you're a sinner," Raph says with a wink as he leaves the backstage area.

Backstage is actually a hidden section of the big top, underneath the stands, where everyone waits until it's their turn in The Sinner's Circus. The elaborateness of the structure stands out from the rest of the carnival grounds, and I wonder if it's a newer addition.

The lights dim, the fog clearing to showcase Raph in his little red outfit, decked out to the nines.

"Welcome to The Sinner's Circus, where it doesn't matter who you are. If you pay, you get to play. Tonight's acts will feature not only our new, *purrfect* sibling duo, but a bonus finale that is certainly... sharp!" Raph announces in his charming way. "Our first act of the night is sure to lift your spirits."

Rowan enters the ring, flanked by Lilian and Reina. They perform a few tricks, Reina dancing and Lilian doing backbends and contortion, before Rowan lifts the two up onto his shoulders.

"C'mon, I think you can hold more," Lilian teases.

They traverse into the audience, looking for volunteers to be added onto Rowan's shoulders until there's four in total. He's probably holding up *at least* five or six hundred pounds, and I'm in awe of his strength.

Once he's finished, Lilian and Reina perform their separate acts, and it's odd to see Lilian without Baelor. I wonder where *The Carver* is tonight.

"This next act is not only looking good, they're *feline* good too," Raph says into the microphone, and I cringe. Raph might not be a father, but he sure as Hel knows how to crack a dad joke.

Yasmeena and Khalid give each other knowing glances as they step into the ring. A large hoop—which I've recently learned is called a lyra and is apparently "totally different" from Rowan's Cyr wheel—drops down from the ceiling thanks to Leo and Lyle, who run our lights, sound, and props.

As Yasmeena climbs onto the hoop, Khalid begins dousing his blades in oil and lighting them on fire with his tongue. The lyra slowly lifts back up into the air, and Yasmeena makes shapes with her body, showcasing her flexibility and strength. I think if she wanted, her body could make the form of any letter of the alphabet. Any symbol. Anything, really.

It's hard to choose who to watch—they're both such incredible performers. I can't help but wonder what it would be like to be in the audience. From this thin crack between the stands, I can only see their backs and a small scope of what the full show appears like to those sitting in the proper area.

The lyra comes back down, and that's when the real fun begins. I've seen them perform together over the past week or so since they joined, but this is new.

Khalid lights the hoop on fire. The bright orange flames illuminate the deep tan of Yasmeena's skin, and my eyes are fixated as she moves her hands and feet to avoid the flames.

I have no idea how Khalid does it. He must be using magic to move the fire, or something. Maybe the fire is magic itself. I thought Draven said none of the half-demons or hybrids had access to magic, but that seems far from the truth.

The level of trust these two have for one another is astounding, but it makes sense. They're siblings, of course they trust one another with their lives. I can't help but wonder if I have a sibling back home. And if I don't, would I want to? Did I secretly wish I had someone to spend my childhood with? To share both my joy and my suffering?

I imagine being an only child would've been incredibly lonely. Everyone here has somebody. Yasmeena has Khalid, Raph has Luc, Una has Po, Leo has Lyle, and even Draven has the girls. And if they don't have siblings, they have spouses. Robyn has Quinn and Rowan, Baelor has Lilian. The whole troupe is just one big happy family made up of smaller families.

And then there's me. I'm truly the outsider.

But maybe I don't have to be? Maybe, even if it's only temporary, I can build a life here. I need to stop wallowing and just enjoy my time. This is just the very odd, very magical version of a semester abroad.

When Yasmeena and Khalid's act is finished, the audience claps and cheers for a long time, and they just stand there in silence, smiling.

"Cat got your tongue?" Raph asks before shooing them out of the ring. "Rumor has it there's a ghost lurking around The Sinner's Circus, but can you find his heads?"

Somehow I have always missed Raph's act. Whether I've been in the bathroom, or I just wasn't watching the show that night, I haven't the slightest clue what it is.

The Phantom.

Poof. Raph's head disappears before our eyes, him suddenly appearing like a headless horseman. Headless ringleader? He's fucking headless. There is no head on his body.

The audience gasps in utter disbelief, and I gasp right along with them. A hand cups my mouth, and I realize I've been so intent on watching the show, I forgot there are other people waiting here with me.

One other person now. Draven.

I try to squirm against the warm press of skin into my face, but he holds me close, the back of my body pushing against him. "Be quiet, pest. The audience can't know we're down here."

He's right. I know he's right. The twins use smoke and fog to cover performers' entries so nobody knows where they're coming from, but it would put everyone at risk if someone figured it out. We don't need obsessive fans in our space.

I'd stomp on his foot, but my feet are bare and I'm pretty sure it would hurt me more than it would hurt him, so instead I nod my agreement, and he finally lets go.

Peeking through the crevice, Raph's head is now replaced by two floating theatrical masks. They look like Comedy and Tragedy split in half.

"Melpo and Thalia," Draven whispers. "Before these grounds belonged to the carnival, it was a sacred theater." His breath caresses my ear as he continues to tell me the story. "Melpo—a dancer—and Thalia—a comedian—performed here every night. They were young forbidden lovers from dueling families who took their lives so they could be together."

"Really?" I ask.

"No," he shakes his head, clearly trying not to laugh. "Raph is simply using magic to levitate masks that Absinthe made."

I let out a breath and listen to Raph's voice come back over the speakers. "Our finale for tonight is sure to make you spin, but watch your step and be amazed because only pretty ladies live."

One of the twins places a single chair in the center of the ring, and Draven crosses towards it, removing his shirt as he walks, and the crowd goes wild. Everyone is screaming and fainting, and I think I even hear someone moan. Another twin is setting up the wheel of death, and I take in some shaky breaths, trying not to let my nerves get the better of me.

The music begins and I come out through the misty fog, my body moving to the sensual rhythms. I am nothing but glitter, sweat, and adrenaline as I take my place.

There are bright lights beaming into my eyes, and the music sounds nothing like the slow glide of the cello I'm used to dancing to every day. This music is faster and sexier. There's brass and even instruments I don't recognize coming through the speaker.

I move, performing my split and flipping my body over to hoist myself up, just like I did yesterday. When my body is finally upright on Draven's lap, I'm acutely aware of the senses pressing into me.

Metal. Piercings. *Oh my god.* Draven has his nipples pierced.

He pulls out a blade and twirls it around in his fingers until it's against my throat, and I bite my lower lip, grinding into him, and I hear someone cheer.

Swinging my body around until I'm straddling him, I flip my hair and he uses the opportunity to suck on my neck as I move. It's not what we practiced, but the audience seems to eat it up.

Finally, Draven decides he's had enough of our little song and dance, and pushes me off of him, my legs moving backwards until he presses me against the wheel and forcefully places my wrist into the first red leather strap. He does my other wrist and then moves down my body, his fingers gliding down the fabric of my costume, and my skin, and I look down to see a bulge in his tight pants.

He's hard, which means one thing: I am not completely alone with these feelings festering inside me.

Or *maybe* I'm being ridiculous and any attractive individual dancing on him would gain that reaction, but for now, I'll pretend my lust is reciprocated. It's the fantasy I'll think about as I touch mys—*nope*. Definitely not going to think about that right now.

Once my ankles are strapped in as well, I take in a deep breath as Draven backs away and winks before throwing the first blade. It lands directly between my open thighs, and a blush creeps across my skin. He throws another, and it hits a section of wood right next to my arm.

"Let's kick it up a notch, shall we? See how this pretty lady handles real danger," Draven says to the audience. I'm guessing only the first few rows can hear him without a mic, but everyone is on the edge of their seat as he spins the wheel of death.

I can't see much, just blurry visions of light, Draven, and the audience as I spin round and round, trying to focus on a spot to avoid getting nauseous. I feel the thud of a blade landing next to my other arm. Another one quickly follows, hitting above my head.

Thud. Cold metal presses against the flesh of my ear, and I fear he's cut it off, or at least cut it open. The wheel slows down, but I feel no pain. Just the dizzy, adrenaline-pumped feeling of performing like this.

Draven managed to land a dagger so close it touches my skin, but didn't actually slice it open. He either got incredibly lucky, or he's an even better throw than I thought. It's fucking *magical* how close it is, and I stay still as he pulls each blade out of the wheel, one by one.

Slowly, he unhooks me from my straps, and we take our bows. There's a cacophony of applause as the audience gives us a standing ovation, and I look over at Draven, beaming with pride, but I can't read him.

He looks somewhere between proud and pained, and it kills me. Just like everyone else in the troupe, Draven works hard. Harder than most, probably. He deserves an ounce of joy, and I don't know what's keeping it from him.

What haunts you? I think as I watch his sweat-slicked body exit the ring.

Sometimes I'm certain the only reason I'm so happy is *because* I lost my memories. I think for some, remembering is harder than forgetting. You have to relive your pain and suffering, which I don't experience. I don't have any grief or trauma. I mean, *technically* I do, but I can't remember any of it.

I follow Draven back to the hall, where everyone is already waiting. Reina comes up and claps me on the back, which is immediately followed by the biggest hug from Absinthe.

"You really did it, girl," Lilian says, and everyone's eyes glitter with pride.

Leo, Draven, and Khalid go over some of the lighting choices and mechanisms, already discussing new ideas for the next show, but I just need to catch my breath.

I take a seat beside Robyn and Raph. "Where's Quinn?"

"With Rowan, tucking the girls in," Robyn says.

Everyone did so well, it was incredible. The side shows are fun, but this truly feels like a performance, and not just something you stop and watch on your way to buy a hotdog.

"Raph, can I ask you something?"

"You just did," he replies, curling the edges of his mustache.

I roll my eyes. "Is your act inspired by The Phantom of the Opera?"

"The what?"

"The Phantom of the Opera," I start. "On Earth it's one of the most famous musicals of all time. The guy wears a mask, a lot like yours, and he's literally called The Phantom. It's been around for thousands of years."

"And you think a demon governor on another planet based his circus persona off of this... old musical?" he asks, obviously trying—and failing—not to tease me.

"Well. It sounds really stupid when you put it that way, but yes," I say. "That is what I thought."

He shakes his head. "Don't feel too bad, they are inspired by something on Earth. Something a lot older than that, though. They're actually from ancient mythology; their names are Melpomene and Thalia—"

"Nope," I say, shooting up onto my feet. "Not falling for that one again."

"Falling for what? They're muses!"

"Fool me once, shame on you. Fool me twice, shame on me," I say, and exit the hall, heading towards my tent.

I need to fucking *sleep*.

THERE'S a man coughing up blood in front of me. He's human, unlike anyone I've seen lately. There's no carnival. I'm not even sure I'm still on Hel. This feels like Earth, or at least what I remember of it.

I am watching a clone of myself. *Do I have a twin?* No, that's definitely me. She has the same little birthmark on the back of her left calf.

My skin feels flushed and feverish as I watch myself hold my grandfather's hand. Tears fall down my face. Not *my* face, but the version in front of me. She's a sobbing, blubbering mess, while the nurses press buttons on the machine and move wires so she can crawl into the hospital bed and lay beside him.

His chest isn't moving anymore, and now I'm crying too. There's nobody else in the room besides me and the medical staff, and my head is pounding, so many memories slamming into me at once.

Nobody else is here because they're all dead. Gone.

I know my parents died in a car crash when I was a kid, coming home from a concert. I remembered that a couple of weeks ago. I also know that my nonna died of breast cancer when I was a teenager, a recent memory that came to me. And here goes my nonno.

A blood-clot induced stroke. It's bewildering that I could ever forget such important, completely devastating memories. These are capstones of my life, heart, and soul. And yet for the last month or so, I've been living in a different reality. One where I could dream of a family I won't get to come home to.

The worst part of all? I still don't remember everything. I have no fucking clue how I survived on Earth. My job, my apartment or house, whether or not I had a boyfriend or girlfriend or partner. I don't know if my favorite color is fuchsia or red wine.

At first, I couldn't believe that my memories were truly gone. Then I was angry, so mad with the world, wondering what I did to deserve this. My anger quickly turned to bargaining, my brain wondering what could have been, or what might be once my memories return, but now all I feel is darkness.

Denial, anger, bargaining... depression.

I'm fucking depressed. I put on a brave face, trying desperately to enjoy this new life I'm building, but my feelings are hollow. Maybe I just need to accept that my memories might never fully return? Or that I might never make it back to Earth?

Maybe I just need to—

Blinking, I peel my eyelids open, forcing myself to look at the ceiling of the tent. It was all a dream. Somehow, I *knew* I was dreaming—knew that I was trapped in a memory, forced to relive one of the most anguishing days of my life from an outsider's point of view.

Before ending up on Hel, it seems my life had become a series of dimly lit rooms, each one darker and colder than the last. Now, every door I open can lead me in a new direction, but the same ghosts continue to haunt me, their silence harrowing.

I just have to keep going until I find acceptance—until the ghosts don't follow me anymore.

Symphony No. 14

Draven

I've never been one to mix business and pleasure, but this human might change that. It's not that I'm completely against screwing around in the workplace, it's just never made sense. There's never really been an opportunity for it.

I joined the carnival when I was sixteen. After I killed my father, Luc took us under his wing. He's never told me why, though I suspect it was to protect us from my father's allies, should they have found out his cause of death. At some point, Luc finally decided we were too much to handle. Or maybe he truly needed to focus on his royal duties. Either way, Phaelyn and I were sent off to different places. Phaelyn went to live with Zada on Luxuria, and I was given to Raph. I fought tooth and nail to not be separated from my sister, but eventually, it became obvious that she needed space from me, and she deserved a maternal figure —someone who could dedicate their time to finish raising her, and Zada was exactly that.

When I joined, Robyn, Quinn, and Aida were already a part of the carnival. There was an exodus of previous carnies—something political that I was too young to understand—and we were vastly understaffed.

After a short while, Raph tasked me with finding new

members, and that's when I found Reina and Absinthe. They were just kids. Reina performing on the street, and Absinthe a petty thief. They became my sisters.

Eventually Lilian came knocking on the gates, followed by Taryn, and we were like a little family.

Baelor was the first person who joined that wasn't significantly older or like family to me. I'm pretty sure he's straight as a board, but even if he wasn't, no fucking thank you. Rowan joined —he's older, ridiculous, and only had the hots for Robyn and Quinn.

Leo and Lyle joined when they were just eighteen years old, and of course, obviously, the younger ones were born into the carnival. We've gotten into a rhythm. We're all a weird, fucked up family, and it works. Even Baelor marrying Lilian—it somehow works.

None of us wanna ruin what we have here. Leo and Lyle haven't even *tried* to sleep with my sisters, which might be why I keep them around. Together, the three of us play wingman, helping our friends find gorgeous and handsome strangers to fuck.

But now? I think our bubble might've popped. There are three very available, very attractive individuals that have just been thrown into the mix, and someone is going to take the bait. I'm just fucking pissed that the human-shaped worm wriggling in front of me looks so delectable.

Gemma decided we need to practice the tango before dinner tonight, and that's exactly what we're doing. Her body is pressed against mine, her breath hot on my skin, and I can't help but allow my eyes to wander down her body, following the way she moves.

"My eyes are up here, Scorpion," she teases, and time seems to still.

Our feet are moving, our hands still clasped, but there's a new spark in the air. The tension is tangible and I want to grab it—I want to grab *her* and kiss those pillowy pink lips.

"Where's Quinn?" she asks, and like I've been in a fog, I drop her hands and look around the room.

The troupe has started filing in, everyone sitting patiently, making quiet conversation. Una is resting her head on Robyn's shoulder, while Po bounces in Rowan's lap. It's nice to be back to a more regular routine after the excitement of rehearsing with someone new.

"They're cooking, but they'll be back soon. The Three Muskets are never apart for long," I answer.

"The what now?"

"The Three Muskets?"

She stares at me like I've got dumbass written on my forehead, her big brown eyes wide, thick brows furrowed. "Do you mean The Three Musketeers?"

I shake my head. "No, I mean The Three Muskets. It's a slang term for a polyamorous triad."

"What are you talking about? It's an old book on Earth. Muskets don't even make any sense, that's a type of weapon." She looks so sure of herself.

"What are *you* talking about? The Three Muskets is a reference to an old demonic tale about preparing for battle."

One corner of her mouth ticks up, and she's clearly amused by my answer. "Why would demons use guns? It's literally a slapstick comedy routine, but alright."

"What exactly is your act?" Khalid's voice interrupts our back-and-forth. Baelor smiles back at him broadly. I hate how much he gets under my skin, festering like a wound.

At least I'm not alone in my feelings, as Reina and Gemma both seem to grimace every time he speaks.

"I'm The Carver. I carve ladies up," Baelor explains, as if we're all fucking idiots.

"I get that, but like—why?"

Absinthe snorts and lets out a giggle. "Because they want to be."

"It releases endorphins," Reina says, and I blink. She's right, though I'd never thought about it until now.

Khalid shakes his head, his gaze piercing as he looks over Baelor and Lilian. "I don't see your wife with any scars—"

"Khalid, that's enough," Yasmeena cuts in.

"No, it's okay," Baelor responds, calm as always. I think he only has two modes: halcyon and horny. "My wife and I have... different proclivities."

"And you're just okay with letting him do that?" Khalid asks Lilian, who is twiddling her fingers, her eyes void of any light, and I grind my teeth.

There are plenty of the populace who participate in all sorts of romantic and sexual arrangements. Take Robyn, Quinn, and Rowan's relationship, for example. There are others that share a main partner, as well as side partners, and they are healthy and happy.

But that is not what *this* is, because it is missing the most important factors: communication and consent. I know in my heart of hearts that Lilian doesn't want this, but she agrees because she feels she must. She's used to being controlled, so she just allows him to do it.

Just like her parents did before she joined the carnival.

The more I think about it, the angrier I get. Except I don't have the luxury to be angry right now. We need to be a united front against everyone—the other demons in power, The Legion, even the citizens of Hel, who one day might turn on us for siding with Luc.

My leg is shaking, sweat lining my brow as I clench my fists when a soft hand presses against the top of my thigh, squeezing it.

Gemma.

She shifts her body, leaning close to my ear. "Take a deep breath. Don't let him work you up so easily," she whispers, and a shiver racks through my entire body.

"Careful, pest," I say in a hushed tone. "Someone might think you actually enjoy touching me."

"Wouldn't that be a shame?" she jests, and I'll be honest, I'm having fun. It's nice to have someone to banter with that isn't my family—nice to be seen and to develop trust with someone new. And with her memory loss, we are getting to know her all while she is getting to know herself.

I find her annoying, bubbly, and insufferable, but I also know that I'd protect her just as much as I'd protect any of the troupe. She's swiftly become one of us.

"Did Baelor ever tell you the story about the famous wasp?" Leo asks, and Lyle nods in agreement.

"That is a good one!" Lyle says.

I fucking hate this joke. Baelor has told it to quite literally everyone he's ever met. When I meet someone, I like to take my time. I learn their quirks and cater the conversation style to their personality. Baelor? Tells the same terrible joke.

"I have not," Gemma says, feigning interest.

Reina and Lilian audibly sigh, which makes me laugh. Even Taryn, who is in her tank talking to Raph, looks over and gives us a proper eye roll.

Baelor cracks his knuckles. "There was once a wasp. He was not like other wasps. He could talk and sing. He even wanted to go to school. In his single month of life, he attended university at a prestigious school—"

"Do you guys have universities?" Gemma interrupts.

"Not currently, no. We used to," Robyn says, now listening in. "It's a shame."

"That is not the point," Baelor says. "This is an old story. Might even be from Earth."

"I was just clarifying."

Baelor squints at Gemma before schooling his face back into a smile. "I ask that you all kindly turn on your suspension of disbelief."

"Suspension?" she whispers in my ear, and I try not to chuckle.

"Just listen to the fucktwat."

Baelor coughs and we all sit up, humoring him. "After graduating with his PhD, the wasp decides to run for mayor. His campaign is successful and he wins. He helps improve the city, fixing many of the roads and infrastructure."

Gemma gives me a funny look, and I widen my eyes at her.

"Once the wasp was done with his term as mayor, he decided to run for governor. He won that election as well, improving the state or continent he lived on immensely. He introduced new laws that helped children get fed and took care of the environment, and when that term ended, he ran for president," Baelor says, his tone dripping like honey.

The human looks less than amused. "I don't really get how all of this would be possible in under a month," she says.

"I might be remembering the story wrong, it might've been a year... or a few," Baelor admits, and that's when Reina decides to go in for the kill.

"Wasps don't live that long," Reina says.

"Really, Reina?" Baelor's face has shifted, his brows furrowed and smile fading. "Anyway, after a great presidency, the wasp decided it was time to become supreme leader of the planet. The devil, if you will. He combined every continent and nation, creating rule books everyone had to follow. They started taxing the citizens, using the money for education and housing, and the entire planet began to thrive. Once the wasp grew old, though, he started to age. His face wrinkled, his wings not flapping as quickly anymore. The citizens of his planet threw him a retirement party! It was fun and full of music. The wasp danced the night away, and he started to feel thirsty, so he went to grab a glass of lemonade, but the line was too long. It stretched for miles."

"Here it fucking goes," I whisper to Gemma, and one of her eyebrows quirks up.

"The wasp said to himself *I don't need lemonade, I could drink punch instead.* He went to go get punch, and that's when he realized there was no punchline," Baelor finally says, a wide smirk spreading across his face to reveal his teeth.

Everyone in the room groans, unamused to have had to listen to this for the twentieth time, but I swear Gemma cracks the smallest of smiles.

The smell of cooked meat hits my nostrils, and I give Khalid a look.

Quinn steps into the hall, a plate of food in their hands, and they gesture for Rowan to get up and help carry some of the other trays. He's on his feet in an instant, a flirty smile forming across his face.

"Eat up, carnivores," I say, stabbing at a slice of meat with my fork.

"Is anyone here *actually* a carnivore?" the human asks, her tone mocking. Yasmeena and Khalid smile, and Yasmeena gives a little wave.

I swear I see Gemma gulp in response.

"I think I'm technically worse than a carnivore," Reina says, grinning in a way that shows off her long fangs.

I wonder if Reina has told Gemma how she feeds. It's something only Raph and I currently know, but with the two of them sharing a tent, I'm sure the human wonders where her roommate goes late at night. Or maybe she doesn't—too submersed in her own head and dreams.

More than I'd like to admit to myself, I wonder what happens in those dreams. Does she dance on a stage, or commit crimes in dark alleyways? Are there beautiful blue skies or dark starry nights? What does it smell like in her dreams? Is she happy?

Or do her dreams look more like mine—nightmares full of bloody hands, clammy skin, and an empty, hollow feeling in her chest from where her heart might as well have been carved out of her?

"I'm an herbivore," Taryn says from one of her many tanks. She only has two portable ones. One filled to the top with four wheels to allow lots of movement for performances, and another for dinners and spending time with all of us. She's in that one now, the water only coming up to her hips, with slits for easier communication through the glass.

Taryn's tent was built with an underwater spring below it so she can swim freely. It's been really nice for her to have that privacy away from her family, but I do live with the fear of what we'd do if she somehow got sick or stuck down there.

"I might as well be. I'm not fond of meat," Quinn says.

Rowan's eyebrows shoot up. "That's funny, you sure liked m—"

"Rowan," Lilian says with a gasp, but Robyn shakes her head, her rich, mauve-colored curls bouncing.

"Absinthe took the girls to go play when Baelor started the wasp joke," she explains.

Baelor shrugs. "The joke isn't inappropriate for children."

"No, it's just fucking annoying, and Una has an attitude," Reina says, and we all laugh.

I might be broken and burned, but there's no place I'd rather be than surrounded by the people I love, and much to my dismay, the infestation of new faces that have begun to grow on me.

Dinner continues as normal, with everyone sharing stories and jokes, and I stop focusing on their words, allowing myself to wander into the mindset of The Spy.

I need to acquire more information on atra and how it's used in tattoo ink, but there's one problem. I don't know many lupion. Most of them reside on Violenta working in fight rings, with the exception of a lucky few.

Theoretically, I could contact Cain Lupine. He's an old friend of Luc and Raph, and he might have the information we need— or know someone who does. I file these thoughts away for later, the gears of my brain turning back into place until I feel like Draven again.

Just Draven. I'll have to be The Scorpion or The Executioner soon, but for these few hours a day, it's nice to be me.

When dinner concludes, Una and Absinthe clean up while

everyone else leaves to get ready. Someone tugs on my sleeve and I turn, expecting Po.

"We need to talk," Raph says. His lips are pursed, his eyebrows slightly furrowed, and there are bags under his eyes. Whatever it is, Raph is worried, and that is one of the few things that actually frightens me.

He glances around the room, ensuring nobody is around. It's the kind of paranoia I see from everyone else, but never from Raph or Luc. "I've been tracking our money," he says, and it's barely a whisper. "Tracking how many tickets we sell to the carnival as well as the circus, I know how much those tickets cost. We are missing money."

"What?" We all know that the carnival is sinking. It's why we hired Gemma, Yasmeena, and Khalid in the first place. We're trying to amp things up, increase interest. But are we miscounting our funds?

"Our overall sales are lower, yes, but revenue is missing," he explains to me like I'm twelve.

I know what he means—I know the words and their individual and combined meanings, but I can't wrap my brain around the type of betrayal this would be.

I shake my head. "It must be Yasmeena or Khalid then, right? I like them, but they're new. Maybe they don't understand the depth of this, or they're upset at the lack of pay. That's a fair thing to be upset over, and we haven't exactly explained it to them," I say, trying to reason with the complexity of the situation.

"It cannot be Yasmeena or Khalid, Draven. It started happening before they got here," Raph says, and he looks pained.

"How long?" I ask, even though I know in my bones how long it's been. I know who it is, and my skin is going hot with rage and denial.

I know it's her. Logically, it *has* to be her because she's the only other new variable that's been added to this equation, but some small part of me still doesn't want to believe it could be the human. I want to find someone else to blame—someone else to put this on, even when I know it's pointless and denying the truth will only bring me more pain.

There's a pit in my stomach where emotions were *just* starting to develop. Friendship—I was actually willing to be friends with the human, but not anymore. We let her into our home, we took care of her. Yes, it's a job, but we've shared some of our secrets and histories and she has the audacity to take from us.

She knows we could all use the money. None of us have enough to access our magic, Aida is trying to get back to her family.

This is why I don't trust anyone, and why I can't let new members in. I'll let them into the carnival, sure. But my heart? Access to it remains closed; the door is shut. Baelor and the boys ride the line, but I was actually considering letting in this fucking pest. Hel, I was going to let Khalid and Yasmeena in, too.

Not anymore.

Raph looks at me, but he's not angry, he's sad and I can't be the one to comfort him. "You were ready to make so many excuses for the felion, are you not willing to do the same for Gemma?"

"The Al-Khalifa siblings are newer, and I haven't trusted them with much yet. I perform with this human—this pest of a person every day, Raph. I trust her with The Scorpion, and with Reina. She sleeps in the same room as one of my sisters every night, and if she's stealing from us? What else could she be hiding? I bet she's one of The Legion's spies after all."

"We should tell Robyn and make a decision. I would like to investigate this more before jumping to conclusions," he says, nervously fidgeting with his mustache.

"After tonight's show, I will confront her and bring you both my findings. Have Reina search their tent during the show. Do not tell Luc, yet. Please," I say, and I'm not sure why.

What am I even pleading for? I knew this would happen all along.

Symphony No. 15
Gemma

There's an intense level of scrutiny in Draven's gaze as he stares at me in the darkness. We're waiting backstage, but the air feels different. It's thick with tension, dripping like tree sap from a broken branch.

Dinner was lovely. We teased each other, sure, but things felt friendly. A little flirty, too. Now? He's looking at me like I killed his cat or told him I hate his favorite movie. I'm not sure what happened in the time between then and now, but I'm desperate to go back.

Despite how heart-wrenching it's been getting my memories back, I *am* enjoying my time here, and Draven is a huge part of that. Raph might be the ringleader, but Draven is the star of the show. He electrifies every room he walks into. I'm not sure how I've fucked up our tentative friendship, but I'd like to mend it—or maybe mend whatever inside him is broken.

Dark tendrils of smoke conceal my entrance, filling my vision with a swirling haze. When the music starts, and he's in his chair, I slink out onto the stage.

Just like we've practiced and performed so many times, I fall into a split before pulling myself towards him, flipping my body until I land in his lap. He grips the skin of my thighs, but tonight it's harder. Rougher. So much so, I think I'm going to bruise.

What the fuck? I think. But don't say it aloud because I'm smiling in the center of the ring, hundreds of demons, half-demons, and hybrids staring down at me—at us. Looking back over my shoulder, I raise my eyebrows at him, hoping he'll let up or give some sort of hint at what's going on inside that head of his. Instead, I'm met with the same callous stare.

This is going to be a long fucking performance.

When he pushes me into the wheel, his anger feels real, losing all the sensuality it normally holds. It's not sexy but a raw, fiery rage. He hooks me into the straps, pulling on the edge of the wood, and I actually fear the blades as they fly through the air towards me.

The first two land perfectly, but the third does not. It slices through both my dress and skin. It's not deep or anything, but I can feel the wetness of my blood, my head getting heavy as he taunts me. Everything feels inside out or upside down, and not just because *I'm* upside down.

He's saying something to the crowd about what happens to naughty girls, a twisted grin across his lips, and I cringe, unable to move or say or do anything.

I honestly don't know what's wrong with me, but by the time he lets me loose and we exit the big top, Draven isn't the only one seething with rage. Reina passes, and she shakes her head at Draven. I don't understand their silent communications, but he seems even more pissed now. He's following me, his long legs easily keeping pace with mine, and I dart into the nearest tent, hoping he won't follow.

I notice all too late that it's *his* tent.

"What is your fucking damage?" I ask as he pushes inside. I'm positive my sweat-slicked hair and bloody clothes aren't the most appealing sight right now, but I'm good and truly pissed, and I don't care. "You did that on purpose," I hiss, pressing a finger into his chest.

He pushes me off, the shove so hard I nearly fall to the ground. "How could you do this to us?" Hurt and rage flash across his face in quick succession. "Actually, I don't want to hear whatever pathetic, piece of shit excuse you have."

"Excuse for *what*?"

"Where'd you hide the money? Or better yet, who'd you give it to? And don't play stupid. You're better off being transparent with me, *now*." My back is against a dresser, and his hands wrap around my wrists, keeping me in place.

"Huh?" He's spewing gibberish questions at me faster than I can process, and it's making my head spin.

"Why are you here?"

"I don't know why I'm fucking stuck here, Draven. I don't know why my own mind seems to be betraying me, or how I ended up on a planet full of murderers and scoundrels, but I do know that I don't deserve this from you. You tried to kill me the first time we met, and I forgave you. I remained kind," I say, willing strength into my voice. I can feel the tears welling in my eyes, but I blink them away, not wanting to let the droplets fall.

"You call this kind? You're a manipulator, and you had all of us fooled. I told myself from the start that you were no good. But you kept showing up. You put in the effort, and I was willing to let you in—to consider you a friend." He shakes his head, his tone wrathful. "It doesn't matter. Whether you're a spy for The Legion or you have your own personal vendetta, you took from us."

I try to shake out of his vise, but he tightens his grip. "I didn't take anything."

"Then explain where the money went."

It's deadly quiet for a moment, because I don't know. I don't know what money he's talking about, who took it, or why he thinks it was me. I'm afraid whatever I say next will determine exactly how my future here will go. "I don't know," I finally say, my voice shaking as the tears finally stream down my face.

Draven doesn't say a word, and I continue, bleary-eyed with despair and rage. "I didn't take any money, I promise. I wouldn't do that, I'm—I know I don't know myself fully, but I know I'm not like that. I-I care about you all so much. I wouldn't do anything that would put you guys in harm's way. I love Reina and Lilian and Absinthe and Una and Po and the rest of you are growing on me and you... you." My voice breaks, the tears sliding down my cheeks. "You're an asshole, but I consider you a friend, too."

He searches my eyes like he can find the answers he's seeking inside them, and his expression softens as he lets go of my wrists, his feet remaining planted.

Neither of us moves a muscle, too lost in each other's gazes as I process all this. The assumption without asking me first, the slicing of my side, the threats and the forcefulness. I'm fucking *hurt*. All the loneliness and confusion, all the loss and grief has built and built and built like a house on sand. I have been a ticking time bomb of volatile emotions, and he just forced me to detonate. Raising my arm, I slap Draven square across the cheek.

The sound seems so loud, but he just barely shuffles back, eyes wide with shock. His hand lifts in return, coming towards my face in an instant, and I brace for impact.

But he cups my jaw instead, pulling me flush against his body, kissing me as hard as I struck him. His hands dance the foxtrot across my skin, fingers moving feverishly down my neck and shoulders. I moan a little, melting into his touch, and allow myself to relax in the embrace. My hands come up around his neck, and he pushes me up onto the dresser, deepening the kiss as his fingers dig into my hips.

From the few memories I have, I believe I've only slept with humans. Is it his half-demon-ness that makes me feel like my blood is made of magic with a simple kiss, or is it him? Although, if I'm being honest with myself, this kiss feels anything but simple. Draven is all-consuming, his tongue meeting mine with a fervor I've never experienced before.

Languidly, he kisses the edge of my jaw before working his way down my neck and onto my chest, and I decide to tease him. I buck my hips up, grinding into him, and he pushes away, his eyes darkening before he reaches down and pulls out a blade.

"Are you taunting me?"

"That depends. Is it working?" I ask with a smirk.

There's a tiny ounce of fear lingering deep within the cavern of my chest. It whispers, warning me to run and hide, that this half-demon is dangerous and might try to kill me again. But another, stronger part of me is tantalized by the recklessness.

If he wants to break me—to tear me limb from limb—I want to let him.

He wields his weapon, methodically slicing the seams of my dress until it's nothing but tattered fabric on the bedroom floor of his tent. I am now naked, completely bare to him, and I like it. His hands roam my body, stopping at the small wound on my side.

"I did that," he says, his brows furrowing. It's not a question, but not an observation. "Hurt me," he commands.

"What?"

"I want you to hurt me back."

I shake my head, trying not to laugh at the ridiculousness of his request. "I did. I literally slapped you."

"No, pest. I want you to make me bleed," Draven demands, his voice gruff. He puts the knife into my hand and wraps his fingers around my wrist.

"Stop," I say, lifting my face into his. His nose rubs up against mine, the septum piercing tickling my skin. "Let me decide."

I consider for a moment all the ways I could really hurt him, but I don't want to. I like Draven. He pisses me off and makes me want to scream, yet I enjoy working with him. The banter is fun, and he's hot and so caring for everyone he loves, despite what he wants the world to believe.

I bite his lower lip. Hard. The metallic tang of his blood coats my tongue, and I smile, licking my lips as I stare back at him.

He's smiling too, fucking giddy over it as he smashes his mouth back into mine, and I hear a clang as the knife drops to the floor. He works his way down my neck and onto my chest, pushing me to lie back on the dresser, fully exposed to him.

"Let me feel that needy little clit of yours," Draven says, his tone dripping like honey.

His tongue makes contact with me, and I let out a sharp exhale, my body instantly reacting to the warm, wet heat of his mouth. He wholly consumes me, bringing his finger up to play with my opening.

"Please," I practically whimper.

If he asked me right now, I'd probably beg for him to fill me. Anything would do. His fingers, his cock, *anything*. I have a desperate, aching need as I rock towards him. Finally, he slips his index finger inside, teasing as he hooks it into me. His tongue continues to work in rhythmic circles, my body overwhelmed with all the sensations.

I'm not sure if anything has ever felt this good. I writhe against his mouth, and I can feel his groans of pleasure vibrate through my body as I come crashing down, every nerve ending exploding in ecstasy.

"You are a goddess among mortals," he says, kissing my inner thigh.

"What does that make you?" I ask, a little breathlessly.

"Lucky."

Quickly, I push Draven's tunic up over his head, revealing the hard planes of his chest and abdomen. His skin is a deep red—taut and muscular—and I stare at the tiny golden bars adorning his nipples.

"How many piercings do you have?" I ask, my eyes roaming over his face. One for each ear, his septum, and one for each nipple. That's five.

"Ten, last I checked," he says, both corners of his mouth ticking up into the cockiest of grins.

"Where are the—"

Before I can even finish my sentence, Draven's pants are on the ground, his hard length jutting out, and I audibly gasp. Not only is his dick thick and pretty, but there are five piercings on the underside.

"Holy—"

His mouth crushes mine as he scoops me up and tosses me onto the bed. Pulling my legs, he wraps them around his body before placing the head of his cock at my entrance.

"Are you going to be good and take my cock?" he asks as he starts to stretch me and I nod feverishly.

Draven moves slowly, pushing his legs against mine until he's filled me completely and I flush. I could feel the piercings one by one as he slid in, just ever-so-slightly.

"That's my girl. You look so perfect, taking all of me," he says, the depths of his voice resonating through my core.

He pulls out, and I whimper, only for him to thrust right back in. If anything, the piercings remind me of a ribbed condom, or the ridges of a dildo. Not too much, but just enough to feel good.

Our bodies are slick with sweat as we get lost in one another's pleasure, my hips bucking as I grind up into him. We're fluid and in tune, like dancers performing a tango, anticipating one another's movements as our bodies press together. The air is thick with passion as he sucks on my neck and I moan with every thrust.

I choose not to think about my memories or my past or the fact that all of this is temporary, but to live in the moment and enjoy Draven's touch. The way he makes everything come to life, my whole body singing out for him.

His pace quickens, and he straightens his back, a devilish grin making way across his features as he stares down at me with those golden, angular eyes of his. His body is perfect, and I close my eyes, falling over the edge once more.

"*Yes, c*ome on my cock, just like that," he groans through ragged breaths before losing himself with me.

Warm liquid fills me as our muscles tense and contract. Draven pulls out and lays down beside me.

Thank fuck for IUDs, I think, and check that off as one of the things my memory has gifted me awareness of. Zero recollection of my favorite foods, but at least I can remember I'm on birth control.

Draven kisses my cheek and stands up to go clean himself off. I take the opportunity to burrito myself in his blanket, loving the soft texture of the blue fabric against my skin.

When Draven returns, he squints and furrows his brow at me. "Share some of the blanket, pest," he hisses, his hands grabbing at the edges to unravel it.

He finally gets a good hold of the blanket and rips it completely off me.

"You frustrate me," I say, cold and unamused.

"Sexually?"

I take one of the pillows and thwack him directly in the face with it.

Symphony No. 16

Gemma

I highly doubt that when I was a little girl, I thought *when I grow up, I want to dance in a circus and ride through the streets of a demon planet on the back of a violent half-demon's motorcycle*. But I can't lie, the last month has felt like a dream. All of my memories are heavy with grief and despair, but the experience I've had here has been genuinely joyful.

It makes me almost not want to go back home. *Almost.*

My hands are wrapped around Draven's waist, pressed against the hard muscles of his abdomen, and I can feel the rise and fall of chest with every breath. His tail curls around my leg, the pressure oddly comforting.

The city around us is so different from the carnival. Everything here is glowing and green—the buildings are mostly modern, if not futuristic, but random structures will come into sight that seem out of place. Imagine a cityscape with skyscrapers and office buildings, with random colosseums and cathedrals tucked in between. If I didn't know about magicite, I'd call this place the City of Emeralds.

Magic seems to permeate the air, fueling everything from the water supply to the electricity lines. It's a tangible force, clinging to me like static.

We stop outside a wide building and park in one of the very few spaces out front. It's strange to see how beautiful and clean this place is, even though it lacks the social structure I'm used to. It's not illegal to litter, everyone just chooses not to.

Getting off the bike, Draven helps me remove the helmet before placing it on the seat.

There's a building with an overhang, held up by columns, and he takes me by the hand, leading me up the steps.

"What is this place?" I ask, but he keeps walking forward. There's a sign up top, but the text has been weathered away with time. All I can see is that it was clearly written in Latin.

"Patience, Gemma," he says, and it catches me off guard. It's so rare he utters my name, but it's starting to occur more and more. I think I like it.

Similar to the theaters and museums back on Earth, there is a ticket box in the front to pay your entry fee, and Draven hands over a few crown before we walk in. Once we're inside the main lobby, nothing is like Earth anymore.

I think it's a museum.

Back home, museums have walls lined with pictures, or glass exhibits showcasing objects from history, and replicas of things from the past. This place is just a long, empty hallway full of uncanny, decorative doors.

The one closest to the entrance is black with red blood dripping down, seeping from the crack between the top of the door and its frame. The one beside it is covered in artsy, short brushstrokes, creating simple white clouds in a sunrise-colored sky. It's pastel and pale, emphasizing the way light changes the atmosphere around it. There are many more doors lining the hallway, each one stranger than the last.

"Choose a door," Draven says, looking over at me. He's wearing black slacks and a form-fitted matching dress shirt. It's similar to what he wears to perform at the carnival, sans the corset, and I like seeing him like this. He's more relaxed, almost human-like.

There's a chilly, eerie feeling to the air around us, and I pause. "Any door?"

"I would advise against starting with the one oozing blood, but sure. Any door will do."

I walk up to the one with clouds painted across it, and turn back to Draven, who laces his fingers with mine. I turn the handle, and suddenly we're stepping into an entirely different place. It doesn't even feel like the same planet.

There are flower bushes blooming on each side of us, and we're standing in the center of a small green bridge. The distinct smell of roses and lilies floods my nostrils, and I take a deep breath, enjoying the fresh air. Draven and I walk hand-in-hand until we see a man with a long, dark beard standing in front of an easel, painting the scenery before him. There are fountains and shrubbery making symmetrical paths before us.

"You're shitting me," I whisper, mouth agape. *Monet?*

"Who do you see?"

My brows furrow. "What do you mean?"

"This exhibit shows everyone something different. It's an illusion. It's supposed to be your favorite painter," he explains.

"So you're not seeing famous French painter Claude Monet?"

Draven laughs. "No, not quite."

Monet continues making languid strokes against his canvas. "Who are you seeing then?"

"Raphael Morningstar," he answers.

"Raph?!"

"No." He laughs. "An ancestor—their great uncle. His style was quite unique. Lots of red and black and use of negative space. He often combined two symbols, and it would look different depending on the angle you were viewing the image from."

I try to picture the art and the artist. I'm sure he has red skin, blue eyes, and wings. I wonder what his horns are shaped like, and what the scenery around us is like from Draven's point of view.

We continue past Monet, making our way through a series of vine-covered archways. "Are those green to you?"

"The arches?" he asks, squeezing my hand.

"Yeah, are they covered in vibrant green vines?"

He shakes his head. "No. To me, they're covered in flames."

A peculiar feeling enters my belly as we make it to a door and open it, leading us back into the first hallway.

Except everything is different. The doors have been rearranged, placed in a completely new order, and there are fewer.

"So, how does this place work?" I ask, counting how many doors remain. *Ten.*

"Nobody knows except Cora, the demon who runs it. The magic inside is older than either of us, I can tell you that."

Slime seeps out from all fissures surrounding a bright green door, the emerald goo surrounding the most horrendous thing I've ever seen. Eyeballs are fixed to the front, constantly tracking our movements as I investigate my choices.

"What's this museum's theme?" I ask.

"It's a cultural museum," Draven answers. "History, art, all sorts of things. You're supposed to learn about Hel as well as yourself."

I bristle, a shiver skating down my spine at his thoughtfulness. "Is that why you brought me here? So I could remember things?"

I glance down to where our hands are still touching.

"That's somewhat the truth. I thought it might be a fun experience, but yes. I know obtaining your memories is important to you. Now you know your favorite painter. Perhaps there are other things to unwrap and discover here."

We continue down the narrow hallway, and I stop outside a door covered in colorful shards of glass. "I want this one," I say and Draven nods for me to open it.

When I step inside, I feel out of place, like I'm standing but there's no ground beneath my feet. Everything is pitch black, the air frigid. A loud clattering crashes in my ears, my head feeling like it might split open from the intense pressure in the air.

Light beams out from every corner in a kaleidoscope of color, and I see small glowing orbs heading towards each other. They slam together like pinballs, fragments of land moving and shifting.

The entire room shakes with the force, and my muscles stiffen as Draven wraps his arms around me, holding my face close to his chest.

"What is this?" I whisper, afraid of what's going to happen next.

"This is The Convergence, or at least, how it began."

I crane my neck up towards his face. "*This* is The Convergence?"

"It's how it would've looked to the gods or a god. An all-encompassing point of view."

My hands tremble, my body shaking as I watch the deafening blows of each planet as it crashes into the next. This had to have hurt. "How many people died?"

"Millions of individuals from different species on every planet passed away from the massive collision," he says, very matter-of-fact, and I close my eyes and try to envision how it would feel for my whole world to be turned upside down like that.

In all honesty, it already was. My experience wasn't as graphic or morose, but everything I ever thought I knew was stripped from me this year. My home, my planet, my memories. Even if they all return, I've been permanently changed. I'm not the girl I was before, but one day I might become an amalgamation of who I once was, who I am now, and who I aspire to be.

I'm afraid of starting over again. I've been absorbed into a new family, and I'm terrified once I leave, that'll be it for me. Leaving who I'm becoming might be worse than grieving who I once was.

All of the planets seem to move at once, creating a huge explosion before us, and I curl into Draven's warmth, allowing him to protect me as the room goes entirely white. My eyes are glued shut, my face smooshed into his chest as loud vibrations slam through my body.

When I open my eyes again, we are back in the hallway, except this time it's narrower. Draven lets me out of our embrace, and I immediately miss the heat of his touch.

One, two, three, four, five doors are left.

The eyeball door is gone, and I shudder in horror at the memory of it staring back at us. There's a golden door, pretty and gleaming. I point to it, and Draven nods.

"That is one of my personal favorites," he says, and twists the knob.

We cross the threshold, entering what appears to be an art museum. It's exactly like one I'd find on Earth. There are framed paintings on the wall, and stone sculptures on stands.

"This is the art exhibit?" I ask. Draven shakes his head, the movement accentuating his horns, and I smile. "Then what is it?"

"The history exhibit. They utilize art to tell our story."

He interlocks our fingers again, my ivory skin pale against the red of his flesh. We walk up to a painting, and the little figures flying through the air are actually moving.

"What am I seeing?"

"Deus, and The League of the Seraphim."

The name rings a bell. It must've been something Raph or Luc mentioned to me. "*Who* was Deus?"

"The first King of Hel. It's all legend, mythology if you will, but some believe that Hel used to be part of a greater system. Sent for their misdeeds, some species had their souls devoured by the demons that resided here," he explains. "Deus wanted to change demon civilization and make it better. He started the League of Seraphim—a small army—and they controlled the populous. A planet that had no rules suddenly had hundreds."

"Let me guess, 666?" I say, trying not to laugh.

Draven nods as if that was the perfect guess.

"You can't be serious."

"I'm afraid you were right on the nose," he says and chuckles. "I guess we're predictable?"

"So what happened to Deus and his army?"

He gently rubs my fingers between his, staring at the painting.

"Others weren't happy, so a demon named Lucifer Morningstar overthrew him and established the first monarchy."

"And that's how Luc became the devil?"

"Lucifer reigned first, then his daughter Lucile for a short time after The Convergence, but Lucile's title was stripped from her the moment Luc was born."

My brows furrow, thinking about the way Raph and Luc look. "Luc is the oldest?"

"No," Draven begins. "Josina and Cavan are twins and the eldest. Josina was looked over for having a feminine essence, and Cavan didn't have strong enough magic. Raph was born next, but their grandfather said he didn't have the right temperament, he had too much personality, and then Gabe was born, and he had too little. This is how Luc was chosen as the successor. They wanted the next leader to be strong but malleable. Personable, but not whimsical."

"And his other siblings?"

"Uri was born after Luc, then Zada, and finally Micha, the youngest. None of them were eligible, because Luc was already chosen, though it's said that Josina and Cavan took the most issue with this," he finishes explaining.

"What's their deal?" I ask. I can imagine if I were Josina and Cavan or even Raph, I would be upset that Luc was chosen over me, but the idea of a monarchy based on birth order is silly anyway. Being the eldest doesn't make you the most suited for leadership. But neither does having too much or too little personality as a child. Children are inherently malleable, and it's wild to place them into boxes at such a young age.

Draven finally looks back at me. "Josina and Cavan believe Josina is the true Devil."

A chill runs down my spine. It sounds like these demons are gearing up for war or at least a fight, and I don't want to be here when all Hel breaks loose.

I start walking down one side of the wall, stopping at every painting that catches my eye. There are buildings in this one, the flags on the poles the only thing moving. I wonder what they represent, and what time period and planet they're from.

I turn and face Draven, who is staring at a painting of The Carnival. It looks a lot more quaint than the one we work at now, but it's clearly the same grounds. The carousel is a little shinier, and the Ferris wheel turns, just as it always does.

Draven Orzath confuses me. He has everything I could ever imagine wanting in this world. A family who loves him and a fun and colorful job that's different and thrilling. He's handsome and strong and his body moves like a well-oiled machine. So why is there always an air of despair to him? Melancholy blooms in his chest like a flower, its stem twisting and wrapping around his heart. I just hope someone can snip it before it's too late.

He places a hand on the small of my back, leading me deeper into the room, but my eyes stop on a peculiar image. It's more of a sketch than a painting, thin black lines scrawled across the paper.

A scorpion. On its tail is a beautiful butterfly, fluttering its wings. *The Scorpion and The Butterfly.*

It's *us.*

"Is this one of those images where everyone sees something different?"

Draven stares at the painting, his eyes fixated on whatever is before him, but he nods.

"What do you see?" I ask, not sure if I want the answer.

"Blood."

I shudder, but continue walking down the pathway until we're in the hallway, this time with only two doors left. A glowing green mystery, and the one seeping blood.

"You're going to choose the blood door and ruin this enchanting evening, aren't you?" Draven asks, though we both already know the answer. "Seriously, Gemma, this one isn't a joke. I don't think—"

I turn the knob and we're taken to what can only be described as something from a horror film. It's dead silent except for the sound of Draven's heavy sigh. There are horned skulls coming out of the walls, and artistic imagery of half-demons and demons being tortured.

"What is this, a medieval fucking torture chamber?" I ask, startled by everything before me.

"Yes, actually. What, did you seriously see a door coated in blood and think, *ooh, this one should be full of rainbows and butter-flies*?" he retorts, taunting me.

Everything is too much, and my gut is telling me to leave. I turn back towards the door, but it vanished. "How do I get out of here?"

"One of us has to put on one of the devices and it'll show us... an *image* of someone being tortured or killed."

"Oh, that is truly awful."

"Here, pick something tame. I think that one is only supposed to hurt if you talk," he says, pointing to a metal contraption covered in spikes and barbs.

"Haha, very funny. Are you implying I talk too much?"

One corner of his mouth thicks up. "Yes, but no. You're not going to put on the device, I am."

"What? Draven, no. I'm the one who chose this door, it's my fault. I should've listened to you." I try to grab the trap from his hands, but he lifts it up into the air, out of my reach. "Give it to me."

"No."

I reach up over him and he places the contraption behind his back with one arm, pulling me so we're chest-to-chest. Our noses are pressed against each others, our chests heaving..

"Have you ever been tortured before?" he asks, his voice a little breathy.

I shake my head.

"Have you ever watched someone die?"

"Yes," I answer, thinking of my parents and grandparents.

His eyes are as golden as treasure troves as he stares back at me. "I don't mean in a hospital. Gemma, have you ever killed someone?"

"No, of course not."

"Then let me do this. Let me withstand this kind of pain for you. Let blood drip before me and it actually *mean* something," he whispers, and it becomes ghostly quiet as he backs away, placing the trap over his head.

Everything happens quickly. There's a snapping sound and a scream and the lights go out and then... we're back in the hallway, Draven smiling beside me.

There's only one door left. The green one.

"Are you okay?" I ask.

"I'm fine, pest. Open the door." He looks normal—better than normal, he looks at peace. It's haunting. I fear he was shown more than an image of torture.

"What is this one?"

Draven rubs the center of my back. "This is the exit. It shows you your greatest desire right before you leave. I think it's supposed to send people out with a purpose."

I swiftly grab the handle and step inside, but for the first time, Draven is not beside me. There is a small sink and mirror in the center of the dark room, and I step closer to it. It's not attached to anything, the mirror floating in thin air, and I turn the faucet handle.

To my surprise, water immediately flows. I splash my face with it before turning it off. Is this my greatest desire? It's just myself. That can't be right.

The mirror begins to fracture, slicing into smaller shards, but they don't reflect myself. There's my parents in one segment, followed by my grandparents. There's one of Reina, another of Lilian and Absinthe and the carnies, and even one for Raph and Luc. I continue scanning, stopping on a young boy I don't recognize, before I stare back at the center to find Draven. Reaching out to touch the broken shards, I cut my finger, the blood dripping down like paint off a brush.

Symphony No. 17

Draven

Leaning against a wall, I wait for Gemma to come out of the last exhibit and try not to think about what the mirror showed her. Better yet, I try not to think about what it showed me.

Big brown eyes are the first thing I spot as Gemma comes into view, her body stiff with tension, but she smiles, not giving any inkling of what's on her mind. It's for the best.

"Where to next?" she asks, brushing off her jeans.

"We are going to The Cathedral," I answer, taking her by the hand and leading her back towards my bike.

The Cathedral is a bar owned by Cain Lupine, famous leader of Pack Escalus. Much like the lycan on their origin planet, Umbra, many of the lupion here have organized into packs. The biggest difference is that on Hel, their packs have taken on a more devious role in society, creating a system of syndicates that deal in death and magic.

This kind of underhandedness isn't unique to the lupion— it's predictable, given the way demons have barred everyone's access to magic. I fear that soon enough, lupion, felion, and other species will use the olden ways of their home planets to become more powerful than the half-demons. *What will we do if our*

demon monarchy is overthrown by someone even worse? What will
become of my people?

I often wonder if the demons even fear being overthrown by
them—by anyone able to wield magic without limitations—or if
their heads are too far up their asses to notice the power slowly
being usurped from their grasps.

Driving down the streets of Haeresis, it's nice to feel the
breeze through my hair and horns. Most everything here is ultra-
modern, but The Cathedral looks exactly how it sounds. A gray,
gothic church, with tall towers topped by sharp spires. The archi-
tecture creates shadows on the road, creating a silhouette of the
skyline.

Cain is an old friend of Luc, and he owes him a favor. Tonight
is about having a good time with Gemma, sure, but I won't lie to
myself, I'm here to ask about atra. One of the many magical
substances mined for on Ira, powderized atra has a plethora of
uses. Drinking it can improve strength and lung capacity,
injecting it is said to give you superior levels of speed and agility.
But I want to know more about these old tattoo practices.

"This place is..." Gemma starts.

"Elegant? Ethereal?"

"Kind of ominous, honestly."

I let out a small laugh. "You won't feel that way when we step
inside, I promise."

The front doors are made of stained glass, depicting a large
gray wolf standing on a precipice, howling at the looming golden
moon. Light from inside the building shines outward, reflecting
the colors onto the street while illuminating the beautiful image.

"Are we in lupion territory?" Gemma asks, and I shake my
head.

"Lupion don't really have territory yet, since there's only one
small pack who resides here on Haeresis. This isn't one of their
dens, if that's what you're asking. The Cathedral welcomes
everyone and anyone, regardless of species."

"Oh, I don't know. I'm not familiar with... wolfy business." She whispers the last two words.

I hold back a chuckle, giving her a cheeky smirk. "Just don't let them hear you call it that."

"I wasn't planning on it," she says as we step inside.

The Cathedral is honestly not my favorite place. It is a loud bar with an unbelievable amount of illegal substances. Mostly magically-derived, but some are just... drugs. Inspired by our human ancestors, beings come here to get drunk or high and to forget their troubles.

Unfortunately for me, there isn't a substance strong enough to take away the burden that troubles me most—making my sister a witness when I killed my father. Phaelyn knows the reasoning, but it doesn't take that trauma away. I'm not sure if she'll ever look at me the same.

"This is... a lot," Gemma says after a long beat of staring out into the crowd.

"Yeah?"

"It reminds me of The Midnight Muse from back on Earth. It was a club I worked at. I just have memories of a fun, wonderful place and how it turned into something nefarious and exhausting, like this." Gemma seems to remember more and more every day.

I shrug. "Demons love their revelry."

We cross towards the bar, and I order us both fruity drinks. The bartender—a lupion who must be in her early twenties—instantly piques my interest. Long, straight, almost-white gray hair cascades down her front and back. Tempest Lupine.

She hands us our drinks, and Gemma takes a sip.

"This is good, but I need a bathroom. Will you watch my drink?" she asks, and I nod. Gemma makes to leave, but I grab her arm, not letting her go just yet.

"Are you sure you're good to go by yourself?"

"Draven, I don't need a babysitter."

I loosen my grip. "Fine, but please be careful."

"I will. Try not to poison my drink while I'm gone," she says with a wink.

When Gemma is out of sight, I wave the bartender down. She ignores me at first, so I aggressively cough, causing one of the other patrons to get up and relocate.

"If you're sick, you should go home," she says coldly.

"Are you Cain's daughter?" I ask, cutting to the chase. I almost instantly recognized her, but we haven't formally met, and I'm not trying to scare her off.

Something wild flashes in her eyes—the color of amazonite—before she schools her expression. "And what if I am?"

One corner of my mouth ticks up. "Your father owes my boss a favor, and I've come to collect."

She rolls her eyes, cleaning an empty glass. "And who is your boss?"

"My apologies for the impoliteness. Let me introduce myself," I say and give a small bow. "The name's Draven. Draven Orzath."

Giving others my name instead of my boss's gives me flexibility. Most know I'm The Scorpion, one of Raph's underlings. A few know The Spy, the one who compiles information for Luc. Almost nobody is aware that I am The Executioner, for he is merely a whispered tale. A ghost story. Sharing my name allows her to process which version of myself she knows *without* revealing to her what she does not. It's a sneaky trick, but it works like a charm. From the look on her face, and the way her brows shoot up, I'd say she knows I'm referring to Luc.

Or at least, the version of Luc everyone has in their head. The evil, vile ruler.

"What do you want?"

"Aw, Tempest, don't rush things. Our conversation was just getting started." Her eyes widen at the use of her name, and my tone drips like honey. If I'm being honest, though, *I'm* the one in a rush. I just hope I can get something out of her before Gemma returns. "What do you know about atra?"

She stiffens, someone else flags her down to take their order, and she heads their way.

I need to find out who exactly is selling atra, especially if it's Pack Escalus. Luc and Raph will have to decide where we go from here—if we need to take them out, or if there's another way to ensure this substance doesn't find its way into the hands of The Legion.

When she returns to make the drink, my eyebrows lift in anticipation. "I have a contact that can get you some, if that's what you're after."

"I'm hearing from some that it can work almost like magicite, permanently granting you access to your magic, like a conduit." I keep my tone curious.

"If you mix atra into ink and tattoo the right rune onto someone, you can give them those abilities," she explains before passing the drink to the other patron. I waggle a finger, signaling for her to come closer. I can't risk someone else hearing this conversation.

"So anyone can become practically immortal?" I whisper.

Theoretically, someone could cover themselves in tattoo after tattoo, becoming even more powerful than demons. That could be a problem.

"No. Too many runes, and their body would deteriorate."

I nod in understanding. "Can you get me that—"

Before I see her, I can feel Gemma's presence as she returns, every eye in the room fixated on her. Tempest backs away, and I realize we look suspicious, especially to Gemma, who is downing her drink.

"He's with me," Gemma says boldly, looping her arm in mine.

"Oh, I'm well aware. Besides, darling, I'd be interested in you, not him," Tempest says with a wink.

Pulling some coins out of my pocket, I hand Tempest enough crown to cover our drinks, plus a generous tip. I didn't even take a sip of mine, but nobody seems to notice.

"Thank you, I'll be in touch about your request," she says and salutes us off.

Gemma and I continue to the front door of The Cathedral, her fingers laced in mine, and she gives me a scowl.

"She'll tell you where to get some *what?* Sex? Drugs?"

I give her a smirk, but she doesn't seem enthused. "Why, are you offering?" She shoves me, and I chuckle. "Magic. She's helping me source a specific type of rare magical substance."

"I thought you couldn't access your magic?"

"It doesn't mean I'm not going to try," I say, and the lie tastes bitter on my tongue. In the beginning, it was so easy to lie to this human, but now I feel desperate to tell her the truth. Or perhaps I'm just desperate for someone I'm *able* to tell the truth to.

The twin moons hang high in the sky, glowing green street lamps the only other illumination. *Magicite green.* I stare out at the empty street, listening for pedestrians or vehicles, but hear nothing. Trams fly by above us, but it's otherwise silent.

They're the perfect conditions.

"Can I show you something I've never shown anyone before?" I ask. I'm not sure what's taken over me, but I don't question it.

Everything I do, I do for someone. Whether it's throwing knives, playing piano, or slitting throats, everything serves the others around me. This is the one thing I do for me. Even though it's frivolous and dangerous. I get a thrill from risking my own life, and for whatever fucking reason, I want to share that with someone.

With her.

"Sure."

I lead Gemma down the street and let go of her hand, gesturing for her to stay put. "I'll return in just a moment, I promise."

Heading back to The Cathedral, I get on my motorcycle and rev the engine. I'm not sure what trick to show her. I suppose I should start with something basic. I don't know why I'm even trying to impress her, but something inside me craves her attention.

Riding towards her, I quickly pop a wheelstand. When the front wheel of my bike makes contact with the road again, I look over to see Gemma's eyes beaming back at me.

Time to bring out my showstopper. Quickly, I shift off the seat and make my way up into a surfing pose, my feet both angled on the bike as I stand upright.

"Holy fucking shit," she shouts, and I flash her a toothy grin, stopping my bike right in front of her.

"Yeah?"

"What else can you do?"

I flip down my kickstand and hop off my bike, pulling her towards me as I hungrily press my mouth into hers. I scoop Gemma up, and as she wraps her legs around me, I get back onto my motorcycle.

Our tongues eagerly explore each other's mouths as her body writhes against me, her hips bucking while I pull her by the loops on her jeans.

My cock strains against my trousers, but I don't focus on that. I'm too enwrapped in her pleasure, determined to be the match that sets her ablaze.

"Draven," she breathes against my neck, and my name sounds like a song—her voice makes the sweetest melodies.

I let out a low, raspy groan as she continues to move her hips, her neck craning back. I want nothing more right now than to tear her jeans off her body in the middle of this street, but I fight the urge. Instead, I get lost in her moans and movement.

Do not fucking come, Draven, I think as pleasure seems to wrack through her entire body, every muscle twitching as she lets out a shaky exhale.

"I can do more motorcycle tricks, too," I say against her lips, and it earns me a giggle.

SYMPHONY No. 18
GEMMA

"Draven, what the fuck are you doing?" I ask, my voice shrill as the motorcycle takes us forward, our bodies lurching at the sudden movement.

"They call it a joyride for a reason," he answers with a wink, but the motorcycle keeps going and my heart jumps into my throat.

"Stop. Stop. *Stop*," I scream, and we finally come to a halt. "You're—"

"Dashing? Handsome? The best you've ever had?"

I fight the smile that threatens to spread across my face. "A fucking menace."

Draven grabs the helmet from the back and places it on my head before helping me off his bike. I get back on behind him, wrapping my arms around his waist.

"Where are we going now?"

He shrugs his shoulders. "A hotel?"

"I have an apartment," I say, and I swear I can hear his mouth open.

"What?"

"Yeah, it's in the residential district." I honestly forgot I have an apartment here. It feels like that was forever ago, even though it's only been three months. I'm sure the food in the fridge has gone rotten.

He turns back to me and closes the visor. "Tell me how to get there."

Once we're inside my apartment, Draven is nothing but skin and tongue and teeth, working my jeans down my legs and my shirt over my shoulders until I'm completely bared to him.

I tug at the dark fabric of his shirt, and we work in tandem to unbutton it until my palms can splay across the taut muscles of his abdomen. My hands graze downwards, his throat bobbing as I grip his hard erection, and I swear his golden eyes darken in response.

"Is this what you most desire?" he asks, and I nod before he pulls me into another kiss.

My mind threatens me with the memory of Draven in the center of the mirror. *If only he knew how real that answer truly was.*

He reaches a hand down and circles my clit until I am dripping and desperate. I want more—*need* more. More friction, more fulfillment, more of *him*.

"Tell me what you want," he demands, his voice low and heady.

"More," I plead as he curls a finger up inside me.

He actually makes a fucking *tsk* sound and I swear I'm going to kill him. "Oh, I'm going to need you to be more specific," he says, just to torture me.

"Please, Draven, I want you to fuck me," I whimper as he removes his finger.

"Good." He flips me, bending me over the couch in one quick motion.

Draven's pants are down in an instant, his cock teasing my entrance.

I am just a mass of sensations as he rocks forward until he's all the way in, my pussy stretching as if it were made for him.

"That's it, love."

With every thrust, his piercings press against my walls, bringing in new waves of pleasure. Whatever memories I thought I'd regained, I fear I've lost again, because I can hardly remember anything except the way I feel right now. My own name is more foreign to me than the feeling of his hands on my hips as he fucks me into oblivion.

His thrusts pick up in pace, and a symphony of moans mixed with the sounds of flesh slapping flesh resonate through the air. I am so lost in our debauchery I don't care about any of the pain I've endured. I don't care about whether or not I get to live here forever or travel back to Earth.

Draven holds my wrists behind my back, and the waves of pleasure finally rise to their fullest heights before crashing down, my back bowing and muscles tightening as I writhe with satisfaction.

He's crashing too, hot liquid spilling out into me as a guttural groan tears from his throat, and I smile.

Lust might just be my favorite sin.

LOCKING the front door of my apartment, I give Draven a cheeky grin. "Show me another trick."

"Out here?" He waggles his eyebrows.

"No," I say, and cross my arms. "Show me another motorcycle trick. I'm sure you can do more than just a wheelie."

"Wheelstand," he corrects me.

"Whatever," I say, waving to brush him off. "On Earth we call them wheelies."

His mouth curls down in a look of disgust. "It's not sexy if you call it a *wheelie*. That's like calling my dick a wiener."

I roll my eyes, discarding his ridiculousness, and stand there, waiting for him to do something. He sighs and hands me my helmet before he hops onto the back of his bike and drives it down the road until he's out of view.

When he returns, butterflies erupt in my stomach.

Draven is doing a fucking handstand on top of his motorcycle, fingers still gripping the handle. His shirt has come untucked from his pants, revealing his defined abs, and I practically swoon.

He sits back atop his bike and gestures for me to get on behind him, and I quickly oblige, excited for our next adventure.

"Were you watching the trick, or just staring at my body? I wouldn't blame you either way," he says, and I can feel the red hot blush spreading down my cheeks, painting my neck and chest.

"I was observing the stunt."

He clicks his tongue. "The stunt wasn't my abs, Gemma."

"Where are we headed now?" I ask, refusing to humor him. My face feels pained from the way I've been smiling and blushing all night.

"Home," he says, breaking the bubble we blew around us.

This entire night has felt like a fever dream. We weren't human and half-demon, attempted killer and victim, or even performance partners. Tonight, we were simply Gemma and Draven.

My hair whisks out from under my helmet, dancing behind me as we drive fast enough to produce gusts of wind. The city is a living, breathing landscape. Trams fly overhead, but I can't make out the details, just lines of vivid green lights moving past my field of vision.

I lift the visor on my helmet, and the scents that hit my nose are just as layered and loud as the city around us—musky cologne, asphalt, and exhaust.

The carnival comes back into view, and it's hard to believe that this captivating place isn't where I belong. Everything here is weird and wacky, sexy, violent, and *fun*. It makes me feel alive, like life has more to offer.

So why shouldn't I stay?

WE'RE SITTING against the tree, right near the edge of the lake, and it's the most serene experience of my life. The stars in the sky are so much more visible here than in the rest of the city, it's breathtaking.

Every star is a soul. A life, a being. All with their own families and stories. There's not enough time to learn them all, but I'd like to at least learn more about the half-demon beside me.

"What broke you?" I ask, disrupting the peaceful silence.

"I'm not broken," Draven says on a laugh, as if this is some sort of joke.

"Your heart. Your spirit. Whatever you want to call it. Everything about your life is wonderful, but you still act like there's a stick up your ass. Who hurt you?"

"Everything about my life is *not* wonderful. I have the most annoying scene partner *ever,*" he says, and gives me a look. "And to answer your question, my father. Or maybe myself." His voice nearly cracks.

I lean my head against his shoulder. "Obviously I don't remember everything, but from what I can recall, my life was full of death," I share. "My parents. My grandparents. It's all too much. I used to yearn for my memories, but now I fear them."

Draven gently kisses the top of my head. "I'm sorry."

"It's okay," I say and shrug. "Why do you say yourself?"

There's a sharp inhale, and for a moment, I'm afraid I've asked too much. "Because I killed my father."

It should be a shocking revelation, but somehow, it isn't. My experience on Hel has been coddled by the protections of Luc, Raph, and Draven, but they've told me the horrors that persist. Murder, violence, treachery. These things are to be expected here, but not from Draven.

He's different. He would kill anyone—even me—if it meant protecting the carnies. They're his family. Maybe not by blood, but by choice. To kill his own father? He must have done something atrocious.

Why? I almost ask, but Draven begins again.

"He had been abusing all of us for years. He was involved in some pretty risky business ventures, and it was all starting to go south. Phaelyn did something to piss him off—I honestly can't even remember what it was anymore. She might've played a wrong note or ate the last cookie or something negligent, but he was *mad*," he says, and a chill runs down my spine.

"Some half-demons were granted access to their magic for work or other causes, and my father was one of the lucky ones, but it wasn't enough for him. Nothing was ever enough for him. He took some experimental potion to enhance his magic, and it had some gruesome side effects. When he went after my sister, my mom intervened, and the force of the blow actually killed her. Magic and rage are one Hel of a mixture."

I try to wrap my head around how someone could do this to their family, but draw a blank.

"The rest of the night is a blur. I know Phaelyn hid. I know he tortured me, ripped my wings out bit-by-bit. And I know that at some point, I stole the ring off his finger and used my magic to kill him."

"Did anybody come to help you? A soldier, a social worker, anybody?" I ask, my heart leaping into my throat. He was so young to go through something so awful.

"Luc. Somehow, word got back to Luc, and he came to help clean up the mess. We were found in a corner, crying and drenched in blood. Everything about my life changed from there. I was just a husk, but Luc and Raph gave me something to live for."

I have never experienced that depth of pain, but I do know what it's like to feel empty. I can't remember who I was before I lost everyone. There are fragments of memories, scattered across the floor of my mind like broken shards of glass.

My legs on the bar as I stretched before dance class.

The curve of my grandmother's body as she tied an apron around her waist.

The scent of my grandfather's cologne—musky, yet sweet.

Whenever I allow myself to sift through my grief, picking up each memory, they cut my hands open, slowly bleeding me dry.

I am tired of bleeding and weeping and *remembering*. I've ached so badly to remember, but now I think I'm better off if I just forget.

The wind rustles Draven's bright white hair, and we continue to talk well past the witching hour. About not only the darkness in our souls, but joyful stories, too.

There's part of me that desperately aches for the past, but there's another new part of me that would rather carve space for new memories. Memories on Hel. Memories with the carnies.

With Draven.

SYMPHONY NO. 19
DRAVEN

I wake up to Gemma in my arms and it is the most at peace I've ever felt, which is a problem of the highest magnitude.

I rely more on facts and statistics than I do emotions, and as I run the numbers, it's not looking good. At the very best, we become fuck buddies and grow platonic attachments to each other, and then she leaves and goes back to Earth. At the worst? She destroys me.

And I am willing to let her. Some sick, fucked up part of me wants Gemma to crawl into my skin like the pest that she is. I want her to detonate, killing us both.

Looking down at her, I brush a strand of hair off her forehead and behind her ear, and lean down to kiss her gently.

Fuck.

I should lock up my heart and throw away the key—toss it into the ocean, never to be seen again. Unfortunately for me, I'm a damn good swimmer.

"Good morning," she says, her voice still a little raspy from sleep. The light of the morning sun illuminates Gemma's face, turning her eyes from deep brown to a near-gold.

It shouldn't draw me in, I see golden eyes every day, in my friends and family, and in my own reflection. Yet, there's something radiant about hers. There's a glittering quality to them like nothing I've ever seen before.

"Good morning, beautiful bug. We should probably head back to camp," I say, even though we both know I'd rather rip her clothes off again. But alas, duty calls.

"Bug?" she says and sits up to stare at me. "I think I prefer pest."

Standing, I brush off my trousers before reaching a hand down to help Gemma up, and we walk back towards the main part of camp, our fingers intertwined. There's a smoky, dusty note to the air around us, and I freeze, searching for the cause.

A barbeque, surely. Or perhaps someone is smoking some sort of magical blend of herbs. But my eyes come up short, and I fear the worst, the tempo of my steps increasing minute-by-minute until Gemma and I are mad-dashing towards the tents.

Flames.

Orange, horrible flames engulf one of the tents, and I barrel towards the small crowd that stands in front of it. Quinn is shaking uncontrollably, while Raph uses his magic to try and stop the fire from spreading. Baelor and Rowan come running, carrying buckets, and the twins help them dump the water onto the tent.

A few of the others are missing, and it wouldn't normally matter, but Robyn's absence strikes a specific chord in me.

I scan the area. "Where are the children?"

"R-Robyn is looking for them. I-I tried, but I can't see anything. My vision keeps going blurry," Quinn says, their voice wobbling on every beat.

"Did you check inside?" I ask, and move before anyone has the chance to answer.

Raph follows my lead without hesitation as we charge into the tent, which is used as a supplies closet. Nobody should be in here, but my gut tells me that isn't the reality we're living in.

The heat feels like walls pressing into us. Wood pops and

splinters, metal groaning and warping in a cacophony of sound as everything seems to melt and deteriorate.

Hardly anything is visible except smoke and ash, and the air seems to suffocate me more with every inhale, but I push past the burnt rubble to find Una and Po collapsed on the floor. Here, they somehow appear even younger than they are. Una is a teenager, but right now she seems like a child.

There are burns marring Una's legs, but Po looks unscathed other than the fact that she's unconscious.

I pick Po up, carrying her like a baby in my arms, her pink skin warm to the touch. Raph gently tosses Una over his shoulder, and we rush back outside.

My lungs are desperate for clean air as I inhale my first breath on the other side, grateful to be out of that tight, searing space.

Quinn and Rowan's faces can only be described as devastation and determination, and part of me is glad that Robyn is somewhere else on the grounds, unable to see her babies like this.

"What are we doing next?" Rowan shouts over the roar of the water flooding out of the hoses they've pulled towards the scene.

"I'm going to fly Una to the hospital, someone will have to take Po," Raph says, and leaps into the air, not giving us a moment to argue.

I look to see Gemma, Rowan, Quinn, and Reina with matching pained expressions. They obviously cannot take her. Baelor says nothing, his face carefully blank.

Leo and Lyle start to speak, but I wave them off as I give Gemma a quick kiss on the lips and haul ass for my bike. The twins have wings, sure, but we all know they don't use them enough for me to trust them with this.

With Po seated in front of me, nestled in one arm, I drive as fast as I safely can, straight towards Haeresis Hospital. The sound of my heartbeat roars in my ears, even louder than the rev of my engine, but I press on.

When I get there, I jump off and drop my bike, not even

caring to push down my kickstand. I don't care about anything except ensuring Una and Po are safe.

Running inside, the fluorescent lights beam down on us. They're white lights, but there's still a faint emerald sheen to everything on this continent. There's machinery buzzing while nurses talk to one another about the incoming patients.

One looks up to see me carrying Po and immediately drops her paperwork, reaching for the child in an instant. I pass Po over and make to follow the nurse, but a firm hand grips my left shoulder, abruptly stopping me.

"Let the professionals handle this," Raph says, and gestures for us to sit in the lobby.

I follow him, taking a seat next to the door. He grabs a magazine off the side table and tosses it towards me. I balk at the front cover—it's Phaelyn. She's holding a violin, her beautiful wings curving out, creating a cave around her.

She looks beautiful. Hauntingly so, and I wish more than anything that I could call her right now, but the last time we spoke, we argued.

You have to let go of the past. You need to stop living in fear.

My sister shared so many sentiments I wish could be true, but look at where I am now. I have one night of fun, and two of the most important people in my life nearly die.

"Hey," Raph says, placing a hand on my shaking leg. "I didn't show you that to make you spiral, I showed you because she is happy. She's achieving all her dreams, and that was only possible because you allowed it."

"Luc didn't give me much of a choice," I say through gritted teeth.

"The girls will be okay. Take a fucking breath."

I place the magazine back onto the table, and cross my arms before looking at him. "How did this even happen?"

"We're not sure. Perhaps Khalid was practicing his magic and made a mistake?" Raph suggests. "I'm positive it was an accident."

And I'm positive nobody was practicing shit in a supplies closet. "Was Una already in there when it caught fire?"

"I don't know. It's possible, or it's possible she went in to grab some of Absinthe's things," Raph suggests. Una likes to pretend she doesn't care about anyone. She's the epitome of teenage angst, but she adores Absinthe. She and Lilian listen to her rambles more than any of us.

"And Po... I'm guessing went in to help Una," I say, though it's pointing out the obvious.

"That seems to be the case."

I just hope more than anything they'll be safe.

FAMILIAR CURLS and strong muscles stride into the hospital, and I swear Rowan almost thwacks a sleeping Raph when the demon governor opens his eyes.

"How're they doing?" Rowan asks, sitting down beside Raph.

"Stable," I say.

"I called the hospital before we left," Robyn shares. "We know they're stable, but how are they *feeling*?"

"They kicked Draven out—said he was hovering like a mother hen—but Po seems her usual giggly self. Una is still unconscious," Raph says, and I swear he's purposefully trying to get under my skin.

"Alright, well you two should go home and get some rest," Robyn says. It's a suggestion, but I know she's requiring it of us.

"Quinn and Reina said they'll be here in a few hours with food," Rowan shares. "Please, listen to my wife."

"Absinthe?" Raph asks, and Robyn shakes her head.

A pang of guilt for anything negative I've ever said about Absinthe's ridiculous props hits my chest all at once. I fucked up. We all did, honestly. Gemma might've been the only one of us to truly appreciate her craftsmanship and how much it means to her.

"She won't come out of her tent," Robyn says.

"I'll check on her when I get back," I reply, and everyone nods. Her birth parents, her wings, and now her prop tent—my heart aches for Absinthe. She's younger than I, and yet her life has been full of such tremendous loss.

We exit through the front doors, and Raph salutes me before taking off towards the carnival grounds. Walking over, I pick my bike off the ground and get it started. The next few days won't be easy, but I've got to get home and help patch things up. When the girls get out of the hospital, I want everything to be as good as new.

The roads are more hectic than when I normally ride, people walking down the street, and the constant sound of the trams from above. Flying and the trams are the most common modes of transportation on Haeresis, but there are cars and bicyclists as well as a few other types of vehicles. Motorcycles of course, hover-crafts. With our general lack of laws, everything can get a little wild, which is one of the reasons Reina doesn't appreciate me riding.

It might sound ridiculous, but there's nothing freer than the wind in my hair, and the small threat of danger as I ride through the city, executing tricks. It feels like I'm performing without the mask, like this is the ultimate version of myself. I'm able to be bare in front of strangers without repercussions or conversations, and it's glorious.

It's better than killing. Hel, it might be better than sex. Not better than sex with Gemma, but definitely with some of the other partners I've had in the past.

I live for the thrill, as well as the rare opportunity when I don't have to be The Scorpion, or The Spy, or The Executioner. I'm simply Draven.

A half-demon flies past me, his body nimble and lithe as he blows me a kiss, and I reach one hand up to catch it.

Haeresis is even busier than usual, and I narrowly avoid hitting a pedestrian who is not paying attention to their surroundings. There's a truck barreling down the road beside me, but I don't pay it any mind until it starts crossing a little close to me, inching its way in my direction.

A demon flies straight into another, and they fall down with a thump in front of the truck. The driver jerks to one side, avoiding squashing them like two bugs.

Time seems to slow, everything happening all at once. There's a bright light and a thunderous sound, followed by the feeling of skin scraping on concrete.

I think a truck came too close. I think my bike slid out from under me.

I—

Symphony No. 20

Gemma

I'm just a mortal. A human mortal. We live to be a hundred, croak, and then nobody knows where our souls go or if we even have one. Demons live thousands of years. I can't imagine what that's like, and yet as I wait for more news on Una and Po, and for the return of Draven and Raph, it feels like a century has passed.

Even without all my memories, I know I've never experienced such an extreme endorphin drop in my life until today. We were enjoying a night full of light and liquor and lust, only to return to a literal nightmare.

This was worse than my nightmares. Full of death, my nightmares show me the trauma of my past. The people I've already mourned, and the experiences I hope to never have again. This is real. We could've actually lost Una and Po, and I'm not sure Draven would've ever forgiven himself.

Reina and Lilian have spent the last few hours comforting Quinn. Absinthe is holed up in her tent, and everyone else has been sorting out other affairs. Robyn let me know that the girls were stable before she and Rowan left, but I fear the entire cast is emotionally volatile right now.

We have no leader. Raph and Draven and Robyn tell us what

to do and when to do it, and when their presence is removed, all Hel seems to break loose.

I overheard Khalid fighting with Baelor and the twins over how the fire started. Aida and Taryn were bickering over how much water usage was actually necessary to put it out. Everything feels upside down, and I want nothing more but to be wrapped up in Draven's arms, listening to Raph tell us all how to handle this.

I thought the carnival had become my new home, but I realize now that it's the people that make it so, not the grounds. It's the way Po and Una laugh, or how Reina and Raph always make sure to check in on me. It's Leo and Lyle's stupid pranks, and Rowan showing off his muscles. Home is Absinthe and her funky props, and Draven always scowling at my antics. These carnies are my home, and there's nothing that could properly replace that.

Raph lands outside the hall, his wings gracefully retracting behind his body as he stares at the chaos erupting before me. He claps twice—quick and succinct—and everyone stills at once. Draven is noticeably absent, but nobody says a thing.

"Leo, I want you to put a sign out front saying we're closed today. Aida, can you and Khalid investigate the source of the fire?" They nod, and he continues. "Lyle, work with Baelor to rebuild that tent. Reina, how about you and Yasmeena make some hot tea and bring some to Absinthe?"

"On it," Reina says, and Yasmeena follows behind her as she heads out.

Raph cracks his knuckles. "Quinn, the girls are going to be okay. You should lie down and get some rest."

Quinn stops to say something, but they leave after a beat, and I stare at Raph.

"Where's Draven?" I ask, and he shrugs.

"I fly faster than he rides," he says. "I'm sure he'll be back soon."

I shake my head. I don't know who here has seen Draven ride, but he's fast. "Not by much." There's a sinking feeling in my stomach that I try to brush off, but it's no use. Something is very wrong.

"It's possible he stopped somewhere to get something. Just give him a little time," Raph says, dismissing me.

I know something's up. I might not be a demon or have magical powers, but my intuition has rarely steered me wrong.

Fuck this. I don't need his permission.

Rushing away from camp, I head through the empty carnival. It's eerie, seeing everything so quiet and empty, devoid of its usual luster. There's no giggling children or sound of metal turning.

When I get up to where Draven keeps his motorcycle, I hope to see him. Some small part of me is sure he's going to be seated inside, leaning against his bike, waiting for me with a sinful grin on his lips.

I push open the rolling door to find an empty room.

"Gem," Draven says from behind me, his voice hoarse, and I practically squeal in response.

Dashing out of the storage unit, I run towards him, ready to leap into his arms, but there's blood everywhere. A dark, metallic taste fills my nostrils and shakes me to my core. His clothes are tattered, torn every which way, and his leg drags as he walks towards me.

"What happened?"

"Slipped and fell," he says, and smiles. "Just a—just a couple of scratches. Not a big deal."

I take one of his arms and wrap it around my shoulders, doing my best to hold up some of his weight. Slowly, we walk back onto the grounds and I yell out for help.

DRAVEN HAS SLEPT for the last three days, only waking when Una and Po finally arrived from the hospital. Similarly to Draven, Una is covered in bandages, but Po looks unscathed.

When Reina and I visited her yesterday, she told us the full story. Or at least, as well as a seven-year-old can tell a story.

No one else was around when the fire started, she said. *It was hot and Una was worried all of Absinthe's props would get ruined, so she ran inside. I waited and waited and waited and then I heard coughing, so I ran in to help and that's when I woke up here, but I feel okay.* Her tight tendrils of curls bounce as she talks. *The yogurt they keep trying to give me is yucky, but really, I'm fine. Don't worry about me. The doctor says Una is getting better too. Much better.*

I've never met a braver soul, willing to walk straight into a fire for her sister without a second thought. It's a relief to have them both back.

The Sinner's Circus has been closed this week, and the carnival is running on bare bones. The twins, Baelor, Lilian, Aida, Taryn, Yasmeena, and Khalid have mostly been keeping things afloat, while the rest of us have taken care of the sick and injured.

We never did figure out what started the fire.

Raph asks me to get something from Lilian, and while I'm on my way to her, I decide to stop by Aida's tent. Without the full crew, the carnival's relatively empty. Even Aida and Taryn, who sometimes attract lines of half-demons that want to see or speak to them, don't have a soul outside their tents.

"Aida," I say, hoping to find just her as I step inside.

"Come in, child," she replies.

For someone who looks no older than forty, her voice sounds ancient. All-knowing. The magic of Hel is classified differently than it was back on Earth, but Aida would be considered what we call *seers.* She can see different potential outcomes before they're played out. They're not exact predictions of the future, but high possibilities.

I have avoided her a bit *because* of this magic. The more I've learned about my past, the less I'm interested in my future, afraid I'm going to end up in a similar place.

Depressed.

But now it's time to face my fears. "Can I ask a personal question?"

She smiles, her henna-covered hands shifting to place the tarot deck down onto the table, before she uses her tail to gesture for me to have a seat. I oblige.

Aida's tongue is moving, but there's no audible sound I can hear. She must be speaking the language of the serpentine.

"I'm sorry?"

She shakes her head. "Force of habit. I switch into Serpenia often in front of clients. It makes me sound more mystical. I would much rather converse in Arabic or English, though. They are more natural languages to me at this point."

"Why do you want to go back to Earth?"

"Why do you?"

I don't. I mean, I feel obligated to, but I'm not sure I *want* to leave anymore. "I'm not sure. I think it feels like I have to."

"You do not. Neither do I, though I wish for the ability to. My twin brother, Adeib, is getting married, and he has invited me to come. We have not seen each other since before The Convergence, and I would like nothing more than our reunion," she explains. Aida amazes me. She doesn't falter, there are no tears welling in her eyes. She just tells it like it is.

"Where does—" I start to ask more about her brother, but there's a voice coming from outside the tent.

"Come in," Aida says, and waves me off. "We may speak another time."

Do I have to go back to Earth? I mean, I guess I could eventually, but does it have to be the next vessel over? What if I ask Luc if I can stay, just one more year. I need more time here. I want to be with the carnies—Hel, I want to travel to other continents, too.

Would it be so bad if this became the place I called home?

Acquiring a key from Lilian, I return it to Raph, who suggests I check on Draven, and I plan to do exactly that.

Entering Draven's tent, I place a washcloth into a small bucket, wringing it out before bending down to wash the scratches on his face. They're starting to scab, but I don't want him to get an infection.

I go to remove my hand, but Draven catches my wrist. "Stay a little while," he groans.

So I sit at the edge of the bed and let him draw circles on my skin with his fingers, his touch much gentler than normal, as if I'm the one injured.

"Where are you hurting?" I ask, his skin warm to the touch.

"Mostly my head," Draven groans, the bags under his eyes much heavier than before.

My muscles stiffen, worry creasing my brows. "Did you hit your head during the accident?"

"No," he starts to say, sucking in a shaky breath. "I get migraines pretty regularly."

"You're stressed."

He lets out a quiet chuckle. "You could say that."

"Draven, you can't afford to keep burning the candle at both ends," I say. I don't know all the ins and outs of Draven's role with Raph and Luc, but I know enough to say as much. He is picking up the burdens that everyone else lets drop.

He kisses the top of my hand. "I have to, butterfly. I have too much at stake. Too many people to protect."

Symphony No. 21

Draven

Gemma is a distraction I cannot afford. I have dedicated my life to serving Luc and protecting the carnies. She might be one of us right now, but she isn't going to stay one of us forever. I cannot risk the lives of my family for the girl I'm falling for.

Frankly, I cannot fall in love at all. So what the fuck is my problem?

Yasmeena and Khalid sit at the table across from Robyn, Raph, and myself. We decided to handle this like we always would, by giving Khalid a fair chance to state his case. Yasmeena says there's no way her brother could've done this, and I desperately want to believe her, but I can't.

"So tell us, Khalid, where were you the morning of the fire?" Robyn asks. She's normally the gentlest of us three, but this is personal. Those are her daughters.

"I was in camp, but nowhere near the supply tent," he explains calmly.

"Let's make this simple—can someone vouch they were with you?" Raph asks, but Khalid shakes his head.

"I was alone."

I glance over at Yasmeena, and there's something off about the way she's looking at her brother, like she knows he's lying. "Yas, tell me how you know he didn't do this?"

She shrugs. "You've seen his magical abilities. He could burn a hair off my head if he wanted to, without hurting a single other strand."

Khalid's eyes scan the tent like he's going to find his answer somewhere. Yasmeena and Robyn continue going back and forth, both of them determined to protect their family. Raph tries mediating, and my head begins to pound, a splitting migraine threatening to develop from all the noise.

They've been getting a lot more frequent lately.

"This is bullshit," I say, cutting through their bickering. "Khalid, can you just tell us who you were with so we can corroborate your story with them and move on to finding the actual culprit—"

"Or cause! It could be an innocent cause," Raph interrupts me to clarify. If this weren't his carnival, I'd probably deck him right now.

"I said I was alone," he lies. Again.

"Let's use deductive reasoning, then. You weren't with Robyn or Gemma. I think you're bisexual, so maybe the twins?" He shakes his head. "Baelor and Lilian are definitely a no. So which one of my sisters are you fucking?"

Khalid swallows, and I swear the felion—who is a nice, golden tan—turns pallid.

"Yasmeena, do us all a favor and go get Reina," I say. I'm finished with amusing this idiocy.

He scratches the back of his neck, uncomfortable being caught in his web of lies. Lucky for him, I'm a scorpion, not a spider. "How'd you know?"

"Absinthe is a lesbian, and Taryn hates fire. Plus, you guys eyefuck each other on the regular. I might not be an inter-planetary scientist, but I'm not stupid, either," I say, and turn to Robyn. "We have a meeting with the devil this afternoon, can you handle the rest of this?"

"Absolutely," she says with a smirk. "I enjoy teasing Reina, anyway."

I cannot imagine thinking I'd be more upset about two grown adults sleeping together than I would be about accidentally harming children, but here we are. I don't care if Reina and Khalid are fucking—I don't care what they're doing at all, so long as they're not secretly members of The Legion. If he hurts her, I'll kill him, but she'd probably finish the job before I even got the opportunity.

Walking towards my tent, I pass Reina and Yasmeena, and I shape my hand into a cat-claw-like gesture. Yas lets out an irritated sigh, but Reina's eyes search me, putting together the missing pieces.

She stops and crosses her arms, reminding me much of how she looked when we were teenagers. "Am I really in trouble for sleeping with Khalid? As if we all aren't aware you're fucking Gemma?"

"You're not in trouble, fangs. We need you to vouch for your little boyfriend to prove he isn't responsible for the fire," I say, and give her shoulder a squeeze. "Relax."

She bares her teeth at me, and I smile in turn.

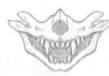

THE ECONOMIC DISTRICT has never been my most favored destination. There are no bars, no carnival, and everything here glows magicite green. More so than anywhere else, it's a reminder of what we aren't allowed to have. I look down at my ring, sparkling in the sunlight—what *they* aren't allowed to have.

I am now part of the exception.

Skyscrapers loom high above, beckoning towards the clouds. I stare past them, up to the clear sky, and wait for Raph's arrival.

When his wings come into view, I open the door to One Haeresis Plaza.

I have strange memories of this place.

"Mi-mister Orzath and," Baph starts, her words slow but intentional. "Mister Raph Morningstar. You may pr-roceed."

We continue down the hall, and Raph presses the button to call the elevator. His hands are jittery, his usual jolly demeanor replaced by a nervous, vibratory energy. As we step inside, orchestral music plays through the speakers, and I try to notate the piece in my mind before we get to Luc's floor. The elevator door opens once again, and we're met with another sterile hallway with a series of closed doors.

Raph opens the one leading to Luc's office and I suck in a breath.

Luc's feet are up on the table, his shiny patent leather loafers practically sparkling, and it honestly makes me want to snap his legs.

I wouldn't, because he's my boss and a royal, but I definitely consider how entertaining it would be for a moment before taking a seat next to Raph.

"Hello Draven, hello brother," Luc says, his tone already coy. "Catch me up to speed, please. What's been going on at our dear carnival?"

"Well, as you know, there was a fire. We've ruled it an accident, but Una and Po were injured. Luckily, both girls should make a full recovery," Raph says with a smile.

"An accident?"

I lower my head, looking up through my brows. "Raph is choosing to call it an accident, but I'm not so easily convinced."

"Oh?" One corner of Luc's mouth ticks up, clearly amused by the growing tension between us, and Raph puts his hands in the air.

"I am choosing not to raise Hel over a spark," Raph says, the end of his sentence pitching up into almost a squeak.

"That analogy would be much more fitting if we weren't discussing a literal fire," I say, hoping they can hear the ire in my voice.

"Is everyone alright? How's Lilian?" Luc asks, and I want to literally rip out his demon testicles.

"Why don't you ask her husband?"

Luc grimaces.

Raph glances back and forth between the two of us and uncomfortably chuckles. "Lilian is fine."

It's said that before The Convergence, there were different classifications of demons on Hel. Some sentient, some less. I know that all the sentient ones stayed on Hel, while all the weaker creatures—like ghouls and shades—died, or perhaps wound up on another planet.

That's what researchers and historians say, and I trust them, but... part of me thinks it's possible the Morningstar siblings are somehow related to those archaic creatures. I don't dare say that out loud—it's probably treacherous to compare royals to the demon equivalent of a mindless, soul-sucking plant.

And yet, damn, do I want to.

"Good. Now, let's continue. After the fire, you hurt yourself on the motorcycle?" Luc asks.

"Yes. It wasn't my fault, though," I clarify.

"Alright," Luc says, but his expression is bored. Distant. He and Raph take a lot of credit for making me into the half-demon I am today, but Luc does fuck-all when he finds out I've been injured.

Perhaps all fathers are the same.

"Why the fuck did you call this meeting when it clearly could've been a phone call?" I ask, and Luc's brows raise in turn, a grin spreading across his lips.

"Yes, Raph, do tell us why you called this meeting." Luc finally takes his feet off his desk, sitting up to look at us properly.

Oh, Hel. Raph still hasn't told him about the money.

Raph twiddles his thumbs, one of his legs shaking as he stares down at the floor, and I honestly feel bad for him. None of the Morningstar siblings asked for these positions of power—except for Josina, who wanted to be The Devil instead of a mere governor—and most of them don't have the personality or composure to lead a continent or planet. These were the cards they were dealt, though, and I empathize.

"I have good news and bad news regarding Hel's Carnival. The good news is that our ticket sales aren't actually dropping," Raph says, and there's a little bit of hope gleaming in his eyes. "The bad news is that I cross-referenced my nightly logs of our funds with the amount of tickets sold each day and evening, and there is money missing."

"I don't understand. We've been so concerned over the lack of sales at the carnival, how could this have happened?" Luc asks, and I consider punching him.

"Someone is stealing the money," I say, giving him a pointed glare.

"Obviously," Luc responds. "What I don't understand is why you haven't been keeping track of ticket sales and profit up until now. We could have nipped this in the bud much earlier on."

I have to give Luc credit where credit is due, he's not always as dumb as he portrays.

"Leo was keeping track of ticket sales, but then we assigned him to the new spotlights," Raph explains.

"If half-demons had access to our magic, he would easily be able to do both at the same time," I state, not giving a fuck if they give me grief over it.

"Not the time, Draven," Raph says nervously.

"When did you find out?" Luc asks, and I grind my teeth.

"A few weeks ago," Raph answers. "But we've been investigating. We've ruled out three suspects."

"How many remain?"

"Three," I say. "Gemma, Yasmeena, and Khalid are innocent. Baelor, Leo, and Lyle are still on the chopping block."

"Am I a bad leader if I say I hope it's Baelor?" Luc asks, and I crack a smile for the first time today.

"Am I a bad hand if I say I hope so, too?"

Raph looks less than amused about Baelor being the thief, but it doesn't matter. Regardless of who it is, it's a betrayal. Especially if it has anything to do with The Legion, which I suspect it does.

"What motives could they have?" Luc asks in earnest.

"Baelor might be trying to get rich quick to impress Lilian's parents?" I offer. "Though it feels unlikely, since Lilian doesn't want anything to do with them."

"And Leo and Lyle?"

Raph scratches his chin. "They've never asked for anything."

"I think, whatever the reason, it's because of The Legion. And for all we know, it could be all three of them," I say. "I can't imagine Leo and Lyle not working together as a team."

"When you're ready, Draven, I want you to set up a sting. Torture them, seduce them, whatever you need to do. Get someone from The Legion to talk, see if they can discreetly tell you who the mole is," Luc suggests, and I nod.

I make to stand, but The Devil gestures for me to remain planted.

"Raph, thank you for your time today," he says, and dismisses his brother.

The only time Luc wants to speak to me alone is when there's a problem I'm expected to solve or if I'm in trouble. Either way, I don't like this. At least he spares me the embarrassment of lecturing me in front of Raph, can't say I do the same for either of them.

The door shuts, and Luc cracks his knuckles. "Someone at Pack Escalus contacted me asking if I'm interested in buying *atra*."

"Did you say yes?"

"I didn't say no. Why did they contact me?" he asks, and a vein pops out in his neck.

"I received some information about rune tattoos from a confidant of mine that tied it to atra and lupion customs. I wanted more information on the substance, especially with everything happening with The Legion. I want to make sure it doesn't make it into their hands," I explain.

"That's all fine and dandy, until you included me. We can't take them out now; it'll be obvious the hit came from me," Luc says, his voice as hot as an eternal flame.

Oh, fuck. "I never used your name."

"But the implication you gave—"

"Suggested I work for you or Raph, yes. You're right. I fucked up." I scratch my chin, plucking the strings in my mind for a song —for an answer. "At the very least, you could ask Cain to not sell to The Legion. We can figure out the logistics of taking out their dealer or cutting their supply chain later."

"Agreed. Have you considered bringing in an additional party or two?"

"For what?" I cock my head to the side.

Luc stares me down, in eyes the color of ice. "For The Spy and The Executioner. I fear you're burning the candle at both ends."

That's the second person who's said that to me this week, but who would I even bring in? The only ones I trust are my family, and I will not put them in harm's way. Not if I don't have to.

I salute him as I stand to leave. "It's Hel, Luc. Everything here eventually burns."

Symphony No. 22
Gemma

Velvet presses against my shoulders as I lean on the base of Po's bed while Quinn French braids my hair. Una is sitting on the bed beside me, pulling Po's tight curls into two buns on either side of her head.

Space buns. That's what we called them on Earth. Oh, the irony that now I've truly been to outer space, at least in some capacity, to get here.

She is the most adoring little being I have ever had the pleasure of spending time with, and a pang of guilt hits my gut knowing our absence could've led to her demise. Or Una's. The what-ifs and endless possibilities of what might've happened if we hadn't returned when we did gnaw at my core, threatening to eat me from the inside out, but I push them aside along with the memory of an injured Draven limping towards me.

It won't help to wallow over what might've been. I spent so much of my life on Earth miserable and consumed by grief. It engulfed me just like those flames engulfed the shed, but I refuse to be a victim anymore. My memories have *mostly* returned, and with them came a serene clarity of what I want out of life.

I want this. I want a family—but more specifically, I want *this* family. With the clowns and demons and devils. I want Draven, and I can't believe I'm saying this, but I want to live on Hel. I like this strange place with limited rules and flexible morality.

I am going to find a way to stay, even if it means making another deal with the devil himself. I am determined to find an excuse that keeps me planted here, allowing me to grow the roots I have always desired.

Una finishes Po's hair, and the little half-demon perks up, standing before the three of us.

"I want to do a fashion show," she announces proudly. "Q, can I?"

Quinn looks at their daughter with a warm expression. "Of course. Show us your best outfit."

Po begins rummaging through a tan leather chest at the edge of their bed, pulling out different fabrics and costumes, until she instructs us all to close our eyes. We oblige, and I can hear rustling and zipping as she puts on whatever she's about to show us.

"Okay," Po says, her voice coming from the entrance of the tent. "Everybody open."

Po struts in wearing a frilly, layered pink jumpsuit of sorts, but that's not what catches my attention the most. *What catches my attention* is the black, oversized jacket she's swimming in.

"Is that my jacket?" I ask, staring in both bewilderment and amusement.

"No, silly. It's my jacket!" Po says, blowing a ringlet of hair out of her face.

Una smirks, cocking a brow as she asks. "And where did you get the jacket from?"

"It's not yours, big sissy. Draven gave this to me," Po announces, crossing her arms. "I know I steal a lot of your clothes, but this one really is mine."

I laugh, and don't say another word. It's *definitely* the jacket I lost when I first entered the carnival, but it'll fit Po eventually. I want to be here long enough to see her grow into it, and the half-demon she chooses to become. I dream of a future where I attend Reina's wedding, where Una goes on to accomplish everything she sets her mind to, and I dream of *him*. Draven.

There are a thousand possibilities for my future. Ones where I'm back on Earth working a miserable joke of a job, or maybe I'm married with a wife or husband and children. But they all sound so unsatisfying compared to the life I could live here, and the things I could wish for. I enjoy living on edge, dancing under the lights of a big top, and hearing demonic applause. It's the only future where I see myself truly happy.

Once Quinn finishes my hair, I give everyone a squeeze before leaving the tent to go find a snack. Or a certain half-demon. Whichever comes first.

The Carnival is still running half-staffed. Raph wanted to give everyone ample time to recover, and none of us felt like arguing. Still, it's strange to walk through camp in the bright light of day, the sun's rays beaming down on me.

There's no sound except for the distant hum of music. Sweat creases my forehead, and there's a weird churning feeling in my gut. *A warning.*

Somehow, my instincts never seem to steer me wrong. I wasn't fearful of Luc when I should have been, and it's the reason I'm here today.

I was afraid of Draven from the start. I'm still afraid of him, but now it's for an entirely different reason—one I'm not entirely sure I'm brave enough to admit out loud. At least, not yet.

I know he won't be back until this evening, but I want nothing more than to see him right now. He shouldn't be dealing with this shit so soon after his and the girls' accidents.

"Ahem," a deep voice coughs, and I'm instantly reminded of that sinking feeling taking over my body. The one I work so hard to avoid.

I turn, thinking I'm going to see a deranged stalker or demonic murderer, but it's just Baelor, eating what looks like a lemon.

"Your skin is glowing," he says, and leans against one of the poles holding a tent in place. I stop in my tracks, unsure of whether or not I should be polite or disregard him.

He could be the thief. Maybe I could weasel information out of him?

"Thank you," I say. "How're you feeling?"

Baelor travels the distance between us in one quick step. His presence is overwhelming, and his breath seems to steal mine, like there isn't enough oxygen for both of us. He's tall, maybe an inch or so taller than Draven, and he looms over me in a way that can only be described as threatening. I'm not cornered, I could back away and run, but my muscles won't budge. It's an all-too familiar feeling. "Like I need to make you my partner."

"What?" Baelor is *married*. To Lilian. Is he drunk?

"The Sinner's Circus. I think we should join our acts," he says, his voice dripping like honeyed poison.

A pang of relief hits me at his words, but it's quickly swallowed by an anxious, itchy feeling that takes over my entire body. I would rather do almost anything than perform in an act with this half-demon. In another life, I might've taken the sweet bait. I might have seen his words as beautiful promises, but that is not the version of me I am today. My past has brought me pain and grief and something else—something more sinister sits under the surface of my memories. "I don't think Draven likes to share." I mean performance partners, but there's an underlying message there, too.

"Draven wouldn't be sharing, baby. You'd be all mine." He runs a hand down my shoulder and arm, caressing me slowly. Though his touch is soft, my vision spins, the feeling on my skin reminding me of a man's tight grip. More memories threaten to break through, but I try to focus on his words instead of my shadowed past. "Raph is looking for acts to bring in more business. Let's show them something truly remarkable."

My body and brain know what happens next. They know exactly how a guy like this will react to being rejected, and yet I stand still. I'm stuck, fixed in place with every fibre of my being on high alert. Sirens blare in the back of my mind, and a scream endeavors to come loose from my throat, but when I open my mouth, nothing comes out. With this terrifying moment comes shocking clarity. Regardless of what's happening now, nothing can scare me away from this place. Not the threat of murder from a handsome pianist, and definitely not a perverted clown with no respect for others' boundaries. I will claw Baelor's eyes out if I have to, but this is *my* home.

And that's when a blade comes flying towards us, and I'm finally able to scream. "DON'T!"

It stops right before Baelor's face, a near microscopic distance from stabbing right through him. The metallic, sparkly scent of magic fills the air, and my ears are met with a thud as the dagger hits the ground.

I'm not sure why I yelled what I did. I don't like, or even pity, Baelor, but I didn't want to be the reason someone takes a life. I couldn't let that burden be mine to bear.

Baelor turns, and it's Draven who stands before us. His eyes are tired, the bags underneath them much puffier than normal, and there's a quiet sort of darkness clouding his golden irises.

Draven pulls another blade from his boot and holds it up to Baelor's neck. "Touch her and I will cut off your fingers one by one whilst feeding them to Luc's helhounds."—He shifts his arm up, placing the metal right against the corner of Baelor's eye— "And if you ever dare to even *glance* in her direction the wrong way again, I will gouge your fucking eyes out. Furthermore, I'll forego my blades for my bare hands, just to make it extra personal. Are we clear?"

"'Crystal," Baelor answers through gritted teeth. His body starts out tense, posturing and angry, but it quickly changes before our eyes. It's as if we can see his vision clear from seeing pure red, and the clown we all know swims back to the surface.

Baelor's ears wiggle, his eyes going wide with shame. To my surprise, Draven releases him, and Baelor darts away, back towards the hall.

I want to focus on Draven and the way his eyes wander up and down my form. I want to ask him about his meeting, and tell him about my day before Baelor, but my mind feels like it's balancing on the edge of a cliff, ready for me to fall into the darkest of abysses.

My memories shift to the sensation of rough hands and quiet whispers. Pain and tears flood my thoughts. The way my girl-friend looked at me when I told her—the way I apologized for it happening.

And then all the oxygen vacates my lungs.

Symphony No. 23

Draven

Gemma falls to the ground, her chest heaving as she struggles to take in a breath. I scoop Gem up into my arms and carry her back to my tent, unsure of what ails her.

Her behavior is erratic and emotional, reminding me of when I was a teenager and I'd wake up from night terrors, plagued by the memories of my late mother and father. She's clearly distraught, and the sight reaches into my chest, plucking every one of my heartstrings.

Gemma was a quiet hum beneath all the noise of Hel's Carnival. She was an accident, an incidental, but never the melody. And yet now I seem to hear her in everything.

I want to hold her, to use my body to shield her from the horrors of this world, but that might not be what she needs right now. Whatever this is, whatever vicious memory has dug its gnarly claws into her, might cause Gemma to require solitude over comfort. All I know is right now, I will become whatever she needs. Whether it be a soft place to land, or a bodyguard standing at the door, I'll be exactly the being she wants.

Placing her on my bed, I take the gray sheets and cover her, tucking her in gently.

I start to leave my tent, but Gemma grasps my pant leg, stopping me. "Please."

I freeze, waiting for further instructions.

"Sit with me," she pleads.

I follow her simple command and sit, running a finger down the side of her arm, and she shifts to lay her head in my lap.

"When Baelor attacked me, it triggered a bunch of childhood and teenage memories," she explains.

"I'm guessing they weren't about a vacation on the beach?"

"Not particularly." There are little dew drop tears welling in her eyes. "When I was a teenager, a man... forced himself on me."

My body stiffens, every fibre of my being on edge, but I keep up with the gentle strokes on her skin. This isn't about me or my rage, this is about Gemma.

"He was older. He'd come hang out at our dance competitions—"

"A coach?"

She shakes her head, her breathing ragged. "No. It was kind of weird. He used to dance? And so nobody questioned his presence. One time I slept over at a friend's house, and her big sister dragged us to this crazy house party. With enough eyeliner, I sorta looked like everyone else. We danced and drank, and he said he was worried about the open drinks. That men could drug us or something." Gemma swallows. "He said he had some soda cans upstairs, but he needed help if he was going to bring them down, so I followed him."

"Was it his house?" I ask, trying not to let the rage simmering in my chest make its way into my voice. Rage won't take her pain away, but comfort might.

She furrows her brows. "No. I'm such a fucking idiot, I don't know why I believed him."

"You're not an idiot. You were a child," I say, trying to reassure her. "You did nothing wrong."

"I know." Her eyes are full of devastation. "Anyway, obviously that was a ploy to get me to trust him. And it worked. I fully trusted that he was a good guy. The rest of what happened should be pretty clear..."

"You don't need to tell me any more, but if there's anything I can do to help you, anything at all, please let me know," I say, and she nods.

If Baelor ever pulls a stunt like that again, his only spot in Hel's Carnival will be in the fucking ground.

"After that, I stopped dancing until my grandparents died and I was desperate for a job. That's when I started at The Midnight Muse." Her eyes shift, her mind seeming to wander to somewhere far or long ago.

"Do you enjoy dancing now?" I ask, hoping for a certain answer.

Gemma gives me a small smile. "I do. And actually, there is something you can do for me."

"Shoot."

She lets out a small, nervous giggle, and I wipe a tear off her cheek. "I want you to teach me how to defend myself."

"It would be my pleasure," I say, and drag her softly into my lap, wrapping my arms around her waist. "I'll train you until you can kick even Rowan's muscular ass."

Gemma laughs, the sound soft and genuine, and it's my favorite song.

I CLICK MY PEN, the scribbles on the page barely legible as I try to formulate a plan for finding our thief.

Torture them, Luc said. But who? Baelor? Leo and Lyle? Or better yet, I could find contacts directly from The Legion.

Seduce them, Luc also suggested. It's not my favorite plan, but it's a Hel of a lot easier. If they don't have the information I need, I could find an out. But where do I find members of The Legion?

Throwing my notebook on my bed, I head out of my

bedroom and towards Reina and Gemma's tent. I try not to notice the smell of vanilla and cherry as I enter, focusing wholly on Reina, rather than the beautiful human making *fuck me eyes* at me.

"Fangs, I've got a question for you."

"Go for it, dirty dog," she says, and Gemma snort laughs.

My eyebrows shoot up. "Dirty dog?"

Reina shrugs her slender shoulders. "I'm trying out some new nicknames for you. You're dirty, you smell like dog. You're a perv. I don't know, I thought it fit."

"*Anyway,* do you happen to have any contacts in The Legion?"

Reina's eyes widen for a millisecond before she completely schools her features. "Negative."

"You're lying," I press her, leaning up against the dresser.

Gemma's lying on her stomach, her head resting in her hands as she kicks her feet with amusement at our interaction.

"I'm not lying, I'm omitting," Reina says with a glare. "But no. Look, I hate Luc, but I don't... we don't have any better options."

"But you know someone who does?"

"Have better options? Yeah, Gemma. Hit me up when you get tired of this cretin. I'll set you up with someone nice."

Gemma smiles ear-to-ear. "But Reina, what if I want you?" She blows kisses, and Reina catches them.

"Alas, I've already been taken by another."

"We could've been the cutest couple. It's a shame we fell for smelly half-demons," Gemma says and winks at me.

"Smelly?" "Khalid is *not* a half-demon." Reina and I say at the same time.

Gemma rolls her eyes. "Semantics."

I let out a sigh. "Are you two always this insufferable? Reina, who the fuck knows someone in The Legion?"

There's an uncomfortable silence before Reina finally responds. "Absinthe. But you didn't hear it from me, dude."

I was afraid she was going to say that. I was hoping she'd tell me Baelor or the twins and we could cut to the chase, but I guess it can't ever be too easy. I salute the two goodbye and exit the tent, heading straight for Absinthe.

After the fire, we rebuilt her small prop tent to hold not only storage, but an entire workshop for Absinthe, Rowan, and the twins.

I enter the space, not having seen it since the start of the remodel, and I'm surprised to find it's already full of stuff. Tools and spare pieces of wood, sure, but there are tons of props here too. Replicas of old ones that got destroyed, as well as new and inventive things. There's a wooden block, lacquered in a glossy chestnut, that seems to secretly separate from another block, and I fiddle it with my finger. It seems to be too small to hold a body, and yet that's exactly what it does. Seams and slats run across the plane, carved neatly into the wood, just wide enough for something to fit through—if you were flexible enough. I picture Lilian twisting and shifting her bones and muscles, contorting every which way to make the trick come to life.

"I watched an old demon film where they sawed someone in half, and I thought... we could totally fake that without killing anyone!" Absinthe explains, popping out seemingly out of nowhere.

"You invented something so you *don't* have to kill anyone?" I ask, scratching my chin.

Her smile broadens, but her white face paint doesn't crease. "Of course. This is for a *family friendly* show. We could use it in a daytime act," she explains.

"That's quite clever of you."

"It's not finished yet. I still have to add the glitter."

I wave my hands. "Oh, I don't think it needs—"

"*Everything* needs more glitter, Draven," she corrects, her eyes making a crazed expression. "Now, brother dear, what are you here for? Do you need..." Absinthe walks past me and does a back-bend before grabbing a rod covered in swirls. When she lifts it, other props fall off, revealing the hammer head underneath. "....a fun new toy?"

Absinthe swings the hammer around, giggling before placing it back on the ground.

"I need to speak with someone from The Legion," I say, unsure of how much I should reveal, for both her sake and mine.

"Who?"

I shrug. "Nobody in particular. I just have a couple of questions."

Absinthe crosses her arms, the colorful pattern of her clown suit rippling with the movement. "No."

"No?"

"I'm not going to give you one of my friends' names for them to wind up dead."

Fair. Honestly, a fair retort. "They won't *die*."

Her nostrils flare at me. "No? Then what are you doing, Draven? You want me to trust you, you've gotta trust me back."

Trust. It's possibly my fatal flaw, but I don't trust anyone. Of all my sisters, Reina is the one I'm closest to, one of the only ones who truly knows the ins and outs of my work, and even she gets shielded from the bulk of it. I put my life on the line for Luc and Raph nearly every damn day, and even with them, I have precautions in place. Traps set up should they betray me or each other.

How could I trust anyone when the person meant to love and protect me tried to kill me and everyone I love? How does one come back from that?

But she's right. I have to trust her.

"I'm going to set up a sort-of sting operation. You're going to invite your friend to an orgy I'm hosting. Tell him to bring some of his Legion friends. Once they're here, I'm going to question them," I explain.

"What's your goal?"

"To find out if Baelor, Leo, or Lyle have any greater involvement in The Legion."

She tilts her head. "And you won't kill Minh?"

"I will not kill your friend Minh. *His* friends, however, I can't promise. It depends on whether or not they're operatives," I say in earnest.

"Fine. I will set up the arrangements. An orgy with the famous *Scorpion,* huh?"

I smile. "I'm not going to actually fuck any of them. The plan is to do enough to get the info I need, and then get the Hel out of there."

"Okay, good, because I've fucked his friend Desdemona and it would be totally weird if we slept with the same person," she says and shivers. "Bleh."

"Wouldn't dream of it. I already have someone."

Someone that's *mine.*

Symphony No. 24

Gemma

"What are you wearing?" Draven asks when I enter his tent, ready for our first self-defense class.

"My outfit for tonight? With sweatpants over top," I say, defensive. We have dinner tonight, followed immediately by The Sinner's Circus. "What was I supposed to wear, armor?"

"I—nevermind. Are you feeling ready?"

"Not particularly," I say, and take a seat on his bed.

Draven smiles. "Good, because if someone ever does try to harm you and I'm not there, you won't feel ready then, either. Now, stand up."

I do, balling my fists as though I'm ready to fight.

"Um. How about you act as though you're walking through a parking lot and you hear a strange sound," he says, and hands me a knife. I grip it in one hand, and start to move away from him, when Draven grabs me from behind.

"What are you doing?!" I say, my voice loud and strained.

"What would you do?"

"I don't fucking know," I say, and stomp on his foot. Draven doesn't move.

"Bend your knees to stabilize your body," he says, talking me through the movement. His arm presses further into my body, his hand wrapping around the back of my arm. "Use your elbow. Push it back and strike me in the ribs."

I do just that, and he lets out a groan. "That's my girl. Now, stab me."

Taking the knife, I swing it through the air, but Draven blocks my blow.

He shakes his head, one arm still wrapped around me. "Not like that. Keep the hand holding the knife close to your body, and make sure you pay attention to your center of gravity." Draven taps the back of my knees with his foot, and I bend them again, not realizing they'd straightened.

"How do I stab you?" I ask, genuinely not sure of what to do next.

"Reverse your grip on the knife handle and strike me somewhere vulnerable. Perhaps the inner thigh? There's a big artery there," he explains, and I go for it, stopping right before I'd pierce his pants and skin.

"Perfect," he says, and then scoops me up, tossing me over his shoulder as I scream for him to put me down. "We'll do more lessons later, it's time for dinner."

My legs traverse the stage for the first time in what feels like forever, my body moving like a flickering flame, lighting up the darkness of night. There are hundreds of eyes on me, but I only yearn for a single pair.

Draven won't be here today. It's odd performing without him, but Reina is with me on the cello, her familiar presence a great comfort.

My body moves with visually effortless grace, muscle memory kicking into place as I perform an old strip routine from back at The Midnight Muse. I shake my breasts, making the tassels whip around in circles, and the audience lets out a thunderous applause.

Lilian performs after me, her back bending in ways I couldn't imagine, and The Sinner's Circus continues on just like it always has.

Once the show is over, we clean up, but I linger a little longer. My eyes scan the area, memorizing every detail of the big top. From the color of the striped fabric to the lights shining down, illuminating the center ring. I remain fixed in place, my mind flipping through memories of different nights and performances.

I find myself wandering around camp, mindlessly meandering past tent after tent. Draven said he would be out late tonight *handling some business*, and most of everyone else has gone to bed by now. Reina is nowhere to be seen, which means she's almost definitely with Khalid. I'm a little lonely, but it's kind of nice to bask in the quiet solitude of this place.

When I first arrived at the carnival, I thought nighttime was creepy. Dead silence, no people or demons, just flickering lights. Now, it brings a sense of serenity.

It's only been a few months, but now I can't envision myself anywhere else in the galaxy. We've done so much to transform The Sinner's Circus, but I think there's more fame and glory to take.

Trapeze, balancing acts, more dancing and fire. There's a million things we can add to our repertoire. I'd love to see Draven do something with his motorcycle. My mind wanders to the way his forearms flex as he tightens his grip on the handles, the way his vehicle moves effortlessly—that would truly be an act to behold.

There's a rustling sound coming from the hall, and I stop dead in my tracks, an eerie chill whispering against my skin as goosebumps prickle down my spine. *Why would somebody be in the hall this late at night?*

I brush off the uncomfortable feeling, positive I'm going to find Raph or Absinthe sitting inside. Or maybe Draven was hoping I waited up for him. It would be like him to sit in the hall, leaving hints so I'd come find him. He's probably sitting in a chair, his feet up on the table, a cocky grin spread across his face.

Entering through the front, I don't find much of anything, but there's the faintest scent of magic emanating in the air—that sparkling, crispy smell. The hall is large and spacious. The noise is coming from Raph's office—one of the smaller offshoots off the main dining and practice area—and I have to school the disappointment from my face.

I like Raph, I do. He's got a fun personality and I honestly wouldn't mind chatting with him, even if just to get my mind off everything, but there was a very particular demon I was hoping to find tonight.

A very sexy half-demon who is good with his hands.

Pushing past the privacy curtain, I yelp. There is a half demon standing before me, but he isn't Draven.

It's one of the twins.

He turns to face me, and my eyes dart back and forth between his brows, looking for the infamous scar, but come up short. It's Lyle, then. Lyle is standing in front of the empty safe. *Lyle* is staring at me like a deer in headlights.

"Gemma, what're you doing here so late?"

Every hair on my arms stick up at attention. "I could ask you the same thing."

He gives me a toothy grin, one fang grazing his bottom lip. It's the same smile he's always had, but there's an uncomfortable edge to it tonight. "Draven's busy with *company,* Raph's out dealing with governor business, I figured I'd double check and make sure the safe was alright."

"They don't keep the money in the safe anymore," I say, my breath becoming heavy.

Lyle stares at me like he wants to tear me limb-from-limb, and just like I did the first day I arrived here, I run like hell—like *Hel.* Faster than Robyn's helhorse, I run out of the hall and into the main part of camp. My feet are flying so fast they barely touch the ground as I dart past tents, trying to come up with a semblance of a plan. I could run into a tent, but what if no one's there? Or worse, what if I accidentally enter one of the children's tents?

My mind tries to map out a way to Draven or Reina, but I'm not sure who is here, and even worse... I'm not sure who else I can trust. Yasmeena, Absinthe, Robyn. But their tents aren't close, and what do I do if I get caught?

Tucking myself behind a bush, I decide to lie low so I can book it towards Draven. Leather boots thud against the dirt, and I hold my breath as Lyle walks past, in opposite direction of where I'm heading next.

With only the sound of my heart thundering in my chest, I take a deep breath and think of Draven before charging for his tent.

The lights are on, and I can hear the faint sounds of a record playing as I run inside to find the most gut-wrenching sight.

Draven is bare-chested and straddling someone. His vow is deep and low as he murmurs something sweet in their ear, the same way he's done to me countless times. There's an entourage of beautiful, feminine demons, shirtless and moaning behind them, and every hair on my arms sticks straight up.

My heart shatters into a million tiny fragments. I want to pick up a shard and flay him with it, make him bleed and hurt just as much as he's hurting me. I want to scream, but my voice is caught in my throat. It feels like all of Hel is frozen, the whole planet no longer spinning on its axis. All there's left is me and Draven and the ice forming deep in the pit of my chest in a last ditch effort to protect my heart.

He turns, eyes going wide as his face flushes, and I'm not sure if it's from lust or fear. Desperately, I want him to say anything, but we just stare at one another as he climbs off the demon's lap.

My mind flashes to Una and Po, the sound of their laughter, and I choose them. I choose them over myself, and I push down all the pain and rage bubbling at my core.

"Lyle is the thief, and I'm afraid he's going to hurt someone if we don't go and stop him," I say matter-of-factly. As much as I hate Draven right now, I love this family more.

The other demons sitting on Draven's bed wrap themselves in his sheets, and I grit my teeth at the sight. I wonder how many of them he fucked tonight. Tears sting my eyes, but I blink them away. I can mourn this relationship later. Hel's Carnival has bordered on a Utopia for me if you forget the beginning and... well, Baelor. It was too good to be true, of course Draven was just using me. Manipulating me for some greater purpose. Why would a magical, powerful half-demon fall in love with a pathetic human? My mere existence at this carnival was practically court-ordered by the King of Hel himself, and my life on Earth wasn't rainbows and butterflies either. It was a miserable, lonesome existence.

How could I ever think he'd settle for me?

Draven swallows and whispers. "Butterfly, I need you to trust me right now."

Symphony No. 25

Draven

The worst moment of my life was watching the light leave my mother's eyes. The second? One might assume I'd say killing my father, or worse yet, when he slowly tore my wings from my body, but they would be mistaken. The absolute look of betrayal in Gemma's eyes as she walked in and found me with these bastards will haunt me until my very last breath.

My hand reaches down to retrieve the dagger from my boot before I turn back towards Minh. "Do you have anything to do with this?" I ask, placing the tip of the blade against the wide, pink column of his throat.

The demon shakes his head, his throat bobbing. "No, we're not operatives."

"You're not Legion?"

"I'm Legion, but only by association. I don't do any of the dirty work, I just fluff their numbers and enjoy the parties," Minh confesses as blood trickles down his muscular neck.

I remove the knife from the demon and stalk towards Gemma, closing the distance between us. A single tear falls down her face, but I wipe it away.

"I have to leave, but I need you to go retrieve Reina and come find me," I say, and plant a kiss on her forehead. "I love you."

She balks as if my words were a strike against her skin, and my heart aches.

I'm aware this isn't the best time for a confession of that magnitude, but I had to tell her, just in case I don't get another chance to. I'm confident in my strength and capabilities, but I have no idea what I'm truly up against.

I needed her to hear the truth directly from the source.

Exiting the tent, I charge through camp, using my magic like a beacon leading me straight to Lyle. My energy reaches across the grounds, thermally feeling for familiar waves of body heat. There are some I recognize, and others I don't, but I ignore everything, homing in on Lyle.

When I finally spot him, he has Lilian pinned in a corner, his tall body hulking over hers. I chuck a blade in his direction, but it stays suspended in mid-air, and an effervescent, bitter magical scent hits my nostrils in opposition to mine.

My mind is racing faster than the staccato beat of my heart as I consider all the possible ways Lyle was able to acquire magic. Runes, magicite, atra consumption. I naively assumed all of these options were too difficult for the other carnies, but I was wrong.

I stand frozen, my feet stuck to the ground, as a vein pops in Lyle's neck. It's taking all his energy just to keep me planted here, and I'm barely fighting back. I can't, I'm too caught up in the devastation from this level of betrayal.

Is Leo in on this, or anyone else? There are strangers on the grounds.

Letting these scoundrels hurt my family would be a fate worse than death. Lyle darts out of my reach, and I allow him a head start.

However much time I gift him, it won't be enough.

"I want you to get Robyn, Quinn, and the children and get out of here. Send Absinthe and Rowan to help us. Take Baelor with you, if you please. He can protect you all," I say, and Lilian nods before spreading her wings and taking flight.

To my irritation and surprise, there are small traps scattered about camp as I make my way towards the hall. Fields of metal thorns and rope contraptions were placed on the ground by some-body—I'd place my bets on The Legion. They're meant to slow or maim, not kill or seriously injure, and they were lazily done, haphazardly throughout the walkways between our tents.

To me, they're more annoyance than anything. If I had wings, I would simply fly to avoid them. Unfortunately, I'm on foot, so I'm stuck dealing with the ridiculous mechanisms.

Turning a corner, I spot Aida. Her tail whips around on the dirt, quickly destroying one of the poorly laid traps. She looks up at me, her forehead beading with sweat, and nods. I continue past, a warm feeling filling my chest.

Pride. If there's one thing I have, it's my fellow carnies. My throat stings a little at the thought of losing any of them, but I shake it off. There isn't time for that right now. Not yet.

Entering Taryn's tent, I take my sai off the wall. There's a splashing sound, and I see the tip of her tail as she traverses deeper into the underground springs. *Good.* Right now, she's safer down there than up here.

A rodent crawls up my leg as a thorn-covered baseball bat nearly takes me out.

Lyle.

My body perks back up, and I stare him straight in the eyes. "Do you expect me to run from you?" I ask, every muscle going still.

When Luc first took me in, I stayed at one of his estates with a giant library. Every day I'd pick up a different book, reading it from cover-to-cover, trying to absorb every bit of information available. Books in English, in Latin, in Vietnamese. He even had books from other planets. I learned countless things: war strate-gies, agricultural mitigation, psychology... Specifically, human psychology.

The doctors from Earth loved to bring up the nervous system and humans' fight-or-flight response. Only some of my DNA is human, but I like to imagine that we half-demons have that same innate sense to fight or flee.

I have always been a fighter. It was my destiny. I had to fight tooth and claw just to survive my own upbringing. I'm not going down because of some punk and his twisted idea of mutiny.

"No, I didn't expect to have to deal with you at all," Lyle says, spitting at me. "But here we are."

I all but snarl as I show him my teeth, and he laughs as he takes another swing.

"Is The Scorpion going to sting me?" Lyle asks, his tone mocking.

I shake my head. "Tonight, I'm The Executioner."

Lyle's golden eyes go wide with shock and confusion, before he schools his features. The Executioner, to him, is nothing but a fairytale. A myth about the demon or half-demon that lurks in Luc's shadow, ready to strike when The Devil gives his orders. Unfortunately for Lyle, I'm the crack in the foundation of his plans, the inevitable cause of his downfall.

He whips past as I use my magic to chuck my blade directly at him. It slices open the side of his arm, but he keeps running, heading straight into the hall. Lyle nearly trips on a vine, but he makes it into the tent.

I follow suit, chasing after him. The hall is a cacophony of sound as we walk into what can only be described as a battlefield. Two of the demons from earlier are fighting with Khalid and Reina, and Absinthe is cornered by another. Minh might not be an operative, but some of his posse most definitely are.

Another demon—one I don't recognize—is going up against Gemma and Yasmeena.

There is more noise coming from outside, and I can feel Raph's magic as he and Rowan battle against whatever else is out there.

I thrust my sai right through the demon harassing Gemma. Blood gushes from his back, and he sinks to the floor. Grabbing a dagger from my other boot, I hand it to Gemma. "Make sure you use this."

Lyle, seeing he has nowhere left to run, charges for me, but I dodge the blow.

I cross the room towards the sound of Reina's yelp, Lyle still on my heels. I hear him cry out in pain, and I can only assume Yasmeena's claws are buried in his back.

Everything seems to happen in an instant. I gut the guy attacking Reina, and Lyle frees himself from Yasmeena's grasp. He finally manages to land a hit, right to the side of my leg.

I yell out in pain, and I'm about to strike back at Lyle when I notice Absinthe struggling against her own foe. Using all the force I can muster—both magic and strength—I knock Lyle to the ground.

"Do you like daggers?" I call towards Absinthe, who is weaponless and narrowly avoiding certain death.

"I like stabbing," she answers back.

Quickly, I throw a dagger in her direction, wielding my magic so that the blade lands perfectly in her hand. I watch as she uses it to gouge out his eye. Blood sprays everywhere, the sound squishy and disgusting as she completely destroys the inside of his socket before starting on the other one, and I try not to cringe at the little giggle that escapes her mouth.

A few wide-eyed stares remind me that my family hasn't seen much of my magic, but if I'm going to use it for anything, it's them. Wielding it, I ensure every person I love is safe or has the weaponry they need to fight. One by one we take down each invader—either killing them or incapacitating them enough to no longer be a threat.

And now, we just have Lyle.

Rowan helps me strap him to a chair with our belts before heading to help Raph with the mess outside. Absinthe is still smiling, but everyone else looks somber as we stare at someone we all once considered family.

There's a rustling at the door and I hear faint voices arguing as

Leo walks in, tears falling from his swollen eyes. In his hand is a blue notebook.

"What is that?" Reina asks as Leo stomps towards his twin.

"His homicidal manifesto," Leo spits. "Lyle has been fucking us over for months."

His voice sounds delirious, completely devoid of its usual qualities, but one thing is for certain: Leo had nothing to do with this.

"I was going to save us, Leo," Lyle says.

Reina punches Lyle square in the face, hard enough to knock a tooth out.

He goes to speak, but Yasmeena shoves a piece of fabric in his mouth. "Oh, shut the fuck up."

Reina crosses her arms. "Save the villain monologue, Lyle. Nobody's watching your pathetic little performance."

"That's exactly what this was," Leo says, shaking as he opens the book. "This all started because we weren't given acts. Lyle was jealous of Draven."

"So then why did he join The Legion?" I ask, scratching my chin.

"They preyed on him." He gestures with the journal. "I read every word. He was mad one night, went to a bar to drink his feelings away without me, and heard them spewing their garbage about Luc. It all spiraled from there. He started attending secret meetings, and they convinced him to steal from the carnival. Gemma's arrival became the perfect scapegoat," Leo explains.

My skin feels hot, my stomach churning, boiling with rage. Honestly? I could still forgive him. This is a terrible betrayal, but the twins are young and naïve. I could see some cult framing themselves as heroes brainwashing him, but there's just one question.

"Who started the fire?"

Lyle visibly stiffens.

I clear my throat, trying not to let my rage bubble over just yet. "Who started the fucking fire?"

Leo stutters, but I wave for him to stop.

"I want to hear *him* say it," I whisper, and Khalid removes the cloth from Lyle's mouth.

For a moment, I'm not sure he's going to speak as blood drips from his mouth, but he clears his throat. "I started the fire. It was intended to look like Khalid caused it by accident," he admits, his voice crazed and eyes bloodshot.

I know there are other people in the room with me. I know Gemma and my sisters are shocked, Leo is hurt and Khalid is angry, but all I see is red.

"What would you have done if Una or Po died because of your actions?" I ask, my voice so low and raspy it's barely recognizable.

"That was the goal. I was trying to kill Una," he says through gritted teeth. "But Po got in the fucking way." There's a chorus of gasps at his confession.

Every moment with Leo and Lyle flash before my eyes. From when they first arrived, to the hours of board games and flirting, to Una and Po bringing Lyle soup when he didn't feel well. I feel sick with rage and disgust as I stare at this scumbag of a being.

He was supposed to be a friend. A brother, even. One of us. Reaching for my Sai, I go to end him, but something stops my arm.

Leo shakes his head, tears streaming down his face. "I'll do it."

"Leo," Reina reaches out, but Khalid grabs her hand to stop her.

"Let him do what he needs to," Khalid whispers.

Raph and Rowan stand by the entryway, their faces distraught and eyes puffy.

Lyle doesn't say anything. He doesn't plead for forgiveness, or beg his brother to stop. His eyes are almost lifeless as he stares at us. I hand Leo the knife. His slender fingers tremble, and we all collectively hold our breaths.

Everyone here has a sibling—either by blood or by choice—and I'm not positive any of us could kill them, but it's deeper than that. Lyle is not only Leo's brother, but he's the other half of him. They're a package deal. Everything Leo did, Lyle did too. They enjoyed the same things, played the same practical jokes. Their hearts beat as one, at least that's how we all perceived them.

But perhaps we were all wrong, and this entire time they were growing apart. Maybe time changed them into something unrecognizable from one another.

Lyle's expression shifts, his eyes widening as he smiles. "Put an end to this charade and we can change Haeresis—we can transform all of Hel. The Legion—"

"Stop. Stop it. The Legion has killed innocent people," Leo says, and it's true.

The Legion wants the monarchy to end. They seek to replace it with a new system, but some of their operatives are willing to do so, no matter the cost. Even if it'll take the lives of little ones like Una and Po, they don't care. They lack the same empathy they accuse Luc of not having.

"Leo, don't you understand? Sacrifices must be made for the future of the greater good," Lyle says, his voice crescendoing into a rage-fueled shout.

"These are *children* we're talking about," Leo says. His voice shakes, but he seems to be willing as much confidence as he can muster.

Everyone is still, not a muscle moving in sight as we all watch Leo stand before his brother.

"They are casualties," Lyle corrects, and I visibly stiffen at his callous attitude. I've killed many beings, many monsters, but very few have been this openly heartless.

Leo's calm demeanor has transformed into something devastating. His eyes are puffy, his brows furrowed and mouth straight as he runs his fingers through the short white strands of his hair. "Why are you putting me through this again?"

Raph and I are likely the only two in the room aware of what *this* is. Leo and Lyle came to us when they were just eighteen, shunned by their parents. For a few years, most of their backstory was a mystery, but I dug into their past just as I always do.

Leo and Lyle aren't twins, but triplets. Their third brother, Logan, was suspected of being a prolific serial killer. When Lyle found out, he took matters into his own hands and executed Logan. Rather than feeling pride, their parents were pissed, and Lyle was cast out from the family. This is what led them to joining our *sanctuary for the strange.*

"When you killed Logan, I chose you. I *believed* you. I left everything behind, our entire family, to come here with you, and now you're becoming the very thing you feared most. You're a monster, just like Logan was," Leo says, tightening his grip on the knife as tears stream down his face. He wipes them away, the gesture rough.

Lyle's smile finally fades. "That's not fair. I didn't kill anyone."

"But you would have," Leo says, torment heavy in his voice. He moves, shifting so that he's behind Lyle.

"I did it all for you. I killed Logan to protect you. I would have given you everything," Lyle says, and Leo flinches as though the words sting like acid.

Leo places the blade against the column of Lyle's throat. "I didn't need all that, I just needed my brother. *You* were my everything. You were enough for me."

In one swift movement, Leo slices open Lyle's neck, blood spraying in every direction as he slumps in his chair, still being held up by the rope. There are winces and shudders throughout the group, and I widen my eyes, refusing to acknowledge the tears that want to form.

A loud thud comes from behind me, and I turn to see Gemma collapsed on the floor. There's frantic movement everywhere. I run to her, cradling her head in my lap as someone else goes to get a damp towel.

Everything feels topsy-turvy for a moment until she comes to and opens those big doe eyes of hers, staring up at me.

"I remember everything."

Symphony No. 26

Gemma

The days following what we're calling *The Incident* were hard and strange. For some of the carnies, life continued on almost uninterrupted. Taryn, Aida, Yasmeena, Quinn, and Robyn seemed immune to everything that happened, returning to more usual routines. Raph was distant, less lively, clearly blaming himself. Everyone else seemed to be mourning Lyle, or processing his betrayal in their own ways. Even Draven was off, stuck in his own head.

But Leo was nowhere to be found.

Baelor and Khalid searched for him—even checked in other districts—but came home with nothing. It was as if he never existed at all.

Yesterday, Raph decided we should reopen and split the cast into two crews for the time being, at least until we get our heads on straight. Half of us will work the carnival, while the other half works The Sinner's Circus.

Draven, Reina, Rowan, Taryn, Lilian, Khalid, Yasmeena, and myself were chosen for The Sinner's Circus. Everyone else was assigned daytime crew. It's strange, continuing on as if everything's normal, and yet nothing feels normal or *right*. We're all just treading water, trying not to drown.

Draven and I haven't spoken much since that night. I was pretty out of it after my memories returned, and there was a lot of cleanup to do. I don't pity whoever had to scrub Lyle's blood off the chair. Maybe they burned it.

Since that night, everyone's been mostly keeping to themselves. Reina and I have been chatting, but other than that, I've been left to my own devices, trying to navigate what my next steps should be.

Before Hel, before all of this, I wanted to die. I genuinely considered taking my own life, embarrassed there would be nobody to notice if I did. I had no one to write goodbye. My rotting corpse would've likely been found by some poor underpaid paramedic after my landlord called in for a wellness check.

So instead, broke as shit and desperate to feel anything at all, I scoured the local listings for something. A job, a lonely broken heart to mend, anything, and found an ad for Augury University: a magical school for brilliant minds and monstrous hearts. The gig boasted high pay but dangerous conditions, which, incidentally, was just what I needed.

The experiment involved multiple types of magic, forging it all together to create a sort of portal in space. The goal was for me to enter and cross over into another lab inside the school.

Worst-case scenario, if shit went wrong, I'd awkwardly end up in the bathroom or on top of a library bookshelf. At least, that's what I was told.

What happened, however, transported me here. Whatever fuck-up they made sent me straight to Hel with no memories and nothing but the clothes on my back.

There's a part of me that wants to be pissed. I want to call up those magical professors and give them a piece of my mind. But another part of me is endlessly grateful for the last four months. I would have never experienced such beauty and strength, and grown to love this family I'm stuck with, and this weird planet I'm on.

Except I guess I'm not stuck anymore. Theoretically, if I got in contact with Earth, they could probably find me a way back. But is that what I want now that I know the full extent of my life before Hel? Now that I know the truth?

If I died on Hel—if I took my life, I'd have so many letters to write. Piles of goodbyes. How can I just let that go? Why would I leave everyone I love behind?

Stretching my muscles, I wait for Draven to enter the hall. We're planning on debuting a new piece of his, and I'm nervous to see him. Honestly, I'm still angry with him. I know we aren't *officially a couple*, but seeing him with that other demon felt like a betrayal—like he was cheating. And maybe that's not fair, but I can't help how I feel. It gutted me.

Footsteps come within earshot, and I still, completely frozen in place. Draven enters the tent, crossing towards me without a word. We're eye to eye, close enough that I can feel his breath across my face, and he cups my jaw, pushing his nose against mine, so close I can feel the cold metal of his septum piercing brush against my skin.

"I owe you an apology for the other night," he whispers. "It wasn't what it looked like."

That pisses me off. Draven was straddling someone while other demons were half-naked and moaning in his bed. There's nothing else it *could* have been.

I back away from him. "There's no point in lying."

"I'm not... Gemma, it's complicated."

"Complicated, my ass. Sorry, I didn't realize there's nuance to throwing an orgy."

He almost laughs, but stops when he sees my grim expression. "I understand the optics of the situation entirely, but I can assure you that nothing was going to happen. It was an operation; I was simply gathering information."

There's nothing simple about this. "Operation? Is that what we're calling it these days?"

"Spy, not surgical," he clarifies, which is borderline insulting to my intelligence.

I give him a pointed glare. "I knew what you meant. Draven, if you're going to ask for my trust, you have to return some. I deserve to know what's going on. Fully."

He reaches for my hand, intertwining our fingers. "You're the second person to share those sentiments with me this week. It feels like a lot of things keep getting repeated to me—"

"Because a lot of people love you and are worried about you," I cut in."

Draven nods, his eyes looking somber. "I know. It's not lost on me. I haven't been open with you or my sisters, and it's not fair, but I want to protect you all."

"It's not protecting us to keep us in the dark."

He nods. "You're right. Let's clear the air."

Draven sits on the piano bench and pulls me into his lap before telling me everything. From what I already knew of his traumatic childhood, to the work he does for Luc, he fills in every gap. *The Scorpion. The Spy. The Executioner.*

Every mask he wears is like a weight on his chest. I just hope by sharing his truth, it eases some of the load.

"Part of me didn't want to tell you because I genuinely believed it would be safer if you weren't aware," Draven starts. "But another part of me simply wasn't sure if you'd still want to be with me once you knew how much blood is on my hands. The kind of monster you're truly dealing with."

"Nothing you can say would scare me away," I say, and his arms squeeze around me before he lets me go, gently slipping me off his legs and onto the bench.

Draven stands and closes the piano lid before he crosses back towards me. He moves between my legs, pushing me up against the keys, and suddenly I'm breathless. All the oxygen has vacated my lungs as he leans in and wraps a hand around my throat.

"Nothing, butterfly? Nothing can scare you?" he taunts, tightening his grip. "What if I told you that you're mine—that nobody can ever touch you again, not like this?"

"Please," I plead, though the words can hardly come out with the pressure on my windpipe.

His fingers loosen, and he kisses me softly. "These are mine." His mouth moves down my body.

The outfit I'm wearing tonight—if you can call it an outfit— is a black fabric dress with a red lace overlay. There are huge cutouts exposing all of my back, as well as most of my stomach and sides. Draven draws the edge of the dress up, pushing the tassels that hang like berries on a vine, until all that's covering my lower half is my little red thong.

He grips my ass, kissing the exposed skin just above my hip. "This arse is mine," he says in that delicious accent of his, and I stifle a moan.

Wrapping my legs around his waist, Draven picks me up and carries me to the other side of the piano, placing me on top of the lid. My legs are spread, and he uses his teeth to tug at the red lace of my underwear, pulling them off of me.

"Most importantly, I want you to know this," he says, breathing between my legs, his mouth coming expertly close to my skin. "*This* is mine."

His mouth finally connects with my flesh as he sucks on my clit. First, he's slow and deliberate, but soon he begins devouring me like a man starved.

Tiny tremors seize my leg muscles as he works me, and I feel him chuckle against my skin. Draven was supposed to show me a song on the piano tonight, but I didn't realize it was going to be the sound of my moans harmonizing with his laughter to create this sensual symphony.

He uses the pad of his thumb to circle my clit while staring up at me with those golden eyes, and just when I think I'm close, he stops.

"Draven," I let out, the sound breathy.

"Oh, I'm not done with you just yet."

He hooks two fingers, pumping them inside me as he licks

and sucks, and the small ember of heat that was growing in my core ignites into a full-fledged inferno. I allow it to consume me.

I allow *him* to consume me until I come crashing over the edge, falling into a chasm of pure bliss. Draven is my ending and my beginning—he might rip out my heart and tear me to shreds, but he'll make sure to put me back together.

One kiss at a time.

Symphony No. 27

Draven

L uc said the way we handled the The Legion situation was satisfactory, and that he was *only mildly appalled* that Gemma was the one to figure out it was Lyle. What he fails to realize is that she was simply in the wrong place at the right time. She wouldn't have been there if she weren't seeking me out, we both know that to be true, but I digress.

Serve the throne, reap your own.

Tomorrow Raph, Luc, and myself, will be traveling to Proditorum for the Morningstar Summit, our bi-annual royal meeting, which feels akin to getting teeth pulled.

Absinthe, in all her glory, has decided that tonight of all nights is the time to call an all-cast assembly. I just hope she makes it quick, because I'd rather spend the night with Gemma.

As we enter the hall, Reina bumps her shoulder against mine and leans in. "They're talking, Draven. It's bad enough Khalid and Yasmeena have their magic. The other carnies don't understand why you've been granted access and they haven't."

"Well, it was kind of an emergency request, given my job," I say.

"Except most of them don't know that." Reina's mouth curves to the side.

"I know. I know. I don't blame them for their frustrations," I say through gritted teeth. Everyone in the carnival knows I'm The Spy, but very few know I'm The Executioner.

"So what do you want me to say?"

"Tell them I'm working on it. I promise. I'm going to get Luc to give them access, I just need more time."

She gives me a sympathetic smile. "Alright."

"Here ye, here ye," Absinthe shouts as we all gather around the dining table. Everyone, even Taryn and Aida, are in attendance tonight.

Everyone but Leo, that is.

I don't fault Leo for fleeing; I'm positive his head is a mess of emotions right now. I know firsthand what it's like to have to take the life of someone you love, regardless of how bad they might be.

It eats away at you, the guilt gnawing on your insides. You blame yourself, because it's easier than blaming the dead. You list everything you could have done to prevent it. When the pain of your mistakes becomes too heavy to bear, you find someone else —someone who wasn't kind enough, wasn't quick enough, someone who should have seen this coming. Maybe it's even someone who wronged you, and you shift the blame to them, allowing them to become the scapegoat of your story.

Deep down, though? Deep down, you'll always know it was them. It was the one you loved that caused this. They forced your hand, and you simply did what you could—what was best.

If I could, I would hold Leo and tell him this, but he's not here right now and I'm not sure he'll ever be again, but I hope he knows we'd welcome him.

We'd welcome him with open arms.

"Tonight," Absinthe says, pausing for dramatic effect. "Is family game night!"

Raph claps enthusiastically, his excitement soon echoed by Lilian, Robyn, Po and Quinn. Reina and I give each other pointed stares, but Gemma nudges me as if to say *humor her*, and

I join in clapping, too. Soon, everyone applauds, and there's a quiet rumble of *woos* that come from Rowan and Baelor.

I glare in Baelor's direction and lean into Gemma's neck. "Just say the word."

She shakes her head. "For now, just let it go. Tonight is about family."

Rowan suggests we play a card game for the girls, and Una sighs heavily when we reject her request for Poker. We opt for board games instead.

Khalid grabs Mancala for him and Baelor while Yasmeena picks out Rummikub for her, Lilian, Aida, and Absinthe. Gemma gets excited about all the games she recognizes from Earth, her face lighting up every time there's something familiar.

"I want to play something different," she says, smiling down at Po. "Can you tell me our options?"

"We have a trivia game called Infernal Pursuit," Po says, and I shake my head.

"No trivia. I have an unfair advantage over you all," I say with a cocky grin.

Po pushes the box back against the shelf and points to another. "Mephistopholy."

"What now?" Gemma's thick brows furrow, and I try not to laugh.

"It's like Hel's version of Monopoly," Reina explains, and Gemma nods in immediate understanding. "They even have a little figure shaped like the devil."

What the fuck is Monopoly?

"There's Lo To Hel, Condemn Four, and Unus. Oooh!" Po pauses on a big box, pulling it off the shelf and plopping it onto the floor. "Let's play Jenga: Tower of Terror."

Reina, Gemma, Po, and I all fight to stack these awful, thorn-covered wooden blocks without stabbing ourselves or making the tower fall, until Reina takes the victory and Po's eyes begin blinking slowly.

"It's time for bed, sleepy girl," Quinn says, scooping Po up and letting her rest on their hip.

"But Q," Po whines.

Robyn shakes her head. "No buts, little missy."

The three exit the hall, followed by Una, and everyone's games slowly conclude. I swear I see Khalid's ears catch fire when he loses to Baelor, much to Yasmeena and Lilian's amusement.

"I can't believe you lost to that clown," Reina says, grinning at the felion, who playfully shoves her.

Absinthe pulls a bell out from nowhere and rings it incessantly.

"Must you be so obnoxious?" I ask, sighing.

"Mhm." She nods. "Can we play a game with everyone?"

"Like what?" Raph asks. "Imitation?"

"Yes!" Absinthe screams, jumping up for joy. "Let's divide into teams."

We split off into two groups of six, everyone shifting around at the table, and Gemma interlocks her fingers with mine as we wait for further instructions.

"Imitation is a lot like Charades except you imitate one another. It's most fun if you're both insulting *and* dramatic," Raph explains.

"And you can speak, which is a bonus," Reina adds, looking back at Gemma and I.

Raph goes up first, and doesn't say a word, just does a back-bend. It's terrible—he's not very flexible—but a smile plasters its way onto Lilian's face.

"Are you me?" she asks, beaming.

"You betcha!" Raph replies and winks at Reina. "Good luck."

Reina walks up and places her legs together, her feet moving in some sort of ballerina position, and for a second I think she's supposed to be Gemma, whose hand shoots up like a child at school.

"Are you supposed to be Taryn?" Gemma asks, and Reina nods, the two of them proud.

"I thought she was imitating you dancing," I confess, and Gemma waves a hand at me.

"She didn't talk enough for it to be me, it had to be Taryn."

Taryn crosses her arms. "The non-talker will go next, please."

We all turn to Taryn in her tank, and she flexes her arms, pretending she has big muscles. "Aren't I the sexiest thing you've ever seen?"

"She must be imitating me," I whisper to Gemma, who snorts out a laugh.

"As if."

Absinthe cracks her knuckles. "Rowan, duh."

"There it is," Taryn says, and smiles.

I go up and imitate Absinthe, followed by Aida doing a hilarious impression of Raph, and the night continues on, everyone falling into fits of laughter after every imitation, until almost everyone's gone up or been impersonated.

"Come a little closer," a deep and familiar voice says from the entryway. "They call me The Scorpion, but don't worry ladies—I don't bite, but I didn't say I won't sting."

It's Leo.

He looks tired and disheveled, the usually slicked-back white strands of his hair messy and unbrushed. It's only been a week since The Incident, but he looks thinner, his frame hungered and frail.

This is the chance I need to tell him how I feel, but the words diminuendo in my mind until they're nothing but a quiet mumble. If he's here to say goodbye, I will wish him well and let him leave. If he chooses to stay, I will tell him then.

He'll be the second person I'll have ever opened up to about my experiences. Not Luc, not Raph, not even Reina. Just Gemma and Leo. The human who owns my heart, and the half-demon whose heart I wish I could heal.

"Look what the cat dragged in," I say, and Khalid gives me a pointed stare.

Everyone crowds around Leo, spitting question after question at him.

"Where did you go?" "How're you feeling?" "Are you staying?" "Did you miss me?"

A weight I didn't realize was pressing on my chest is instantly lifted by his presence, and I smile, giving him a pat on the back. Grabbing Gemma by the hand, I lead her out of the hall to allow everyone else to enjoy some time with him.

I hope he stays longer than tonight.

"You leave tomorrow?" Gemma asks as we walk through the dirt-lined pathways of camp.

I nod, falling into step beside her. "Yes. Raph and I will be gone for a day or so."

She squeezes my hand. "He's finally going to pay everyone. Are you excited?"

The question shouldn't throttle me, but it does, because I am acutely aware of what this means. It's a way out. For Leo. For Aida. Hel, perhaps even for Lilian, if she wanted to leave that arse.

And Gemma. It's probably enough crown for a ticket back to Earth. And even if it's not, I think she knows she could get the rest if she wanted to. Luc and Raph would give it to her in an instant, and even though it would destroy me from the inside out, I would too.

I would give her anything.

"Not particularly," I say, desperate for a change in topic.

Now that I know life with Gemma by my side, I don't want to imagine it without her. A song without a melody. A silent symphony, the instruments left to gather dust. Life would become meaningless, and I would be an empty husk made of flesh and bone, but nothing more.

She has ruined me.

Gemma's hip bumps against mine, and I knock my body back into hers. Like sunlight, she bursts into laughter.

"Quit being grumpy. Leo is back, we've at least temporarily

scared The Legion away, and the carnival is thriving. Life is good," she says.

It's a weak attempt to cheer me up, as she doesn't mention her plans for herself, but perhaps she's still undecided. At this point, it's my only hope.

"I'm not grumpy. Simply... lost in thought," I say as we enter my tent. A half-truth.

Gemma bites her lower lip. "Let's get lost together."

Symphony No. 28

Draven

Twice a year, every year, the Morningstar siblings travel to Proditorum to meet and discuss the comings and goings of their continents. The only beings allowed in the room are the Morningstars themselves and their plus ones. It can be a spouse, a hand, an assistant, whomever they need.

I am Raph's plus one of choice, as I'm the only citizen of Haeresis that fully understands what goes on behind the scenes of our governmental processes.

As *The Spy* and *The Executioner*, I act as Luc's second in command, but Luc has someone else as his plus one, on a technicality.

Beelzebub Morningstar, Luc's helhound. Prior to The Convergence, there were no dogs on Hel, only a type of wolf. Wolves who mingled with demons, and later humans, became lupion. Wolves who mingled with demons, and later dogs, became helhounds.

Short legged and fluffy, Bub looks like an adorable, sweet pup —until you piss him off. His true form reveals a large, muscular body of shadows with not one, not two, but three heads.

But you'd never guess it based on looking at him.

Raph, an expert on teleportation, brings us to the large continent, where we're shortly greeted by Lucile Morningstar at the door of the palace. She's red, like Luc and Raph, with raven-black hair and ocean-blue eyes, but unlike Luc, there are distinct wrinkles at the corners. She's a thicker, taller woman, with a broad smile.

Luc's mother looks pleased to see us, but there's something pained about her expression, too. Her smile doesn't quite reach her eyes. Beelzebub waves his tail excitedly at her, and she gives him a good pat before waving us off.

Staff escorts us to the grand meeting room, and we take our seats as we await the other guests to arrive by boat and plane.

Gabe is the first to arrive, punctual as ever. He brought an assistant—a beautiful, lively younger woman. A felion, maybe, though it's hard to tell with the amount of plastic surgery she's clearly undergone. It seems in order to work at Gabe's clinic, you must undergo the knife yourself. He nods as he enters, both he and his assistant taking a knee.

"Our Infernal King," they say in unison, rising and taking their seats beside Raph.

There's a long stretch of silence before Raph finally asks. "How many surgeries have you guys performed this year?"

Gabe and Raph fall into polite conversation, but Luc and I sit in silence. Paradoxically, it's both a comfortable and uncomfortable sort of silence. Comfortable because it's us, but uncomfortable due to what is next to come.

Micha is the next to join us, though he's entirely alone. "The husband said this meeting was too much of a drag for him to join us this time around," he announces before slinking into the chair beside Gabe's secretary.

I let out a quiet cough, and Micha jumps to his feet, quickly taking a knee. "Apologies, my Infernal Majest—"

"King," Raph corrects.

"Right. My Infernal King," Micha says. It's faint, but I can hear the slightest bit of embarrassment in his tone, and it brings me great joy.

Being the youngest of the eight siblings, Micha exudes spoiled brat energy wherever he goes. He's so cocky he makes the rest of us look like hens. Pulling out a tablet, he puts on a pair of headphones, pulls a hoodie over his dark, shaven head, and promptly ignores us.

"Don't," Luc says, aware of my dismay towards the little prick.

I can practically see the nervous energy emanating from Luc as we wait for who's next. We both know the twins will be here any moment, and Luc is fiddling with his fingers under the table, though I'm not sure what he expects.

Josina and Cavan hate him, sure, but they aren't going to bloody attack him. Not on neutral territory. Not with everyone watching. And especially not with Raph and me here.

They wouldn't want witnesses, and they wouldn't want a brawl. If Josina and Cavan ever try to take Luc out, it'll be short and sweet.

Twenty minutes must go by when the twins finally march in. They don't bring in assistants, likely because no one on their continent would agree to come. That, or they're too disgustingly obsessed with one another to ask anyone else. I have never seen anything nefarious go down between the pair, but there's an incestuous sort of energy between them that makes my skin crawl.

The two pink-fleshed demons take their seats at the opposite end of the table from us, not saying a single word to anyone.

"You're supposed to take a knee," Micha says, as if he's suddenly the expert.

Luc waves him off, acting as though he doesn't mind. He does, but there's a sort of confidence in pretending you don't care, rather than letting everyone know what affects you.

Uri walks in and immediately takes a knee. "My Infernal King."

He doesn't have anyone accompanying him, his lanky arms

carrying just a notepad and stopwatch. Uri isn't like the rest of the family. Though he might have the most in common with Gabe, Uri is... particular. Everything must be done at specific times and in a specific order. He is deeply satisfied by the act of crossing things off a list, and even more satisfied by telling people no. He might be a bit peculiar, but I honestly think he would've been a fantastic leader.

He's well-organized, logical, and polite. Too bad our options were Bitch One, Bitch Two, Raph, fucking weirdo *Gabe*, or Luc... our devil. He's doing his best, and it's a damn better job than Josina could do. If Josina were The Devil, everyone I love would be dead. She'd allow a famine if it meant keeping her power.

"What is taking her so long?" Josina whispers to Cavan, who doesn't answer.

"It's possible she is busy working. Luxuria might be experiencing difficulties," Uri says reasonably.

"Busy doing what, sucking dick?" Micha laughs.

Four heads snap over to him at once. Luc, Raph, Uri, and myself. We all share the same disgusted glare.

Micha's eyes widen, his shoulders shrugging. "What? Did I say something wrong?"

Finally, Zada walks in, flanked by Phaelyn, and my heart stampedes in my chest like a herd of wild horses.

Though she's my only biological sibling, my relationship with Phaelyn might be the most frayed of all my sisters. After the dreaded night I took my father's life, Phaelyn could hardly look at me. She said she didn't blame me, but she couldn't remain plagued by horrific memories.

It's the reason she went with Zada in the first place. That, and Zada was better emotionally equipped to raise a teenage girl than Luc or Raph. She was able to shape Phaelyn into a well-rounded half-demon.

Now, Phaelyn works as a violinist, as well as Zada's informant. Our lives are so similar, and yet the lines are parallel, never crossing.

"Hello, shitbags," Zada says, looking around the room before taking only a partial knee due to the length of her dress. "Hello, my Infernal King."

Phaelyn follows suit, taking a half-knee beside her. "My Infernal King," she whispers.

They're both effortlessly beautiful. Zada has long, white hair that cascades down her back in waves, and eyes a deep, ocean blue. Her body makes the shape of an hourglass. Phaelyn could almost be her biological daughter, if it weren't for her eyes of gold and the horns atop her head.

Every demon and half-demon in the room has wings except for me and Gabe's assistant. At Hel's Carnival, we're all different —different species, different abilities. Many of us have scars and missing parts, but we're a family. Here, all my differences feel... obvious.

Once everyone is seated, Luc clasps his hands together. "When Uri lists the continent you're responsible for, please provide us with updates on the economic, social, and infrastructural considerations."

Uri nods. "Limbus."

Luc clears his throat. "Horace informed me there are no updates regarding Limbus. Everything with the magicite coves is as it should be."

"Luxuria."

Zada smiles. "Economically, we are in peak season. Business is booming."

"More like boning," Micha says under his breath.

"Would you like to say that to my face?" Zada snarls at her younger brother, fire flickering at her fingertips.

Magic manifests differently in different beings. My magic allows me to perform psychokinesis. Raph can shapeshift and teleport. Luc has some of the strongest magic of any of the Morningstars, his shadow tendrils able to both control and destroy things at will.

Zada? She has fire. But unlike Khalid, hers isn't a localized controlled burn, it's an all-out wildfire. She is the flames of Hel that one only hears about in myth.

Phaelyn's eyes widen in my direction, but I shake my head, hoping she can read my expression. *Let the siblings handle themselves.*

"No ma'am," Micha clarifies, his bravado act simmering into nothing but a scared little bitch. *Good.*

"Our infrastructure is fine, no updates there. Socially, we're mostly the same, though my informant has heard whispers of The Legion making its rounds in some of the brothels," she shares.

"There are conversations about uprisings and mutiny, but they're not in reference to Luxuria," Phaelyn says, her voice much quieter than Zada's.

"Who are they in reference to?" Gabe asks.

"Mostly Ira and Violenta, but also Avaricia. The citizens speak of famine and harsh punishments, claiming Josina and Cavan are cruel leaders. Micha's issues are more about economic equality," Phaelyn explains. "And then there's Luc. Many want a new leader."

"This wouldn't be a problem if Josina were granted her rightful place as The Devil," Cavan says in an irresponsible outburst.

Beelzebub, who has been quiet so far, begins to growl, but Luc soothes him.

"The Legion's top complaint is that their leadership is a demon monarchy, chosen by blood, not that their leader is Luc. The citizens want a vote," I say, and look down the table to Josina. "And they sure as fuck wouldn't vote for you."

"I'd like to hear more about The Legion," Gabe says, and his partner nods her agreement.

Uri shakes his head. "It is not time for Haeresis. Let's move on to Gula. We are doing fine. We experienced a slight issue with a pipe in one of the main restaurants a few months ago, but it has since been fixed. There are no further updates at this time."

"That's wonderful to hear," Raph responds, smiling at Uri.

Uri smiles in turn. "Avaricia?"

"Our infrastructure is top-notch. Economically, we're doing great. No complaints here," Micha says, a shit-eating grin spread across his face.

"Well, that's a bunch of bullshit," Gabe says with a laugh. "According to her reports, your citizens are unhappy."

Micha shrugs. "They claim we're fudging the numbers at the casino, but it's simply untrue."

"It's ironic that the one trying to slut-shame me is unable to keep his population happy. Mock me all you want, Micha, but my citizens are paid and pleasured."

"Well, next is Ira," Uri says, staring down at his timer.

Cavan takes in a deep breath. "Mineral diving has been quite successful this year." He continues on, breaking down the depths his workers have swum, as well as the amount of each mineral they've been able to mine, and what they're all worth. I zone out of the conversation, only listening in when he mentions atra. "We're still mining atra. It's what's allowing the felion to continue diving without the need for oxygen or other expensive equipment."

He doesn't mention selling it to other sources, nor does he bring up Pack Escalus. Luc shakes his head, and we both remain silent.

Uri looks our way. "Haeresis."

"Well. While all of you pretend to have no issues, I'll be open and honest. A member of my inner circle was stealing from the carnival. The thief has been taken care of, but we're all feeling the betrayal heavily," Raph confesses.

He is confident, completely unafraid of how everyone is going to react. Some will see this as weakness, but all I see is strength and a governor who isn't afraid to admit his faults or ask for help.

"I am sorry to hear that," Zada replies.

"My condolences." Uri adjusts his tie, grimacing at the both of us.

"I have personally experienced a run-in with The Legion

recently," I say, and everyone's eyebrows shoot up. "Many were executed, but the few who got away will likely go into hiding. I will keep Luc updated as things progress."

"It makes sense that they'd keep their base mostly on Haeresis, since their issue is with the monarchy itself," Zada notes.

"If I were going to overthrow someone, I'd keep my base out of sight," Micha says.

"Good to know," Luc says, and Micha balks.

"I don't actually have any plans—"

"Relax, kid," Gabe interrupts. "We know you don't have the capacity for an operation of that extent."

Micha is a grown male, much older than I am. Hundreds of years old, to be exact, but to these near-immortals, he's just a child.

"Shall we move on to Violenta?" Uri suggests.

Josina nods, taking a cue from Raph, and is open about her continent's current affairs. She claims many of her citizens are *unruly* and that the lupions are *giving her trouble*. On a continent where the most stable money must be made by fighting, I'm sure the wolf demons are sick and tired of the violence.

Josina doesn't care. She doesn't provide them with alternatives, opting for those unwilling to starve instead. She and some of the others are operating with an archaic mindset. They make me sick.

A servant comes in and whispers something to Luc, who gets up and leaves, and Josina continues speaking until Uri cuts her off.

Gabe goes after, telling us about all the successful surgeries on Fraus, but I tune him out. My head spins, my mind fixated on thoughts of Gemma and what's next for us.

In a world full of smoke and mirrors, all I want is something real.

Gabe concludes his statistical analysis of rhinoplasty to breast augmentation ratios, and Luc returns. Everyone, even Josina, stands up.

"Our Infernal King," we all say in unison as most of us take a knee once more.

"Apologies, I had an important call to take," Luc says and then locks eyes with me. I cock my head, but he doesn't explain further. "Now. Let's discuss a reallocation of resources."

Symphony No. 29

Gemma

That same day.

With Raph and Draven gone and the cast split in two, my availability today is wide open. I want to explore the different districts of Haeresis, and do some fun sightseeing, but unfortunately there's something more important on my agenda.

I have to contact Earth.

Slipping on my only pair of jeans and a tank top, I walk past a still-sleeping Reina and make my way out of our tent. If Draven were here, I'd ask him to take me on his motorcycle to the entertainment district, but he's not here.

And I'm not sure I want him to be.

Walking the streets of Haeresis in the daylight is strange. At night, this place looks like something out of a cyberpunk film—neon green lights filling the space, fast demons flying about, and even faster trams passing overhead. During the day? It's almost normal, earthly.

The entertainment district is like any other major city, with fast-walking businessmen—*business demons?*—and the low rumble of trams and other vehicles buzzing about. Everyone seems to be on some mission, knowing exactly where they're going and what time they need to get there.

I, in contrast, feel sloth-like. My movements are lazy as I meander through the streets of Hel, wanting to avoid the inevitable.

The problem is, I do want to speak to the scientists from Augury University and tell them I wound up here. I want them to know I'm alive and that the experiment worked.

Well, sort of.

But I'm terrified that contacting them means going home. I know it's nonsensical, and I know that no matter how dreary my life was, there's truly no place like home, but I just don't see it that way anymore.

A home without family, without *love,* is just wood and concrete. It has no meaning, no life in it.

That is why I'm standing outside the Earth embassy, hoping for some sort of sign that this is all going to work out. What if they take me back to Earth and I can't remember anything from Hel? What if I go back to being the same woman I was before, someone full of emptiness and suicidal ideation, or worse—what if I remember every moment of my life here?

How am I supposed to swallow down the loneliness eating away at me like necrosis if I know there's a better life for me somewhere far away, practically unreachable?

I press the call button on the small speaker, and nothing happens. Maybe nobody is working today? It could be a holiday I don't know about. I almost turn away when the glass doors open, and I quickly cross the threshold and make my way inside.

It looks exactly how I remember it, cold and sterile, but well lit. The same demon sits at the reception counter, an unamused expression spread across her face.

"Can I help you, Ms. Marino?" she asks, and I'm jolted by her use of my name.

"You... remember me?"

"Yes. I keep track of all of Earth's property that makes its way onto Hel," she explains, and I furrow my brows.

"I'm not property," I say, my voice pitching up at the end.

She sighs. "Technically, I guess not, but my job has never had anything to do with humans. I work exclusively handling resources."

"I can tell," I answer, a little annoyed. "I'd like to place a call to Earth."

"For what purpose?"

"To let the government know I'm alive?"

She cocks her head. "Your government keeps track of who is dead or alive?"

I exhale. "Yes."

She hands me what looks like one of those vintage wired telephones, but it's made of chrome, shiny and green. I dial the number, recalling memorizing it from the initial flier.

Ring. Ring. Ring.

My heart feels like a jackhammer in my chest, and I'm afraid no one's going to pick up. Even the scientists responsible for this probably don't care about what happened to me.

"Dr. DiSanto with the quantumagic lab at Augury University speaking," Dr. DiSanto says into the phone.

"Hi, I'm not sure if you remember me, but my name is Gemma Marino," I reply.

"Holy fucking shit. Heather, contact Dr. Taylor and Dr. Palmer immediately! Tell them Gemma is alive!" he screams, his tone laced with excitement. "Are you okay? Where are you? We thought you died. I thought—I blamed myself. Oh my God."

He sounds almost like he's crying, and guilt festers in my chest. "I'm okay! Hey, I'm okay. I've been stuck on Hel."

"Hel? I need to sit down." There's the sound of a chair

squeaking against a hard floor. "What do you mean you're on Hel?"

I tell him everything. Waking up on Hel with almost no memories, fearing for my life, making a deal with the devil and joining the circus, all of it. We discuss how traumatic and emotional events seemed to trigger my memories returning, and I can hear the scribbling of pen to paper on the other end.

"This is a fucking miracle," Dr. DiSanto says, and I smile. The receptionist is reading a magazine, ignoring the conversation happening beside her.

"Well. I just wanted to let you guys know I'm okay," I say, hoping that'll be the end of the conversation.

"We have a few options. We can work to try to create another portal to have you return through, or we can pay for you to board a ship back," he explains. "What would you prefer?"

"I'd rather not have my memories wiped again. There's a ship that comes here once a year, but the tickets are expensive."

"We might be able to arrange for a quicker ship, since they won't need to carry any heavy cargo. Can I contact you about it later this week?"

"Sure," I say into the phone. "This is the Earth Embassy line. I guess call here and ask to be transferred to Raph Morningstar."

"And who would that be?"

"He's the governor of the continent I'm on, as well as a friend," I say in earnest. "Oh! And one more thing."

"Anything."

I lean against the desk. "Could someone come with me back to Earth? Or like... could I send someone in my place?"

"Hmm. Why do they want to come to Earth?" he asks.

"She has some family there she wants to visit."

There's a long pause on the other line. "Yes, that should be fine. As for sending someone in your place, is it your intent to stay there?!"

Yes. I want to scream yes at the top of my lungs, but there's something holding me back. I know what I want. I know it more than anything, this is where I belong. These are the first group of people—of beings—that made me feel welcome. They gave me a purpose and showed me friendship. For the first time in my life, I wasn't lonely or ostracized, I wasn't the weird, broken girl. I was simply me.

Gemma Marino. The Butterfly.

But this isn't exclusively up to me. This isn't my planet or my carnival. I can't force Raph or Draven to want me to stay.

I take a breath, steadying myself. Deep down, I know nobody will want me to go. Right? Saying goodbye would just bring everyone pain, so why not stay? Why run now when I have a life to keep building here?

If my stay isn't temporary, I have to figure out what's next. Am I even *allowed* to stay on this planet? I'm not from Hel. I don't know all the laws or understand all the customs. I've barely seen much outside of the carnival, but it still feels like staying is the only reasonable choice when the thought of leaving riddles me with nausea.

If I go back to Earth, I might as well be orchestrating my own funeral. Before Hel, before the carnival, my life was nothing but pain and misfortune. Grief, my only friend.

Panic settles into my chest, my hands shaking, but I steady my grip on the phone as I prepare to answer. "I have spent a lot of time here, and it has... grown on me. I intend on staying."

There's a quiet gasp over the phone. "I understand. Actually, I do not understand, but I respect your wishes. Could you get permission from the king to ensure we're not starting an inter-planetary conflict with Hel, though?"

Of course he asked that. I guess I get it. Luc allowed me to stay in the first place, it makes sense I'd have to contact him in order to be granted permanent residence.

"I can do that," I say, having no idea if it's true or not.

"We'll speak again in the next few days in regards to your friend, and you can let me know then if you change your mind and want to come home. You'd be a hero here. Everyone at

Augury was distraught over your death—or, rather, assumed death. There are many people here who'd love to see you again."

They're kind words, but they're meaningless. The people of Augury don't know me. I showed up to a lab a few times and then they accidentally sent me to Hel. I'm not returning to Earth to ease their guilty consciences.

"Bye, now."

I hang up the phone, and the receptionist puts her magazine down. "Did you get everything sorted—"

"Yep," I shout over my shoulder, already exiting out of the embassy and barrelling towards One Haeresis Plaza.

Luc's office building is so different from Luc and the carnies. It is sterile and authoritative, but it's perfect if it enables me to stay here.

Baph sits at the front desk, slowly pressing a stamp into some paperwork, and I can barely contain myself as I walk up to her. "Hey! Hey, um. Is Luc busy right now? The Devil. King Luc. Sorry, I forgot what the fuck I'm supposed to call him, but is he available?"

"The Devil," she starts, her words slow as ever, and anxious energy threatens to consume me. "He isn't he-here right now."

Where is he—oh, *fuck*. Luc is at that meeting with Raph and Draven.

"Could you call him?" I know that's unreasonable. I know that the king of this entire planet has no reason to take my call in the middle of this important meeting, and that I'm being a selfish bitch, but I don't care.

I can't think, can't hardly breathe right now. I just need to know that this is my home and that he's not going to ship me back to Earth the second they all get back.

She picks up a phone and presses the first button, and I hear it start to ring. The thundering applause of my heart in my chest crescendos and I freeze, every muscle in my body rendered unmovable.

"Baph, honey, sweetie, I'm in the middle of the summit.

Who's asking for me?" he says, and it's unlike how he speaks to anyone else. There's still an air of sarcasm, but his tone is much more gentle.

"Gem—"

"Hand over the phone."

Slowly, Baph hands me the green, glowing device, and I place it against my ear. "Luc? Um. My Inferno King or whatever."

"Infernal," he corrects me, and I might throw up. "This must be important if you're calling me right now."

Luc has been nothing but kind and understanding with me since the moment I got here, but I know that I've been a pawn in his game with Draven. It wasn't obvious in the beginning, but it became clear to me over time. That's why Raph pushed us to perform together. It's why he had me share a tent with Reina, the sister Draven is the closest with. Every decision was deliberate, but I'm afraid of being calculated out of the equation. If my presence is no longer beneficial to the carnival, will Luc allow me to stay?

"It is," I say. *Fear is a shadow that fades when you create your own light.* My grandfather's words repeat in my head. "I would like your permission to live here."

"Did you hit your head? We made a deal months ago granting you permission to live here so long as you did your job."

Ah, yes. My deal with the devil. "I know, but that's not what I mean."

"Then what do you want?"

"I want to become a citizen of Hel. A real one. Whatever that might mean. I contacted Earth, and they offered me a way home—"

"Are you considering taking it?" he asks, his voice a little frantic.

"No," I say, and shake my head, even though he can't see it. "No. I'd rather fucking die than go back there."

"Then stay. I will grant you immunity, even if you decide to leave the carnival," he says.

"Wait, really?" Relief floods my chest in waves.

"Why not? Plus, it's made things interesting. My scorpion finally cares about something other than himself," Luc says casually.

Both corners of my mouth curl down, my forehead creasing. "Draven cares about all of the carnies."

"Yes, because they're his family, an extension of himself. He would let a stranger die for them in an instant, except you. You're different, and that intrigues me," Luc admits. "I have to get back to the meeting, but congratulations and welcome to Hel."

SYMPHONY NO. 30

DRAVEN

Everyone says their goodbyes, the end of the meeting going more amicably than any of us expected. After arguing over resources, Uri brought the topic back to The Legion.

Nothing brings everyone together quite like a common enemy.

Luc and Raph exchange kind words with their mother, and we pack up our things, preparing to teleport back to Haeresis.

"Don't be a stranger," I say to Phaelyn as she and Zada get ready to leave.

Both corners of her mouth tick up. "Don't be strange," she says softly, giving me a tight squeeze before they're off.

It's not quite the heartfelt sister-brother reunion I'd have liked, but we'll work on it. I can't rewrite our past, but I can rewrite our future. One step at a time.

"Aw, wasn't that nice," Luc says, breaking the silence.

"Luc," I say, recalling how he left in the middle of the meeting. "Who called you?"

"Oh, it was nothing," Luc says, his tone casual.

Luc's tone is rarely ever casual. Cocky, sarcastic, silly? Absolutely. Casual? That's a rarity, and I'm not buying it. Not one fucking bit.

"Who called you?"

"Draven," Raph says, his blue eyes wide as he scoops up Bub. "Can this wait until we get back?"

"I suppose," I say with a sigh, and let Raph's magic wrap itself around us.

Teleporting feels like riding a roller coaster while on a mind-altering substance. It's fast, dizzying, and it turns your head into melted goop.

We land back on Haeresis, and I breathe in the cozy, stale air of Luc's office before steadying my feet. I can't explain it, but I feel more in control here. My magic is no different anywhere I go, so long as I'm wearing my magicite ring, but I feel grounded on my home continent. Everything is *right* here.

"Now, who the fuck called you?" I say, refusing to let him off the hook this time.

"A lady."

"Well, we know it wasn't Lilian," Raph jests, putting Bub down on the ground, and I fight back a laugh.

"*Luc.*"

He smirks, one eyebrow shooting up. "It was your human. Something about flying back to Earth. I'm not sure, I told her I was busy."

"Brother," Raph begins to say, but the office door closes before I hear the rest of the lecture.

I am dashing through the halls and down the stairs, forgoing the elevator and hurrying straight to my bike. My footfalls land in a syncopated rhythm, my stomach lurching into my throat as I throw on my helmet as fast as I can.

Riding down the streets of Haeresis, I don't care about the accident or the danger I'm putting myself in again. I don't care about limits—not the ones on my bike speedometer, and definitely not the limits I place on myself.

My heartbeat races like a song stuck on a crescendo measure, getting faster and louder each second with no descent in sight. It is relentless, and I'm starting to feel woozy, but I press on until those bone-shaped gates and fences come into view.

Parking my bike, I rampage through the carnival until I'm at camp. Night has settled into the sky, the dirt paths illuminated by lanterns and lights, and I practically push Quinn and Rowan out of the way as I dart for Gemma and Reina's tent.

Reina is carrying her cello, walking out of another tent when I spot her.

"Where's Gemma?"

"She left this morning, but I'm sure she'll be back soon."

Fuck.

There's no concern lining Reina's eyes, not even a hint of sadness or *anything* lingering under the surface, so either Gemma left and told no one, or she's still here.

I run into their tent, greeted by two empty beds, and I'm sick.

No, I'm *scared*. Genuinely afraid, which is an emotion I thought I trained out of myself. Even when dealing with Lyle—Hel, even when handling prolific serial killers, I don't get scared. My adrenaline kicks in, sure, but I know my abilities. I know how hard I've trained and how many styles of martial arts I've studied throughout the years.

I know how many lives I've taken.

But this is different. It's out of my control, and even if I could control it, I wouldn't want to. She has to decide her fate, even it affects mine. Without her, I am a fugue with no final cadence, but she might be an entire symphony on her own. She might not need me or Reina or Po or the rest of the crew, but so help me, I hope she wants us. I hope this place has become a refuge for her, because she's become a refuge for us. For me.

Exiting the tent, I head down towards my own, deciding I'm better off waiting for her there. Tears well in my eyes, but I blink them away, refusing to acknowledge this all-consuming level of torment that's taken over my entire body, shaking me to my core.

Gemma is exactly what Hel's Carnival needed, even though I

hated her. I tried to fucking kill her, and now the thought of living without her makes me want to—no. I can't think like that. Not now. Not when there's still a chance I can convince her to stay.

But I shouldn't have to. I'll get on my hands and knees and beg for her forgiveness. I'll even beg for her pleasure, but I will *not* beg someone to love me. That is a level of desperation I refuse to fall into the pits of, even for her.

And she didn't say it. She didn't say that she loves me.

Relief and anguish swirl in the pit of my stomach as I step into my tent and find her on my bed, waiting for me.

"You're still here," I say, letting out a breath I didn't know I was holding as relief floods my chest.

Gemma stands and plants a soft kiss on my lips before tugging me onto the bed with her. "I'm not going anywhere," she says.

The tears finally fall, but she wipes them away, her touch gentle.

"Luc said you called, and you were flying back to Earth."

She shakes her head. "Oh, he was totally fucking with you."

I sit straight up. "I'm going to kill him."

"Isn't that treason?"

"Do you think I give a damn?"

Gemma laughs, and the sound bursts through the air like rays of sunshine, destroying any lingering tension. "No, I guess you don't."

"Please clarify what is actually happening," I request.

She sucks in a breath. "I contacted Earth to tell them I'm alive, and they offered me a way home."

"But?"

"But I told them my home is here. On Hel. With you." She looks at me with those big brown eyes of hers, and every moment of my life, even the horrible ones, instantly becomes worth it.

"Gemma," I say, and pull her hand to my mouth, pressing a kiss to her knuckles.

"And then I called Luc and asked for permission to stay, and he gave it to me."

I furrow my brows. "Why? There are no laws that say you can't live here."

"Wait, seriously?"

I grin from ear-to-ear. "It appears Luc screwed with both of our heads today."

"He gave me permanent immunity, though. Which is nice."

I push her down onto the bed, getting between her legs

"I don't want to hear another name on your lips tonight," I say, and place my mouth against her neck. "Or ever."

I capture her mouth with my own, and suddenly we become a tangle of limbs as we remove each other's clothes, unable to keep our hands off one another. It's hard to tell where her body ends and mine begins as I take my finger and languidly stroke her clit.

This is unlike we've ever been before. I know how to fuck, and I've fucked Gemma well, but this transverses that. Love is a word, but this is the action of that.

Dipping a finger inside, I pump into her, reveling in how wet she is. Just for me and nobody else. She is *mine*. I don't give a damn if the way I feel is toxic or possessive. I would kill for Gemma—Hel, I would *die* for her, and showing her that is all that matters to me.

I remove my fingers, and she moans, clearly wanting more. Turning my body, I lift one of her legs and push the head of my cock into her.

She's a hot, panting mess. Her cheeks flushed pink, hair damp with sweat, and it's the second most gorgeous thing I've ever seen. The first being the way her pretty pussy takes me so well. I look down to watch her stretch around me.

Gemma is everything I've ever asked for. She is someone I can not only trust, but rely on. Someone willing to fight by my side, or hold back and cheer me on.

I thrust into her, dragging us closer to the edge with every movement.

"Draven, please," she moans, and I give her exactly what she asks for, pounding into her from head to hilt.

She cries out in pleasure as I come inside her, feeling her muscles spasm around me. In this moment, our bodies are a combination of notes and rhythms, creating the perfect song, and we lie like that for as long as she lets me.

"I love you." Gemma's head is resting on my chest, her body in the crook of my arm, and my heart swells with joy.

"Why does it sound like there's going to be a but?"

"Because all deals are conditional. Even love."

"I love you without conditions," I say, and it's the truth.

"Would you love me if I sang really loud and off-pitch?"

I smile. "I would, but I would judge you."

"What if I collected castrated testicles?"

"You'd be a fucking weirdo, but I'd still love you," I say. I don't tell her I'm curious if she meant post-mortem or not.

"There are always conditions to love, even if we pretend there's not. We expect the ones we love to show us kindness and stability. It's human nature," Gemma says, and I arch a brow.

"Except I'm not human. I crave reciprocity, sure, but I do not require it."

She smiles in turn, and it's a big, wide one that shows her teeth. "What if I looked like Baelor?"

"Alright, now you're pushing it," I say, and we both chuckle. "What's your condition?"

"You can't keep doing everything by yourself. You have to learn to trust your family and loved ones," she lectures.

"I trust you."

Gemma sits up and shakes her head, a single brown tendril falling down the front of her face. She tries to blow it away, but it falls right back, and I tuck it behind her ear. "You have to not only trust us, but actually rely on us."

She's right, and I hate how often I find myself admitting that lately.

"How?"

"I want you to develop a team. These masks you wear, you don't have to do it alone," she says. "I could be The Spy, and Reina, The Executioner."

I'm not opposed to developing a team, but I refuse to be the reason Gemma or any of my sisters die.

I shake my head. "Absolutely not. I'm not putting you in any dang—"

"Trust. Trust and rely. It doesn't have to be me, or just me, but I want to become a team. You cannot carry all of the load. The blood can't just be on your hands alone, Draven. Please," her tone is pleading. "And besides, Reina needs the blood supply."

I inhale deeply, forcing my staggering breaths to calm. This could be good for me as well as Luc. More eyes and hands on deck can mean a quicker turnaround on information and contract kills.

"I would want at least two of you per role, mask, whatever we're calling these positions," I say, and she nods. "Absinthe could be the other Executioner. She loves killing."

Gemma almost flinches, but she schools her features. "Right. And what about The Spy?"

"Hmm." I ponder this. Taryn, Lilian, Rowan, none of them are the right fit.

"How about Yasmeena or Khalid?"

"Yasmeena could work, and Khalid can be our additional layer of protection on the ground if we're ever off on a job."

Gemma's practically beaming. "So Team Draven is a go?"

"Yes," I say with a laugh. "You're all going to be acting as the masks I wear for Luc, so how about: The Devil's Masquerade?"

"I love it."

"I love *you*."

SYMPHONY NO. 31
GEMMA

The first month or so after *The Incident* felt like the entire carnival was riding with training wheels. We were down two cast members—Lyle, of course, and Aida. Even if only temporarily while she visits her brother, she was one of our stars. Everyone came to learn their fate.

I was glad she was gone, though. Aida never spent as much time with the rest of us because she was constantly busy, bombarded by long lines almost daily. She deserved a break. Augury University sent a special ship, just for her, as a way to make things up to me. What they didn't realize is they changed my life for the better.

I am eternally grateful for this strange planet and this fantastical life I've built. Things are still changing, too. I moved into Draven's tent, and Khalid moved in with Reina. Baelor even apologized to me, promising not to make me uncomfortable again.

Everything's beginning to slow down at Hel's Carnival, and The Sinner's Circus has lost its luster for many. Now we're looking for new ways to reinvent the wheel.

Leo asked to stay, and we said yes, so we were set on technical work, but we needed to bring new life in. A fresh spin on things.

Absinthe has been learning to ride a motorcycle, and Quinn freshened up on their stilt work. Khalid discussed doing more joint work with Yasmeena, and even Reina was thinking of unique ways to play the cello. Everyone seemed to be doing their part to liven everything up, but then there was us.

Draven, Reina, and I had a good daytime act—everyone loved it—but we still decided to tweak it. Everything can always be better. Now, we rotate between around ten different songs and sets of choreography. In one of the newest routines, Draven begins on piano with Reina on cello, but eventually he gets up and tangos with me. It's romantic and sexy and fun, and the whole crowd goes wild.

Robyn debuted a new daytime act, too. She taught Una and Po how to vault on Nox, and it seems to be a fan favorite, especially little Po.

But that's all Hel's Carnival. The Sinner's Circus still needs its makeover, and I'm determined to be the one to bring it. Reina and Khalid are working on an act together, and Draven and I are trying to come up with something as well—something all of Hel has never seen before.

My head is sitting in Draven's lap, our bodies cushioned by the flowers and grass. He's leaning against an old tree, with birds chirping overhead. The sun is still low in the sky, and it rises with every passing moment, the beautiful peaches and pinks transforming into bright blue.

"What about a completely new act? No knives, no piano," I suggest.

"What do you have against the piano?"

I crack a small grin. "Nothing, but we're trying to be...."

"Innovative?"

"Yeah," I say, and think of the circuses and performances I saw on Earth. "Have you ever heard of hair hanging?"

"No. Does it involve you being naked?" Draven says suggestively.

"No, asshole. It's really cool. You're suspended by your hair."

He looks down at me, cupping my face. "That sounds like an incredible... way to get scalped."

"Only if you do it incorrectly. I knew a girl on Earth whose aunt did it professionally," I share, thinking of my childhood friend Emma. I spent a lot of time at Emma's house before her mother died and her Aunt Peggye adopted her. Since she was in a traveling troupe, they sold Emma's house, but I still think about her sometimes. They both taught me so much. I think that's why The Sinner's Circus always felt a little safe, a little familiar. Deep down I think I knew someone who once loved me also loved a place as wild as here.

"You went to circuses on Earth?"

"Yeah," I say. "There's a lot of rich history about them. Just like Hel's Carnival, historically circuses were a sort of sanctuary for those who were different. There's a lot of discussion about how they used to mistreat animals. Circuses also profited off of exploiting the marginalized and disabled. Over time though, circus culture shifted, and now they're more speculative and theatrical, focusing on artistry and storytelling."

"My oh my." Draven shifts, forcing me to sit up. "Were you secretly obsessed with the circus and schemed your way here? Is that why you showed up that night?"

"No," I say and laugh. "I thought this place was a sanctuary."

"Why do you know so much about circuses, huh?" Draven says while tickling me, and my muscles tense as I giggle hysterically.

"I—I—" the words can't come out, my voice caught in my throat as he continues to torture me with tickle attacks. "Draven!"

He finally lets up, and I suck in a breath.

"I was terrible at science and math. And I wasn't like you, I didn't spend hours reading and learning about everything possible. I hated school. But dance, music, circus, and commedia dell'arte? I loved all that shit. I'd watch videos of different performances for hours," I shared, and Draven looked genuinely interested, his golden eyes sparkling with interest.

"What's one of the most magnificent things you've seen?"

I think on it for a moment. "Oh, definitely the Globe of Death. I've only seen it once, but it was amazing."

"Explain to me how it works."

I make like I'm holding a ball in my hand. "Essentially, there's a giant metal sphere, and motorcyclists all circle the inside of it at the same time, usually in groups of three to four."

"Fucking Hel, that'd be terrifying," he says.

A lightbulb goes off in my brain, the light just as bright as the risen sun, whose rays are beating down on us. "Draven, *we* could do the Globe of Death."

He gives me a look as if to say *are you dense?* "You don't know how to ride a motorcycle...."

"No, I would stand in the middle while you ride around me."

"That's bonkers. Congratulations, you've officially upgraded from pest to clown," Draven says, his eyes wide and eyebrows shooting up.

"I'm serious," I say, and stand up. Looking down, I pace back and forth as I work out the logistics. "It would take a few months to build, but we could put the globe next to the big top and get bleachers for the audience to sit in."

"Gemma, I got into an accident just a couple of months ago, and you think I should be performing stunts, potentially risking your life? Absolutely fucking not." He stands up now and puts his hand in mine. "Let's head back to camp. Conversation over."

"No," I say, and let go of his hand. "Nope. You have got to learn trust. Trust me, trust my abilities, and trust yourself, Draven. You are fantastic on a bike, and you genuinely enjoy it. Why not try something new?"

"Okay, Butterfly." He takes my hand again, this time bringing it up to his mouth and planting a gentle kiss. "I'll think about it."

WITH BLOOD, sweat, tears, and a little bit of Draven's magic, our Globe of Death was built in just under a month. Draven spent weeks practicing in it. Hours of fun, but equal measure hours of torture. Falling and having to get back up time and time again.

Unlike with dancing, Draven's falls could be deadly, but he managed to perfect our routine, just like I knew he would. Now he just has to nail it in front of an audience.

Tonight is the night we'll finally debut our new act. The Devil himself is rumored to be in the audience, so I expect the turnout to be large.

I just hope we don't mess this up.

Walking up to the metal globe, which stands around three times my height, I step inside the sphere. Panels of steel come together to form lattices, their shadows landing on the audience and forming the shape of a mechanical moon. Flecks of red, blue, green, and silvery-white light come in through the metal intersections, beaming down on me.

I stand in the center. Draven is already in there on his bike, and I try not to pay attention to anything else as the music starts. It is loud and electronic, unlike the beautiful symphonies he and Reina normally play, but it's fitting.

Tonight we are daring to do something unheard of on Hel.

My mind takes me back to watching the circus on Earth, and seeing the motorcyclists gather to prepare for the Globe of Death. It was thrilling to watch people perform like this, risking their lives, but it's an entirely different experience being at the heart of it.

I can feel the beating in my chest like a thunderous applause as I swell with pride, because we're actually here, we've practically made it.

I wanted to take my life, and now I'm living the kind of life I thought only happened in dreams. Fairy tales, really.

Electricity courses through me as he revs his engine, and that's when the show really begins. Draven begins zooming, circling me, keeping his distance as he whirls around. The sphere becomes a kaleidoscope of light and sound as rubber clangs against metal, the colorful beams creating an angelic glow around me.

Throwing my arms up, I move my body sensually, hoping the audience can see me.

Tonight's outfit fits me like a glove. Boned and blood-red, the corset cinches me into someone worthy of every demon's eyes. At the top of the bodice, the fabric curves into sharp and deliberate bat-like points, sculpted across my chest as if ready to take flight. Lacy fringe drapes down against my hips, accentuating my subtle curves.

In a cage full of metal and motorcycles, I'd expect the room to smell like gasoline, but Hel is constantly surprising me. Draven's bike is fueled by a specialized magicite solution, creating that sparkly, crisp smell I receive on every inhale. The first time I experienced it, the scent shocked me, but now it's familiar. It's *him*.

Adrenaline pumps through my veins as Draven shifts closer. His speed is slowing down, but he's angling his way towards me, putting an arm out and grazing my waist as he spins over and over again.

I am hotter than a live wire as his gloved hand caresses my back and side, and the audience cheers, clearly just as excited.

We fucking did it.

It's wild to consider how far we've come and how much we've both grown. I went from running from this half-demon, fearing my demise, to trusting him with my life. This entire world was foreign to me. Exciting, but terrifying. Now? I couldn't imagine going back to Earth. Working at The Midnight Muse, or worse, a corporate job.

This moment feels like the perfect culmination of everything we've worked for. I have someone who loves me, and we get to perform together. When our show is over, we're going to celebrate with our strange little family of contortionists, acrobats, and clowns.

I willingly left my entire life behind for this talented demon who I just know is wearing a shit-eating grin under that helmet.

We're truly a match made in Hel.

Symphony No. 32

Gemma

Six Months Later

"Tyrus Lupine must be executed," Draven says, looking at the three of us.

A lot has changed since The Devil's Masquerade formed. Though the rules for greater half-demon society are the same, Luc has seen the necessity for us to have access to magic, and gifted Reina and Absinthe pieces of magicite. My lack of magic actually benefits me as The Spy, because demons don't smell any magic on me, so they don't view me as a threat.

This is a mistake.

We've executed at least four violent members of The Legion, as well as formed friendships with other members. The Legion, apparently, has different factions.

There is a faction that wants to kill everyone, no matter the cost, and another faction that just wants a change to our systems. The larger faction on Haeresis—the one run by a half-demon named Malo Gaultier—has been doing business with Pack Escalus, and more specifically, Tyrus Lupine, the pack's main Possessor. Tyrus deals most of the drugs, potions, and minerals that make it out to the public here on Haeresis. Luc was fine leaving him alone, but not anymore.

Anyone working directly with Malo is *to be terminated immediately.*

"Do you believe Malo will be at Sinner's tonight?" Yasmeena asks, but Draven shakes his head.

"No, he'll send one of his underlings." Draven's hand is interlocked with mine as we exit the hall, heading for the big top.

All of us are wearing different masks tonight. Draven's in his typical mandible mask, which is sexy as ever. Yasmeena's is the top half of a cat skull. Reina and Absinthe's are more obscure— Reina's mask is dark and vampiric, whereas Absinthe's looks like the face of a harlequin puppet.

And then there's mine. *The Butterfly.*

"When Tyrus and the other pack members leave to follow Gemma, you two are going to pounce on them," Draven instructs Absinthe and Reina, who nod. "Yasmeena, make sure you keep up with Malo's underling and the case of atra."

"On it," Yasmeena says, and Absinthe gives a half-hearted salute.

Reina rubs her belly. "Good thing I'm hungry tonight."

We continue walking, planning to enter as if we're audience members.

"Where will you be tonight if you're not joining in on the fun?" I ask, bumping my hip against Draven, who seems to be lost in thought.

"I have another contact I'm meeting with," he says curtly, his eyes darting around nervously.

Yikes. Whoever the contact is, I don't want to meet them if they have Draven acting like *this.*

We get in line behind a group of twenty-something-looking half-demons and grab our tickets, before taking our seats. The Sinner's Circus begins with Raph's usual spiel, and I quietly wait until I spot Tyrus.

When the show is nearing the end, I get up and decide to

make my move. Lilian is doing an amazing job with contortion, and it'll hopefully keep Malo's underlings busy long enough for us to take out some of Pack Escalus.

Carrying a drink in my hand, I pretend to trip accidentally and spill it onto his pants. Tyrus stands, scowling, but calms down once he sees my face.

He is tall and strong, even broader than Draven. With icy gray hair and cold teal eyes, the lupion is a force to be reckoned with.

"I am so sorry," I say, and bat my eyes at him before taking his hand. "Here, let me clean you up."

I make sure to wiggle my hips as much as possible as we walk, and he completely takes the bait. Two more lupion flank us, their ears on high alert, and I see Reina and Absinthe hang back.

As we travel through camp, I take a turn and hear a masculine scream from around the bend behind us. The girls must have gotten the other wolf.

Draven has been training me to fight, but I can't take Tyrus out. I just need to distract him. He pushes me up against a light pole and I kick off my shoe, catching it and jamming the stiletto into his right thigh.

"Fucking bitch," he says, his voice deep and full of a murderous rage.

Absinthe rounds the corner swinging a big bat covered in thorns, and makes her way toward Tyrus. He dodges, pushing her, but Reina comes up the other side and sinks her fangs into the side of his waist.

I flinch. Reina's entire face and chest are already covered in what must be another wolf's blood. The entire fight makes me nauseous. Unlike Draven and the girls, I might never get used to the sight of gore and blood, but I'm still an asset.

Draven says I'm good with *seduction and information acquisition*, and that's good enough for me. Heading back towards the big top, I get a cold, eerie sensation running through my body. Goosebumps cover my arms, every hair standing at attention.

Entering the tent, all the lights are off except a single spotlight on the piano. Draven sits at the bench, soft music coming from the soundboard.

I walk down the dark aisles, toward the center of the ring until I am standing next to Draven, and allow him to finish. It's Totentanz, one of my favorites.

The Dance of Death.

"That's a piece from Earth," I say. The song is thousands of years old, so it's possible it came to Hel during The Convergence. Luc likes Liszt's music, so I wouldn't be surprised.

"From your recital, right?" Draven asks, and I nod in confirmation.

"Yes, haha."

He reaches out a hand. "Dance with me."

I do, and we wrap our arms around one another, beginning a slow and sensual tango. There's no music anymore, just the sound of our feet circling and stepping on the ground, but it's weirdly soothing.

Draven and I don't need music to dance, we have the songs and rhythms of each other's bodies. With every movement, I feel more and more like I was made not only for this, but for him.

"Gemma," he says, his voice quiet, and my feet abruptly stop. Our bodies shift into a slow sway, like one you'd see from two people who cannot dance, but simply want to enjoy each other's company.

In a way, it's even more intimate than our tango.

"You are my solace. My devil-gifted solace," he begins, and I rest my head on his chest. "I am nearly twenty-eight years old, but my life only began a handful of months ago. Every moment before you was simply the prelude."

Draven is full of a lot of things, but sweet words are not typically one of them. He's grumpy and sarcastic, encouraging and thoughtful, but this is more. There's a deep meaning underlying his words that I can't quite decipher.

I look up, wanting to see his expression, and it shakes me to my core. Draven looks youthful. Nervous, desperate energy clings to his features, and I get the urge to want to hold him in my arms and tell him everything will be okay. That I'm here, and I won't let anyone hurt him.

"Marriage on Earth is a pact between two people. It's a promise to be together forever, but you all can get divorced. Hel doesn't work the same way. There are no financial benefits to marriage, and no limits to the number of people involved. Whether you're a couple or a polycule doesn't matter, but you're bound to them for the rest of your lives. There's no paperwork or take backs, but a magical bond that forms, connecting you forever," he explains.

My mind shifts to Robyn, Quinn, and Rowan. The triad is happily married, and it brings me great joy to know that even their souls are intertwined.

Rustling comes from the tent's entrance, and a long-haired demon comes barreling towards us, baring her fangs. I don't recognize her, and my heart quickens from its already jiving pace, when Draven pulls out a dagger and flings it straight for her heart.

She drops to the floor, blood pooling beneath her limp body.

"What the fu—"

"Nevermind her." He shakes his head. "I never wanted to marry. Trust is a commodity I've had little success in obtaining, and I'd rather eat my own heart than give it away to another," Draven says, and his words sting like citrus on a cut lip. I yearn to be the exception.

He grabs my shoulders, squeezing them softly. "That was until you. It was terrifying and cruel, but I fell in love with you so quickly. I knew you were the only being I'd ever settle down for the minute I laid eyes on you in those butterfly wings."

"You hated me," I say, my heart rate stampeding in my chest, faster than even the helhorses.

Draven shakes his head. "No. I hated how badly I needed you. I felt pathetic with how desperate I was to make you mine."

"And now I am."

"In word, but I want you to be mine in name and in flesh. I researched Earthly matrimony customs, so I hope I'm fucking doing this right," he starts, getting down on one knee. "Gemma Marino, will you marry me?"

I could travel through space and time, live a thousand different lives, but nothing could top the way my chest fills with warmth, and the absolute peace I feel looking into Draven's golden eyes.

"Obviously." I laugh through my tears.

He places a ring on my finger, and it is the second most beautiful thing I've ever seen. Yellow gold with a red, heart-shaped ruby as the gemstone, the entire thing sparkles under the spotlight. There are tiny diamonds creating a halo around the center gem, with other shard-like gems coming up and out of the top, making a sort of crown.

The most beautiful thing I've ever seen is a half-demon known as The Scorpion. The ring is beautiful, but everything will forever pale compared to the sight of him.

Draven pulls me in and kisses me, and somehow it is like no kiss I've ever felt before. It feels like floating.

"So, when would you like to have the wedding?" he asks, and I kiss him again.

"I don't know. Can't we enjoy being engaged first? It's only been like thirty seconds."

Draven picks me up and throws me over his shoulder, and I remember a time I would've fought this. There was a time I would've gone kicking and screaming at this half-demon manhandling me like this, but not anymore. Now, my cheeks heat as he carries me out of the big top and towards our tent.

"Oh, you're going to enjoy being engaged, Butterfly. And it'll be a Hel of a lot longer than thirty seconds."

I don't know much, but there is one thing I know for certain: no matter what happens to me in this life, even if one day my memories are somehow taken from me again, there is *nothing* that could make me forget the sense of belonging I feel on this planet full of emerald-colored cities and mischievous demons.

Even if my memories were lost again, I would find my way back here, because Hel's Carnival is where I belong. It's home.

Draven is home.

CODA

This is only the beginning. Not just for you, dear reader, but for The Devil's Masquerade. We've taken the life of a member of Pack Escalus, and now we must face the consequences.

The monsters lurking in the shadows won't stay hidden for long.

AUTHOR'S NOTE

Thank you so much for reading Dance for Demons! I hope you love this world as much as I do. I would like to emphasize that this is a trilogy. Though each book features a different couple, these are not standalones. Every couple will find their happily ever after, but the overarching story will continue. More magic, murder, mystery, and political intrigue will ensue.

See you in Hel!

Xoxo,
    Rose

GLOSSARY

The Convergence: a magical collision of multiple planets (Barac, Earth, Hel, Loria, Umbra, and Moonflower), resulting in changes to Earth, as well as those prospective planets, including magical beings living on Earth and shifts in our geographical and sociological features.

Earth: the human planet.

Hel: the demon planet. The nine continents are: Haeresis, Limbus, Luxuria, Violenta, Ira, Gula, Avaricia, Fraus, and Proditorum.

Haeresis: one of the nine continents of Hel; home to Hel's Carnival.

Hel's Carnival: a carnival whose revenue acts as the spectacle-based economic resource that provides for the citizens of Haeresis in place of a tax system.

The Sinner's Circus: Hel's Carnival's night act; a sexual, violent circus.

Carny/carnies: members of the carnival troupe/family.

Helhound: a demon dog

Helhorse: a demon horse

Demon: a magical being from Hel with an extended lifespan; origins widely unknown.

Cambion: Earthly term for a half-human, half-demon from the planet Hel.

Hybrid: a being descended from multiple magical races.

Vampire: a being that survives off blood; from the planet Umbra

Augury University: a university on Earth where mages can study and further develop their magic.

Magicite: a green crystal that can act as a magical conduit.

Atra: powderized magicite.

ACKNOWLEDGMENTS

Hi <3 thank you for reading. This book has been in my head for the last two or three years and I'm so excited and grateful to have brought it to life.

That being said, there are so many people who go into this process and make publishing possible, so I want to thank all of them.

Thank you to all the wonderful companies/organizations out there who aided in my success. Haus of Fables, BibliOddities, The Word Weavership, Book Marketing with Courtney, and Inkventory, who are all amazing and helpful resources.

Thank you to anyone who has helped me in this process, but especially friends like Ruthie, Meg, Emily, Amber, and everyone who listened to me or advised me over the last two years on all the things. Whether it was publishing advice or proofreading my pronunciation guide, all of my friends came through for me and I love everyone dearly.

Thank you to all the artists who have worked on pieces for Dance for Demons, but especially Amira Naval, Eternal Geekery, and Fallnskye. The three of them are some of the loveliest humans I know, and they helped to make this book the beautiful thing that it is. I seriously couldn't have picked a better team!!

Special shout outs are in order for Jess Wisecup and Emilee, who both have helped me at very strange and random parts of this process. I'd throw a few chapters at them every now and then, or ask them for help with something (like proofing my art poses), and both of them would assist with all my silly questions. I am forever grateful, as they (alongside Ruthie, Amber, and Rae) are some of my very first bookish friends.

Speaking of special shout outs—thank you to Clio Evans, who I'm giving the title of The Great Unstucker. The ideas for this book were ruminating in my brain for so long, I really didn't know what to do with them. Clio helped me through the worst writer's block of my life, and is generally an amazing friend, so thank you to them.

Thank you to my alpha/beta *(what are we in, an omegaverse?)* reader Liz who was so stinkin' helpful throughout my entire writing process. She is amazing and lovely, and deserving of the title The Great Vibes Checker.

Thank you to my husband, Alex, for driving to our high school on your motorcycle when we were teenagers. You were inspiring me before you even knew it.

Shout out to my dog Luna for inspiring me on the idea of helhounds. IYKYK. She's a menace.

Thank you to Heather, who edited this entire book and put up with me (someone with an English degree) who still doesn't understand anything regarding capitalizing royal titles. Not even the ones I've made up myself. Thank you for being my friend, for making me sound more descriptive than I naturally am, and for supporting me even when I write books that include cum. You're one of my favorite humans alive and I love you.

Lastly, thank you to Rae. You're my best friend, and you've probably listened to more voice memos about this book than there are words in the English language. You're my rock, my ride-or-die, and the other half of our shared brain cell. If this book blows up, it's because of you (does that mean I can blame you if it bombs? LOL, kidding). But seriously, I probably wouldn't even still be an author if it wasn't for all of your love and support. Thank you for believing in me.

ABOUT THE AUTHOR

Headshot by Cody Kreiger

Rose Santoriello is an author, chaos bisexual, and karaoke connoisseur. Begrudgingly residing in Florida, they spend their free time at the zoo (their house), time traveling to the 14th century (the renaissance festival), and exchanging peasantries (yapping to friends). Follow them on socials (@rosesantoriello) for stories full of queer joy, bleeding hearts, and neurodivergent/chronically ill fiends!

www.monsterromanceauthor.com

ALSO BY ROSE SANTORIELLO

Coming Soon

Hel's Carnival #2

Hel's Carnival #3

Available Now

Hook-up To Holidate

Sweet Summer Serpentine

Haunt Me Baby

Setting Up Love

www.ingramcontent.com/pod-product-compliance
Lightning Source LLC
Chambersburg PA
CBHW050153120726
47903CB00002B/610